MAGIC HIDDEN
THE MAGIC OF THE HEART SERIES

MISHA McKENZIE

Published by Misha McKenzie

Library of Congress Cataloging-in-Publication Data

McKenzie, Misha
Magic Hidden / Misha McKenzie
     p. cm.

ISBN-13:978-0-9912002-5-2
ISBN-13:978-0-9912002-6-9 (ebook)
I. Title

Printed and bound in the United States of America

10 9 8 7 6 5 4 3 2 1

PROLOGUE

Lindsay cradled the weight of her unborn child—the last living, breathing reminder of her dead husband—and ran as fast as she dared.

At eight months pregnant, panicked flight wasn't safe, but she was out of options. They'd found her. Again. She had to get away. She had to hide. She had to survive.

Lindsay risked injury and precious seconds to assess the progress of her pursuers. *Shit!* They stalked her like a pride of lions on the hunt. And just like the hungry felines, if they caught her, they would kill her. Steven's father wanted only the baby; Lindsay was of no use to him. Expendable.

Her compressed lungs labored, the spasm in her side making every breath torture. Her expectant body just wasn't capable of this kind of exertion. She'd never outrun them like this.

She needed help.

An image flashed into her mind like a beacon—mossy green eyes, hair black as midnight, and a face which would rival that of any cover model.

No. She couldn't involve him. *Wouldn't* involve him.

She saw an alleyway up ahead where people ate, drank, and laughed while they took a break from shopping the busier part of town. Could she get lost in the crowds? She'd tried keeping to less-populated areas, but she hadn't been able to ditch the men following her.

Taking a chance, Lindsay ducked into the alley, deliberately slowing her pace as she threaded her way through to the other end.

She emerged from between the buildings and into the flow of tourists visiting downtown Charlevoix. Another quick backwards glance told her she'd finally gained some ground. Her trackers had fallen behind, helpless to navigate through the people-packed lane. The seas that had parted so easily for her had closed back in, hindering their pursuit.

Lindsay turned left towards the drawbridge and the hiding places she'd scouted when she'd first arrived in town.

She'd taken no more than three steps towards safety when her feet came to a skidding halt. There, a few blocks away, stood the very man who had just occupied her thoughts.

Was it a sign? Was a greater power guiding her to overcome her fear, leading her towards salvation? If what she'd heard about him were true, he may be her, and her baby's, only chance of survival.

Still, Lindsay almost dismissed the idea. She couldn't risk someone getting hurt because of her. She'd already lost too much.

But there he stood, just when she needed someone most.

Would he help her?

She started forward again but was blocked by a stream of elderly tourists as they exited a café. They slowly made their way to a tour bus parked at the curb.

Lindsay's mind raced. If she waited for them to pass, her stalkers would surely find her. If she barreled through the crowd, it would cause a scene and draw their attention to her anyway.

Left with only one choice, she darted into the middle of the group. She pulled in her petite frame in an effort to appear inconspicuous and moved along with the group onto the waiting vehicle.

She took a seat near the front and ducked down. The lions, finally free of the horde, stopped and scanned in all directions. A short conversation followed before one took off to the right, while another crossed the street. The last predator turned the same way she had come and searched the crowd as he neared her hiding place.

Lindsay sank farther down into her seat, hoping he didn't decide to search the bus.

She held her breath as he passed within ten feet of her. When he was well out of sight, she drew in a deep breath and sat up.

"I don't think you're supposed to be here, my dear," an elderly gentleman told her.

"What?" Lindsay looked around, as if she'd just noticed her surroundings for the first time. "Oh my gosh. You're right. I'm so sorry," she added with an embarrassed smile. "Pregnancy brain." She stood and made her way to the door, sure to keep an eye out in case one of the lions circled back. Lindsay cautiously exited and headed in the direction she'd last seen the man she hoped would be her savior.

The man, if she were right, was an honest-to-God witch.

1

"They want my baby. They'll kill me to get it."

The conviction in the words, more than the vise-like grip on his arm, caused Aiden to turn.

What he found was a woman with long, wind-whipped blonde hair and gray-blue eyes the color of storm-laden skies. She wore a canvas backpack and had one arm wrapped protectively around her very pregnant belly.

At six-one, Aiden towered above her. She couldn't be much more than five-foot- four. She looked young—he'd guess mid-twenties.

And he'd seen her before.

"Lindsay, right?" Aiden gently pried her fingers from his forearm. "You work for Charlie at his restaurant. I saw you the other night."

Instead of answering, she scanned everyone up and down the sidewalk. She grasped his arm again and tried to pull him back into the store he'd just left.

When he stood his ground and wouldn't be moved, her stormy blue eyes came back around to look up at him. "Please, we have to get off the street. I need to talk to you."

Curious in spite of himself, Aiden let her draw him back into the boutique. "What is this about, Lindsay?"

"I've heard things about you . . . about the Marquands," she whispered.

Just those few words caused a shockwave of alarm to shoot through his body.

"What do you mean? What kinds of things?" he demanded, shaking off her grip a second time. "I know you were watching me that night at Charlie's. What do you want?"

Before she could answer, something out the front window of the store caught her attention. Her hands encircled her belly protectively, as if to shield her baby, and she stepped backwards, retreating deeper into the interior.

Aiden followed her gaze but didn't see anything other than tourists. Whatever she'd seen had scared her. She looked poised to run.

This time, it was Aiden who took hold of Lindsay's arm.

"Hey." His sharp tone cut through the space between them and snapped her eyes back to him. "What is it? What did you see?"

She whispered something that Aiden swore sounded like 'lions,' but that couldn't be right. He repeated his question.

When she finally looked up at him, there was fear in her eyes. "I thought . . . nothing. It was nothing."

But it *was* something. By the way her eyes kept darting back to the scene through the glass and the tension he could feel under his fingers, Aiden knew the latter half of fight-or-flight still simmered just beneath the surface.

"What's going on, Lindsay?" Aiden asked again. "What did you need to talk to me about?"

When her focus finally centered back on him, he withdrew his hand. Maybe now he could get some answers.

"I've heard the whispers. I know your family has gifts— powers. You have them too, right? Even though you weren't raised here?"

Aiden's eyes narrowed at her, but he didn't answer. And he wouldn't until he knew what she wanted from him. Not many people knew the truth about the Marquands.

"What is it you want, Lindsay?" The words barely made it through his clenched jaw.

Another nervous glance out the window before her gaze swung back to his. "My husband was like you. He had gifts. And so does this baby." She ran her hands over her swollen abdomen.

"Okay, but you still haven't explained what this has to do with me."

"His family's ruthless. They want my baby, and they'll kill me to get it. I need your help."

Regardless of Aiden's decision, they couldn't continue to have this discussion here.

Most people didn't know the world of magic even existed, so the middle of a busy store, where anyone could overhear, wasn't the place to talk about it. He needed to get them some place more private.

He took hold of her upper arm again and started to guide her out of the boutique.

"What are you doing?" She dug in her heels and pulled away. "I can't go out there! They're still looking for me. I managed to lose them so I could find you, but if I step outside, they'll see me."

She looked genuinely afraid that someone was chasing her. On the off-chance she was telling the truth, Aiden scanned the clothing racks around him and grabbed a hooded jacket.

"Hey, Tanya," he called to the salesgirl. "I'm buying this jacket here." At her nod, he tossed enough cash on the counter to cover it and pushed it at Lindsay. "Put this on."

"You have powers, right?" she said as she stripped off her backpack and donned the jacket.

A few of the shoppers turned and stared.

"Not here," he ground out between his teeth as he reached down and lifted her bag off the floor.

"I'm sorry." She lowered her voice again. "But I need to know if you can even help me."

Fuck. He so didn't need this right now. He'd had more than enough bombs fall on his life in the last month. Wasn't he entitled to a little downtime to sort out where his life was headed?

Hell, yes, he was.

Once she had the coat zipped, Aiden flipped the hood up and dragged her out of the store. "Keep your head down."

The only reason he'd come to Charlevoix today was to run some errands and say goodbye to his cousin. Marissa and her fiancé Jack were headed back to Detroit after spending a few weeks with the family.

And now this.

Aiden came to the end of a row of buildings and spotted a narrow alley. With a quick look to make sure no one was there, he ushered her in and turned her to face him. "Now what do you mean, they're after your baby? Who is 'they'?"

"My husband's family." Her gaze never wavered as she explained it to him again. "They want to take this baby away from me."

"Why would they do that?" he asked, still skeptical of her story.

"It's their last link to their son—my husband."

"Why do you need *my* help? Have your husband deal with his own family."

Grief flashed in her eyes. "He can't. He's dead. He was killed six months ago."

Aiden felt like an ass. "I'm sorry, Lindsay. I really am, but I still don't understand what you think *I* can do."

Her eyes, a moment ago dulled by sorrow, turned a clear and sharp steel-blue with frustration and determination.

"You have to help us. You're the only one who can." Her voice rose in her attempt to make him understand.

"Settle down. Getting upset isn't going to do any good. Just explain what's going on."

She took a deep breath and got her emotions under control.

"My husband and I were together for four years, and during all that time, he never had any contact with his family. He was very adamant that I not contact them in any way, for *any* reason. I had always hoped that whatever had gone wrong between them could be fixed. Especially when we found out I was pregnant. But that never happened," Lindsay told him. "I even honored his wishes after he died, but somehow they found out about the baby, and now they want it. The closer I get to my due date, the more unrelenting their pursuit becomes."

"Again, I have to ask—what does this have to do with *me*?"

"I told you." The aggravation was clear in her voice. "Steven's family is magical. They have powers, powers like yours and your family's. *I* don't happen to have any myself, so my chances of surviving this—and keeping my baby—are somewhere between slim and none. I thought I'd run far enough this time. I'd hoped we were finally safe, but they've found us again.

He didn't like the sound of that. "What do you mean, again?"

"The men Steven's father sends after me. Three of them chased me through town today, but I lost them when I hid on a tour bus full of senior citizens."

He couldn't quite wrap his mind around what she'd had to do just to survive.

"How did you know about my family?"

She hesitated slightly. "I've been in town just over a month. I've heard things about the Marquands, things that wouldn't make much sense to anyone else. But since I know magic exists, I understood. The Marquands are witches, and they have some pretty impressive abilities, and even though you have yet to admit it, that means you do, too."

He knew he shouldn't get involved in her troubles, but something inside him was telling him he couldn't let her go. He didn't know if it had anything to do with his new powers as a witch, or if he were just being pulled in by her fierce blue eyes. There was desperation in them, but there was also boundless strength.

Aiden had a feeling that if he didn't help her, she would disappear. If that happened, he knew he would always wonder what had become of her and the baby.

Even though he still had reservations, he made his decision. He just hoped it didn't come back to bite him in the ass.

"I was just getting ready to go back to the manor. Why don't you come with me? I'll see what I can do to help."

At her nod, he placed his hand at the small of her back and guided her out of the alley. "What about Charlie's?"

"I can't go back there," she told him, pulling the hood closer around her face. "When I saw those men watching me, I knew my time here was finished."

"All right. Have you at least told him you won't be coming back to work?"

"Yeah. I told him I had a family emergency and had to leave town. It's not really a lie, and that way if someone asks him, he won't be able to tell them where I've gone."

"You sound as if you've done this a few times," Aiden observed.

"You have no idea," she agreed. "Almost as soon as I put Steven in the ground, they came after us. I've had to learn fast in order to protect my baby. After a month here, I thought I'd finally lost them for good, that we'd found some place we could settle. I was wrong, and now they're here. I hated to ask anyone else to become a part of this mess, but I just couldn't do it by myself anymore. And then, there you were."

She'd put all her faith in him and his abilities. Aiden wasn't sure how he felt about that. She clearly didn't know his powers had reawakened only a few weeks ago.

Thanks to his new family though, and a lot of practice, he'd gotten a pretty good handle on his inheritance again. But if he decided to help Lindsay, he'd have to explain the rest very soon. She'd based some pretty important decisions on the assumption he knew what the hell he was doing.

He just hoped he did.

"Okay, let's get you to the manor. You'll be safe there until we can figure out what to do next. We can come back later for the rest of your stuff," he said, holding up her pack.

"That's all I have. I've learned to travel light. I was already on my way out of town when I saw you and decided to ask for your help."

Aiden shook his head and turned her towards the docks to wait for the ferry that would take them back to Beaver Island and Marquand Manor.

~~~

Lindsay still wondered if she'd done the right thing as she followed Aiden across the street.

But what other choice did she have? She needed help, and Aiden was her best hope.

They'd just stepped onto the opposite sidewalk when Lindsay's thoughts abruptly halted. A sudden gust of wind came off the water and whipped around her, plucking the hood right off her head. She quickly pulled it back up, worried about whether or not the lions had spotted her.

Face hidden again, she cautiously looked around, her steps slowing as she scanned the area. When she noticed Aiden's longer stride had already carried him down the stairs leading to the waterfront, she picked up her pace.

And in that moment of inattention, someone grabbed her from behind. A hard hand clamped over her mouth, rendering her mute. Holding her tightly against him, her attacker turned and quickly headed in the opposite direction. She had no way of alerting Aiden to the danger as she was pulled into the
~~~

shadows.

Lindsay fought and tried to slow him down, but her feet did nothing but slide on the smooth concrete. On the plus side, she didn't see either of his partners. They must still be searching elsewhere. If she could find some way to get away from this one, she might have a chance of getting back to Aiden.

He'd forcibly dragged her out of sight behind the amphitheater when, suddenly, she was free. Regaining her balance, she turned to find Aiden holding a baseball bat and her attacker lying on the ground, out cold.

The weapon winked out of existence, and Aiden grabbed her hand. "Stay *with* me, damn it!" He pulled her back in the direction of the docks, ignoring the unconscious man at their feet. "I don't think he saw me come up behind him. If we can get you onto the boat without anyone else seeing us, maybe they won't know who you're with or where you've gone."

Luckily, the terminal building sat between the main road and where the ferry docked, obstructing all views from the street. She and Aiden quickly boarded, and he guided her to the lower deck where fewer people were seated. "The boat circles around and passes right through town," he explained. "If anyone is looking, we won't be seen down here."

She couldn't see much from where they sat, but she held her breath until she felt the vibration and hum of the craft, signaling their departure. When the engines revved a short while later, she breathed a sigh of relief. That meant they were past the draw-bridge and clear of the channel, heading out into Lake Michigan. And away from those men.

Aiden lapsed into silence beside her. She tried to engage him in conversation a couple of times but gave up when all she got in response were one-word answers.

Lindsay rose and went to stand at one of the windows. She watched the mainland disappear and then turned her gaze to the place that would soon become her sanctuary.

By the time they reached the island, she was in love with it. It was stunning and serene. A safe haven away from life on the run.

She wondered what it must look like in the fall, when the leaves turned varying shades of yellow, orange, and red.

She loved autumn. For her, the colors and smells set it apart from all the other seasons.

Having been born in October, she'd had some great birthday parties. There was always cool stuff going on that time of year—hay rides, corn mazes, pumpkin-carving contests, and hot apple cider with fresh donuts. Fall in Illinois wasn't plagued by the heat and humidity of the summer months, nor the bone-chilling cold of winter. For her it was the perfect time of year. She would have to make it a point to bring the baby when the colors were changing.

Lindsay resumed her seat next to Aiden as the ferry approached the island.

Aiden waited until they came to a complete stop before standing. He lifted her bag by the strap and swung it over his shoulder. Turning back to her, he reached out to help her to her feet. "You ready?"

"Yeah."

Aiden kept his hand on her elbow to steady her as they made their way off the boat and down the walkway to the parking area.

He removed a ring of keys from his front pocket and hit the button on the key fob. Lindsay saw lights flash on a white SUV.

Seeing the truck, she wasn't sure how she was going to hoist herself into it, but she needn't have worried; Aiden was there to offer a hand.

Once she was in and settled, he closed her door. He rounded the back of the truck and, after tossing her bag in the rear cargo area, he slid behind the wheel and started the engine.

Since he still didn't seem inclined to talk, Lindsay turned

her attention to the scenery outside the window.

Pulling out of the lot, Lindsay marveled at how quiet and peaceful it looked here. Maybe no one would know where she'd gone, and she could enjoy a little of that tranquility.

When Aiden slowed after a few miles, Lindsay knew they must be getting close to where he lived. She didn't know what to expect—probably something similar to the rest of the houses she'd caught sight of—big and beautiful.

She was unprepared for what greeted her when he pulled into the drive.

"Holy shit!" she exclaimed at her first look at Marquand Manor, then promptly slammed her hand over her mouth. "I'm so sorry," she mumbled behind her hand, embarrassed by her outburst.

It helped when Aiden smiled and admitted his reaction had been very similar.

This was by far the largest and most beautiful home she'd ever seen.

It was two stories constructed of large gray stones. It had a huge central structure with wings traveling out from either side. And windows! Man, she'd never seen so many windows on a residence in her life.

As Aiden drove around one side, a row of four garage doors came into view. He pressed a button on the overhead console, and one started to rise. He pulled into the cavernous opening and parked.

She was pretty sure the garage alone was larger than the house she'd shared with Steven.

Before she could even reach for the door handle, Aiden was there, opening it.

He held her arm as she slid out of the seat. Once her feet were firmly on the floor, he led her into the house.

2

Aiden knew firsthand what evil would do to possess power. But even that knowledge hadn't completely convinced him of Lindsay's story. Until someone had plucked her right off the street.

Some force must have been looking out for her, though, because if it hadn't been for that hanging plant falling off the lamppost and directly into his path, he wouldn't have stopped. Wouldn't have noticed that Lindsay was no longer behind him. As it was, she and her captor had already been rounding the back side of the theater shell. Another few seconds, and they would have been gone completely.

Aiden had taken off running, conjuring the bat as he'd rushed to catch up. He'd slowed his pace and approached with silent steps so as not to draw the assailant's notice. Within range, Aiden had reared back and swung for the fences.

What did it say about what she'd gone through in the last six months that almost being kidnapped had hardly fazed her? Aiden was still having a much more difficult time coping with her near-disappearance, and he barely even knew her.

Since it looked like she was telling the truth about someone following her, chances were she was also being honest about the danger to her baby.

Her situation seemed eerily similar to what had occurred within his own family. Aiden had been lucky, all those years ago. He'd had someone to protect him. So now, he would become the protector. And he'd be damned if he'd let evil get its hands on this child.

Aiden had hoped he and Lindsay would have a chance to talk alone before the rest of the family descended. But as luck would have it, his younger sister Amber was in the family room when they entered.

She was curled up in one of the overstuffed chairs, an open book in her lap. When she heard them come in, she looked up and smiled.

"Hey. Back already?"

Her focus shifted to the woman beside him and took in her very obvious condition.

In the short time he'd known Amber, he'd come to realize two things about her: one—she was loyal beyond death to those she loved, and two—she lived to tease.

Him especially.

A mischievous gleam sparkled in her green eyes, and he knew she was going to nail him again.

"Is there something you neglected to tell us, big brother?" The syrupy sweetness in Amber's voice didn't fool him for a minute.

"No, there's not." He grinned back at her. "This is Lindsay. She's been working at Charlie's for the last month or so." He turned back to Lindsay to finish the introductions. "Lindsay, this is my sister Amber."

"Oh yeah, I remember now," Amber said as the memory clicked for her. "You seated us the last time we were all there. How are you?"

"I'm fine," Lindsay returned. "Nice to see you again."

"So, what's going on?" Amber asked speculatively.

"Not what you're thinking, brat." He needed to stop her before she got warmed up. "Lindsay's in trouble and needs some help."

"Yes, I can see that." Amber grinned up at him, unrepentant. "Is it your trouble?"

"I swear I'm going to knock you right out of that chair if you don't stop." He tried to sound stern but ruined the effect by laughing. Taking a deep breath, he tried again. "No, the baby isn't mine. It's her husband's—her *late* husband's," he amended. "And his family wants to take it away from her."

"Why not just go to the police?" Amber asked.

Lindsay took over the explanation. "They can't help. Only someone like Aiden, or like you, can help me."

Amber looked at him with an unreadable expression before turning back to Lindsay.

"What do you mean, someone like us?" Amber set her book aside slowly.

Lindsay's gaze never wavered. "Someone magical. Someone with power."

"What do you know about magic? Do you have abilities?"

Aiden let Amber go ahead with her questions. She'd need to assess the threat to the family in her own way, and Aiden needed his own time to process the information.

"No, but Steven's family does. He did also, and so does this baby. That's why they've pushed so hard to take it from me. I've been running ever since Steven died six months ago. But being so far along now," Lindsay rubbed her hands over her belly, "I'm out of time, and hope, that I can outrun them. Until I met Steven, I didn't even know this world existed. What kind of chance do I have against someone with magic?

"When I got to town," Lindsay looked up at Aiden and moved her hands to rest on her lower back, "and started hearing about you and your family, I thought this could be the answer. It had never occurred to me before to seek out someone like you—like them—for help. After I'd been here for a few weeks with no further incident, I thought I was safe and dismissed the idea completely until today. When his men found me again."

By the way Lindsay rubbed her lower back, Aiden guessed that the weight of the baby made standing for long periods uncomfortable.

Amber seemed to be satisfied with Lindsay's answers for the moment, so Aiden stepped into the silence, gestured to the other empty chair, and motioned to her.

"Why don't we sit down while we figure this out?"

Lindsay looked at the chair longingly and laughed. "As comfortable and inviting as that looks, if I sit down in it, I'll be stuck there forever."

"Don't worry," he told her with a smile. "I'll help you up when you're ready. I just want you to kick back and relax. You've been running long enough."

He waited for her to get settled and more at ease. "Tell us everything you can about your husband's family, starting with their names. Maybe Amber or our parents know them."

Something he'd just said caused her to panic. She started to struggle to regain her footing.

"God, why didn't I think of that?" She turned fright-filled eyes to his. "What if they're good friends or something? They'll tell him I'm here. I can't stay here. I've got to go."

Aiden lunged forward and caught her as she fell in her haste to stand. "Whoa, hold on."

"Let me go—I've got to get out of here." She fought against his hold on her arms. "How could I not think that they might know each other? The magical world can't be all that big. I'm such a dumbass!"

Aiden was trying not to hurt her, but she wouldn't stop wrestling him.

"Lindsay!" His voice snapped out more harshly than intended, but it had the desired effect, and she stopped to look up at him. "Take it easy. No one is going to tell anyone you're here." He looked deep into her blue eyes, hoping she would believe him. "I told you—you're safe here."

Amber's voice broke the silence. "If your husband's family is as bad as you say, I can't imagine our parents having anything to do with them. It's okay, just tell us their names."

Aiden read the uncertainty in her eyes and understood all too well her reluctance to trust them. "Hey." Releasing his hold on her upper arms, he let his hands slide down to hers and grasped them in his. "I promise—no matter who they are, or how well my family knows them—I won't let anything or anyone endanger you or your baby."

He waited as she studied his face and eyes, trying to decide if he were just telling her what she wanted to hear, or if he were telling the truth.

He was committed to doing whatever he could to help her now, so he knew she wouldn't find anything but sincerity in his expression.

When she found what she was looking for, she took a deep breath, slid her hands out of his, and sat back down on the edge of the seat cushion. Splitting her focus between them, she spoke. "Their name is Donnelly. The last I knew, they lived in Chicago."

Out of the corner of his eye, he saw Amber stiffen.

"Carl and Margaret Donnelly?"

"Oh, God, you *do* know them," Lindsay gasped, as if her worst fears had just been realized.

"Yeah. And you were right to stay away from them," Amber assured her. "There's nothing good about them. Or maybe I should say there's nothing good about *Carl*. I've never heard anything specifically about Margaret, but he's every bit as bad as you think. Steven was right to keep you away from him. That man is corrupt."

Amber stood and started out of the room. "I'm going to find the rest of the family to let them know what's going on." She stopped in the doorway and looked back at Lindsay. "Don't worry; we'll help you. Carl Donnelly will *not* get his hands on either one of you."

With that, she left the room.

"She told you the truth." Aiden tried to comfort her as she sat in silence in the wake of Amber's departure.

"Now that we know what, and who, we're up against, we can make plans." He squatted down in front of her. "Try not to worry."

"Yeah, right." It was hard to miss the heavy dose of sarcasm lingering in her tone. "How can I not worry? Your sister," she made a sweeping gesture towards the door with her hand, "just finished telling me that the people after my baby are even worse than I thought they were. And here I am, bringing not only you, but now your entire family, into my mess."

"Don't worry about them. They're a tough group of people. I've seen firsthand just how talented they are. Carl Donnelly has met his match with this bunch."

"But what if something happens to one of you because of *me*?" Her eyes were swimming with unshed tears. "What if . . ."

"Let's not play that game, Lindsay." He took her hands in his again. "Whatever's going to happen will happen, but at least now, with us behind you, it'll be a fair fight. Which is just what you were looking for when you came to me, right?" He paused, but she didn't say anything. "Look, we'll figure out what needs to be done, but in the meantime I think you should try to rest. Do you want anything? Something to eat or drink?"

She sent him a tentative smile and settled back into the chair she'd fought so hard to get out of a few minutes before.

"Water would be great, if it's not too much trouble."

"Water it is then." He walked to the bar and pulled out two bottles from the mini-fridge beneath it. He'd just handed her one when Amber returned with the rest of his family in tow.

~~~
~~~

The two men who entered the room looked remarkably alike. Lindsay had heard they were twins, and now she could see it. The women with them, though, were as different as night and day. One was tall and blonde—the other petite with hair as black as night.

She could see where Aiden had gotten his stunning looks. Hair and facial features from his mother, green eyes and stature from his father.

When Aiden began to make the introductions, the manners her mother had drilled into Lindsay kicked in, and she tried to heave her bulk out of the chair to properly meet his family.

She'd done no more than shift her weight when one of the men waved away the gesture; there was no need for her to stand when they were all just going to seat themselves anyway.

Lindsay hoped her relief didn't show as she settled once again.

Aiden continued the introductions. "Lindsay, this is my father and mother, Conner and Becca, and my Uncle Ben and Aunt Mia. Everyone, this is Lindsay. You might remember her from Charlie's. She's having some trouble, and I told her we'd help."

After everyone was seated, Conner was the first to speak. "Why don't you explain what's happened, and we'll see what we can do?"

She glanced at Aiden first for encouragement, and at his nod retold her history with Steven and who his family was.

"I take it Steven's death was the beginning of everything that's going on now?" Becca asked.

"Yeah, you could say that," Lindsay agreed. "Soon after I turned down their *very* generous offer to take my baby away from me, I noticed that someone was following me, and then I found notes asking me to reconsider, or else. When I ignored those, I began to get phone calls at all hours. Some would be silence on the other end, but with others, someone would tell me that I should rethink my decision if I knew what was good for me. I couldn't take it anymore, so one night I just left. I've been trying to get away from them ever since, but they always seem to find me. The closer I get to my due date, the more merciless they've become. I'm afraid that if they get their hands on me now, seeing as how I'm almost full-term, they'll just kill me and take the baby."

Ben was next. "Why don't you just go to the police? If you can prove Carl has been threatening you, I'm sure they could put a stop to it and protect you."

"I tried that when the letters started to get more explicit about what would happen to me if I didn't cooperate. I kept every last one and showed them to the officer that came. He took everything I had, said he'd look into it, and left. It was the next day that I started to get the phone calls. The very first one told me the police wouldn't help me."

Lindsay recalled the shock she felt at the realization of just how much trouble she was in, and how alone she truly was.

"He was obviously in Carl's pocket and undoubtedly destroyed the evidence. I've been running ever since and, without any kind of proof, or knowing how far his reach extends, I can't take the chance on calling them and revealing my location."

Her attention was drawn to Conner and Ben as their eyes tracked to each other and stayed there. She could see that some kind of silent communication was taking place between them. She waited in tense silence for what would happen next.

3

The quiet seemed to last an eternity, but in reality only a few moments had passed.

When Aiden's father and uncle brought their attention back to her, Lindsay held her breath.

Conner acted as the family spokesperson. "We'll help you. And you're more than welcome to stay here until this gets resolved. He can't get to you here, so you can concentrate on keeping you and the baby safe and healthy."

Lindsay had been on her own since Steven had died. She'd fought, every day, to push the fear and hopelessness away. To know these people she'd only just met were willing to help, had emotions swelling inside of her.

"Thank you," she breathed in relief, her eyes watery in appreciation.

As she sat and listened to the conversation go on around her, she felt some of the tension, some of the fight, leave her body. She was surprised to discover just how tired she really was when she let that go.

The subtle movement of Becca resting her hand on Conner's leg caught Lindsay's attention. Observing Aiden's parents, she saw a look pass between them before Conner turned to his son.

"Aiden." Conner held his son's gaze for a moment. "Why don't you take Lindsay upstairs and show her to one of the guest rooms? Let her get settled in."

Some type of silent exchange had just passed between Aiden's parents, and now between Aiden and his father. But before Lindsay could ask about it, Conner continued.

"Go on up and try to get some rest. You've had a busy few months, and I remember, all too well, what it was like for my wife when she was eight months pregnant. We'll finish this discussion once you've had a chance to take a break."

As much as Lindsay wanted to stay and figure out what had just happened, she didn't want to be rude to Aiden's family.

"Thank you again," Lindsay addressed everyone, "for helping me."

As Aiden assisted her out of the chair and across the room, she thought over the last few minutes in her head.

They were halfway up the stairs when she thought she'd figured it out. "There's something going on they don't want me to know about, isn't there? Something about Steven's father."

Aiden stopped on the stairs and turned to look at her. "No. Why would you think that?"

"Because something happened in there. First between your mom and dad, and then between you and your father. They wanted me out of the room and out of the conversation for some reason. I won't be left out of any plans that are made regarding the safety of my baby, Aiden. Something's going on, I know it is."

"That's because you're a very perceptive person," Aiden admitted. "But it's not what you think."

"What is it then?"

"You're exhausted. We could all see it. You were slowly sinking into that chair. What you saw was Becca telling my father that the rest could wait, and then him passing that message on to me. I guess he figured you would be less likely to argue with him, so he made the suggestion that you rest."

She wasn't sure she believed him. "You and I both know that the discussions aren't going to stop just because I've left the room. This is my life and my *baby's* life. I won't be shut out, Aiden."

"No one is shutting you out of anything, I promise. They will probably talk about what they know of Carl Donnelly, but nothing will be decided without you."

"Don't you think I would be better prepared to deal with him, if I knew exactly what he was capable of?"

"Yes, of course. And you will. But you've been running for too long, and your baby needs you to rest."

She knew he was right. With her pregnancy so far advanced, her stamina was pretty much non-existent. She knew she needed to lie down for a while, but she didn't want her life decided for her while she was sleeping.

"I'll make you a deal," Aiden tried one more time. "After I get you settled into a room, I'll go back down and see what's happening. Then later, I'll recount everything that was said. But you have to promise me that you'll at least try to relax for a while."

"You'll tell me *everything*?" she pressed.

"Yes." With his hand on her lower back, he started up the stairs again.

~~~

Something inside of Aiden kept telling him to keep her close. That feeling had yet to be wrong, so he steered her away from the guest quarters and into the family wing.

Bypassing his own door, he stopped in front of the next one, the room that adjoined his. He took a minute to show her where everything was and asked if she needed anything. When her answer was no, he excused himself to go back downstairs.

The conversation going on in the family room was just as he'd told Lindsay it would be. His father and uncle were compiling everything they could remember about Carl Donnelly.
~~~

He took the chair Lindsay had vacated and listened to what they had to say about the man who threatened her.

"He was always pretty ruthless," Ben remembered. "It didn't seem to matter what he decided he wanted; he would do anything to get it. And that included the removal of people he felt were in his way. There were even rumors that he killed his own parents." Aiden heard the disbelief in his uncle's voice. "How he ended up so sick and twisted is beyond me. Mom always said his parents were the nicest people she'd ever met."

Amber, who'd resumed her seat, added, "Luckily for Lindsay, it sounds like Steven dodged whatever gene screwed Carl up. Thank God."

"If that baby is the focal point of Carl's obsession," Aiden's mother interjected, "then she's right. She doesn't stand a chance without our help. We all remember what it's like to lose our children. We can't let him do that to her. We have to help in any way we can."

"And we will," Aiden told them. "That's why I brought her here. I knew I could count on all of you."

An hour later, he was headed back up the stairs. Needing to make sure Lindsay was okay, he stopped at her door and knocked lightly. Not getting an answer, he slowly opened the door.

She lay on her side, in the center of the bed, sound asleep. He didn't want to disturb her, yet he wanted to assure himself that she was resting comfortably. As he approached, he picked up the throw that had been laid across the foot of the bed.

He'd just draped it over her legs, when he caught movement out of the corner of his eye. His gaze tracked to her rounded stomach.

A few seconds later, there was another ripple as the baby rolled in her womb. Amazed, he knelt beside the bed and reached out his hand.

~~~

Lindsay dozed despite the rolls and nudges of the baby inside her. Until one particularly strong kick brought her fully awake.

She slowly blinked her eyes open and found Aiden kneeling beside the bed. She was about to speak when he silently reached out and laid his hand on her stomach. With all his focus centered on the mound of her belly, Lindsay laid still and just watched him for a few moments.

Aiden was a very handsome man. And as opposite from Steven as anyone could be. Where Steven had been fair-haired and fair-skinned, Aiden was the epitome of tall, dark, and handsome. He had jet-black hair and olive-toned skin that looked like it would tan to an even richer hue in the summer sun.

And he had the greenest eyes she had ever seen. A true green without a hint of blue or hazel. Just a clear, crisp green, like new leaves on the trees in the spring.

He was the complete package. Even with the great looks and—okay, she'd admit it since she wasn't *dead*—killer body, he seemed to be a genuinely nice guy. Hadn't he agreed to help a woman he'd only met one other time, and take on the responsibility of protecting her unborn child?

His hand still rested on her rounded abdomen where he could feel every nudge and hiccup.

Her gaze moved back up to his face, and what she saw there touched her heart.

Absolute bewilderment.

Here was a man who could wield magic with only a thought, and he was awestruck by the little human inside of her.

Lindsay knew the feeling. The first time she'd felt an actual kick and could see the movement from the outside, she too had been amazed. And she was sure she'd had the same sappy
~~~

grin on her face that Aiden's wore now. When she heard him whisper to the baby, she had to bite the inside of her cheek to hold back a laugh.

"I can't believe your mom is sleeping through all this dancing you're doing. You might want to keep it down a little though, so you don't wake her up. She needs all the rest she can get."

No sooner had the words left his mouth, than the lamp on the bedside table started blinking on and off.

Startled, Aiden jerked back and gawked at the lamp.

His expression was priceless, and Lindsay couldn't stop the laughter from bubbling out of her. "That would be the baby telling you it didn't appreciate being told to what to do."

With amazement in his voice, he swung back around to look at her. "When you said the baby had powers, I assumed you meant they would start after it was born—not that it already has them *now*. How is it able to do that? Are all magical babies like that?"

"I don't know, since this is the first one I've ever carried. I think your mother or your aunt would be the ones to ask about that." She couldn't help but smile at the wonder still heavy in his voice.

Then a flush started to creep up his neck and face.

"How long were you awake?"

"Long enough."

Was he embarrassed to be caught touching her while she slept? She pushed herself into a sitting position against the headboard.

"I'm sorry for waking you," he mumbled in apology. "I came in to check on you, and then I saw the baby move. The next thing I knew, I had my hands on you. You probably hate it when people do that."

"There is something about a pregnant belly that just calls to people to touch it." She laughed and rubbed a hand lovingly over the swollen bump. "Especially older women, grandmotherly types. They can't seem to keep their hands to themselves. But don't worry about it—it didn't bother me. And other than not liking you telling it what to do, the baby didn't seem to mind either. Occasionally if someone comes near me, the baby will make it known if it doesn't like that person."

"How?" Aiden seemed fascinated.

"It'll make things happen like the lights, or something will crash to the floor nearby."

"The flowers," Aiden nodded, looking a little shocked.

"What flowers?" Lindsay asked him.

Aiden dropped his gaze to the baby. "When that guy grabbed you today, a pot of flowers fell from a lamppost right in front of me." He switched his focus to Lindsay. "If I hadn't stopped when I did, I wouldn't have seen where that asshole was taking you. I had wondered who was looking out for you, and now I know."

Lindsay rubbed her hands lovingly over her baby. "That doesn't surprise me. I've learned to watch for all kinds of signs from this little guy in here."

"Little guy?" Aiden rose up from the floor to sit on the edge of the bed. "So you know that it's a boy?"

"No. Steven and I had agreed to wait and be surprised. I wanted to stand by that, so every time I go to the doctor, I won't let them tell me."

"With you being on the run, when was the last time you were seen by a doctor?"

"Just last week." Lindsay was a little miffed at his assumption that she didn't take care of herself, or her baby. "Wherever I am, I find an OB/GYN. I even carry my medical files with me, so each doctor I see knows my history. I'm not going to jeopardize my or my child's health. I know how important prenatal care is."

Aiden held his hands up in surrender. "Sorry, none of my business. I'll butt out."

"No, I'm sorry." Lindsay felt like an ass. "It was a logical question, and I'm sorry I bit your head off. I've had only me to rely on for so long, I'm not used to anyone questioning me."

"What about your family? Isn't there anyone who could help you?"

"I'm still in touch with my mom and dad, but I can't go to them, or Carl will find me. We have to keep it limited to brief phone conversations. It's hard, and I miss them terribly, but right now that's all I can do. Needless to say, they're very worried."

"Do they know about Steven and his family being magical?"

"Yeah. Steven and I explained it to them. They know the baby will have powers, too. They were a little freaked at first, but I know they'll love this little one no matter what."

"So they know who's after you and why?"

"Yes, and, understandably, the closer I get to my due date, the more concerned they become. They'll be as happy as I will when this is all behind us and we can get on with our lives. That's why I hope you and your family will be able to help."

"There's no question there. We're going to help you." Aiden kept his promise and spent the next few minutes filling her in on everything that was said in the family room.

"How does someone get to be that twisted?"

"I don't know. From everything that was said, his parents were pretty normal."

"Were?"

When Aiden shifted his gaze away from her and rose from his seat on the bed, Lindsay knew there was more to the deaths of Steven's grandparents than he wanted to tell her.

She followed him across the room to where he stood in front of the window overlooking the front lawn.

She placed her hand in the middle of his back. "Aiden, tell me. I need to know."

He was quiet for so long, she wasn't sure he would. Finally, through her touch, she felt him draw a deep breath into his lungs and release it.

Lindsay dropped her hand when he turned to face her. "Carl's parents died when he was in his early twenties. There was talk that he killed them. It was never proven, but it's pretty much common knowledge that he did it."

She was stunned that someone could be so heartless.

"I just can't wrap my head around something like that." She turned to walk back across the room. "I'm not naive. I know there are bad people in the world, but I never thought I would have to fight for my life against one." She turned back to look at him before she continued. "I know you didn't want to tell me that, but I need to know what I'm facing. You can't hide anything from me if I'm going to get through this. I have to know what he's capable of, so I can prepare myself."

"I know you're a strong woman. You've had to be, to have made it this far on your own, but you're not alone anymore. You don't have to lead the fight."

"Do you think I *want* to be on the front line?" she asked him. "I would much rather hide behind the scenes and let someone else take care of this for me. But I don't have that luxury. I'm just trying to keep us alive." She held her stomach protectively in her hands. "If Carl gets his hands on this innocent child, its life will be filled with hate and cruelty instead of unconditional love and caring. I don't even want to *think* what a life like that would be like."

"I understand that," Aiden told her, his green eyes flashing with the intensity of his feelings. "But you came to me for help. Now it's my responsibility to see that you both get through this in one piece. I'll warn you right now—I intend to do whatever I feel is necessary to do that."

Lindsay opened her mouth to argue, but Aiden continued before she could utter a sound.

"But I also know you're right," he reluctantly admitted. "It's safer for everyone involved if we're all on the same page."

"Thank you," she breathed, grateful to have that settled.

They stood, face to face, staring at each other, neither saying a word. Lindsay started to feel that things had gotten a little too intimate.

Aiden must have picked up on her unease.

"Look, it's getting close to dinner time," he said as he moved around her to cross to the door. "Do you want to get freshened up and join us for something to eat?"

"That would be great. I'm starving." When the lights blinked again, she grinned and changed her answer.

"We're *both* starving."

"Well, we can't have that." Aiden smiled. "Go do whatever you need to do, and let's get you both something to eat."

4

When they walked into the dining room, everyone was already seated. Aiden showed Lindsay to the empty chair next to his.

Once she was seated, he took his own.

"Did you rest well?" Mia asked.

"Surprisingly well, thank you," Lindsay told her. "I didn't think I would be able to, but I fell right to sleep. I guess I needed it more than I thought." Lindsay paused, "I just wanted to thank all of you."

"We'll help in any way we can. That man won't get his hands on either one of you."

The vehemence in Becca's voice surprised Aiden, and when he glanced at Lindsay he saw fresh tears swimming in her eyes.

Aiden touched her clenched fist beneath the table and rubbed the back of her hand until it relaxed.

Conner's voice broke into the emotional silence. "Why don't we put all this business aside for now and enjoy dinner?"

Throughout the meal, Aiden kept an eye on Lindsay. He didn't like how quiet she'd become. Was she still tired? Was there something else she hadn't told them?

The longer her silence went on, the more he needed to know what was going on in her mind.

Aiden leaned into her and whispered. "You've been awfully quiet. What are you thinking about?"

"Nothing much. I'm just amazed that your family would be so quick to help me. They don't even know me."

At the same time, Aiden heard a small, child-like voice, *"She's thinking of running away."*

Aiden was so stunned, he missed most of Lindsay's answer.

He looked at everyone else in turn, trying to figure out who said it.

"What?" Aiden asked.

"I was just saying . . ." Lindsay started to repeat what she'd said, but Aiden wasn't listening. He was waiting for the other to speak.

"She's thinking of running, so she doesn't endanger your family. You can't let her do that. She needs you. She won't survive without you. And neither will I."

Aiden glanced around the room again, only to realize no one else had heard it. The voice was inside his head.

"Aiden, are you okay?"

His mother was concerned, but he didn't acknowledge her question. He needed to know where the voice was coming from and what it meant.

"Who are you?" Aiden demanded.

"Who is who?" His dad was worried now too. "Aiden, what's wrong? Who are you talking to?"

"Aiden, what just happened?" his mother asked him.

"I'm not sure," he finally acknowledged as he tried to figure it out.

Why would a small child be talking inside his head, and where was it coming from?

His gaze dropped to Lindsay's swollen stomach. "No way."

"Aiden?" his mother called to him. "What's going on? Are you okay?"

"Yeah. Yeah, I'm fine," he assured her, but he didn't have time to explain right now—he needed to get to the bottom of this.

"I need to have a little chat with Lindsay. If you all will excuse us?" With that, he ushered Lindsay out of the dining room and up the stairs.

Aiden had barely reached the upper floor when he couldn't hold it back any longer. He spun her around to face him.

"You're thinking about running, aren't you? You've got some foolish notion that you can't endanger my family?"

The shock and dismay on her face was affirmation enough.

"How did you know that?" she demanded, jerking her arm free from his grip. "Can you read my mind? Is that one of your powers?"

"No. But I think someone else we know might be able to do that, and more."

"Someone else?" She wasn't happy. A crease developed between her furious eyes, and her arms folded over her breasts. "Who? Did someone else in your family invade my thoughts? Who was it?"

Aiden tried to explain again, since she still didn't understand what he was trying to tell her.

"Someone did read your mind, Lindsay. But it wasn't anyone from *my* family."

"What are you talking about? Your family is the only one here."

Aiden tried a different tactic. "The reason I knew you were thinking of running away, was because I heard a voice in my head telling me so." He paused to let that sink in. "The voice I heard was that of a child—a *small* child, Lindsay."

She stared at him a moment longer, confusion plain on her face. Aiden saw when it finally clicked. Her gaze shot down to her stomach at the same time her hands reached for it. "No!"

"Yes," he told her. "That baby in there just told me what you were thinking. And it said that I couldn't let you leave. That you won't survive. That neither of you would."

"That's not possible." Lindsay gaped at her abdomen,

stunned.

"Oh, I can assure you, it happened. I heard your baby's voice in my head," he told her. "Was it right? Are you thinking about taking off?"

"The thought had crossed my mind," Lindsay admitted.

"Why?" Aiden didn't bother to hide the irritation in his voice. "I thought we'd already settled this. My family can handle anything Carl wants to dish out. He can't be any worse than the last evil bastard to mess with us, and we took him out of the picture altogether. I thought we'd resolved this already; why is this becoming an issue again?"

"I like your family, okay?" she shouted in frustration. "I don't want anything to happen to them. You just got them back, Aiden. I think I would rather die than take the chance of something happening to you, or your family, because of me."

"Well I can't let you go." He tried to express to her the certainty he'd heard in the baby's voice. "According to that little one in there, if you don't have my help in this, neither of you will make it out alive. I'm not willing to take that chance, so I say we do what it says and stick together."

"Aiden—" Lindsay started.

"No arguments." Aiden didn't want to hear what she was about to say, so he tried to reason with her. "Linds, your baby spoke to me for a reason. It obviously knows something that we don't, and I, for one, am going to listen to it. I suggest you should, too."

She stood silent as she thought it over. "I'll consider it."

"That's all I ask."

Lindsay's eyes dropped to the mound of her stomach as her hands moved restlessly over it.

"What is it?" Aiden asked gently.

"Why did *my* child speak to *you*? If it's able to do that, why hasn't it spoken to me? Why you? A total stranger?"

"I don't know. Maybe it's because I also have powers."

It wasn't all that hard for him to figure out what could be causing her distress. Her next statement confirmed his guess.

"Yeah, but you're not the father. So how, and why, was it able to speak to you?"

"Like I said, I don't know." He tried to allay her fears. "Who knows why babies, and kids in general, for that matter, do what they do."

"Yeah, you're probably right." She didn't meet his gaze, and her hands still held her belly protectively.

"Are you going to be all right? I need to let everyone in the dining room know what just happened. They're probably all in there right now trying to figure out if I've gone crazy."

"Would you mind if I sit out that conversation and go to my room? I have a few things to think over. Be sure to let them know I appreciate everything they're doing for me, and that I'll see them in the morning."

"Will you?" Aiden felt he needed to press his point. "I'll let you go if you promise me you won't run tonight. If you still don't want to bring my family into this, we'll come up with another way, but I'm not leaving you to go through this on your own. That baby and I both agree that you need me to get through this. If it would make you feel better, maybe you and I can go somewhere else to make our stand against Carl."

"I'll go over what you said, and I promise I won't run." Lindsay reached up and hugged him. "Thank you for this." When she stepped back, she added, "I'll see you in the morning."

"Good night, Lindsay."

Before she could walk off down the hall, Aiden bent down so his face was at her belly and said, "And good night to you, little one." He lowered his voice to a whisper. "Keep me posted if your momma comes up with any more crazy ideas, okay?"

"Okay," Aiden heard in his head and smiled.

"It happened again, didn't it? It spoke to you," Lindsay asked incredulously.

Still smiling, Aiden confirmed, "We came to an agreement. Don't worry about it." He turned and started back down the stairs.

"Aiden?"

He turned to look at her.

She paused and looked down. "Never mind."

"What?" Aiden asked.

"It's nothing. Forget I asked."

"Lindsay, I can tell there's something bothering you. What is it?"

"The voice."

"What about it?"

"Could you tell if it was a girl's voice or a boy's?"

Given their previous conversation, he understood instantly; it clearly troubled her that he might know the gender of her baby. He grinned, glad he could put her at ease. "The secret is still safe. It was just a little kid's voice. When they're small, they all kind of sound the same. I honestly couldn't tell."

She thanked him and started down the hall to her room. His smile now gone, he watched her until she was out of sight. Turning, Aiden descended the stairs, trying to block out what it had felt like having her lush body pressed up against him when she'd hugged him.

Thoughts back on track, Aiden headed to the parlor off the main hall where everyone usually gathered after dinner. When he entered, they all looked up expectantly. His father was the first to speak.

"Everything okay?"

"Yeah. There were some things I needed to discuss with Lindsay," Aiden admitted as he crossed the room to take a seat in one the chairs adjacent to the couch.

"Where's Amber?" he asked.

"She said she had things she needed to do tonight, and that she would be back late," Becca answered a little too casually.

Aiden caught the subtle implication and wondered what it meant. "Is something wrong?"

Becca threw a dirty look at her husband. "Your father doesn't seem to think so, but something is definitely going on with your sister."

Aiden was really curious now. "Like what?"

Conner stepped in before Becca could continue. "She doesn't know, and it's probably nothing."

Becca rounded on Conner. "There *is* something. She's been too quiet and mysterious about what's happening in her life. She's hiding something. I can feel it."

"She's a grown woman, hon. She really doesn't have to account for every move she makes. She probably just met some guy and isn't ready to share that with us yet," Conner tried to reason with her.

Becca wouldn't be swayed. "It's more than that. I know it is."

"Is there anything I can do?" Aiden offered.

"No," Conner told him. "Amber's a grown woman; she can take care of herself. She also knows we're all here for her and will do what we can to help if she needs it. If there's something wrong, she'll come to us when she's ready. Now, let's get back to you. You looked a little disconcerted when you left the dining room. I take it there was a problem?"

"That's why I came looking for all of you. There are some questions I need to ask." Aiden's gaze took in both couples.

"Earlier, in the dining room, Lindsay's baby spoke to me," he told them, still not believing it himself. "I heard its voice inside my head, and I have to say, it caught me completely by surprise." He split his gaze between his parents and aunt and uncle. "Has that ever happened to any of you?"

His mother was the first to respond. "Neither you, nor your sister, ever spoke to me while I was carrying you. I can imagine it being a bit of a shock the first time something like that happens." She paused. "What did the baby say? Obviously, it was something that upset you."

"What it did was piss me off." Aiden sat forward and rested his elbows on his knees. "The baby told me that Lindsay was thinking about running away. And if that weren't enough, it also said that if she *did* leave, neither one of them would survive."

"My God," Becca breathed.

"Yeah. That was pretty much my reaction, too," Aiden agreed. "And that's why I hustled her out of the room. I wanted to find out if it were true and, if so, why."

"What did she say when you confronted her?" his uncle Ben asked.

"She admitted she'd thought about it, and then asked how

I knew. Accused one of us of reading her mind, but I told her exactly what had happened. She didn't believe me, of course, but after everything she's witnessed, it wasn't long before she realized I wasn't lying."

"Is she leaving?" Becca asked.

"I don't know." Aiden released a frustrated breath and reclined back in his chair. "But I told her to think about it tonight and to let me know what she decides."

Even though his parents might not understand the next part, he had to be truthful with them. "I may have talked her out of running off alone, but she and I may still have to leave."

"Why?" Becca asked.

"She's afraid of one of you getting hurt. She'd feel responsible if anything were to happen to you."

"Well that's just nonsense," Mia interrupted. "Why should she feel responsible? We all agreed to help her. It was our decision, and if anything were to happen, it wouldn't be her fault."

"*I* know that," Aiden agreed. "But she has it in her head she can't take that chance. I asked her to sleep on it and that we'd talk again tomorrow. I told her whatever she decided, I wasn't going to let her go through this alone. I hope you can understand that."

"We do, son," Conner said. "And we wouldn't expect anything less. She definitely needs help, and I'm glad you'll be there for her."

Aiden repeated his earlier question, turning to Ben and Mia. "Becca already said we never spoke to her from the womb, but did either of you ever hear Gideon or Marissa speaking to you?"

Ben was the only one to answer. "Yes. Gideon spoke to me a couple of times, and you're right—it is a little unnerving at first to hear that little voice in your head."

"So this is normal for a magical baby?" Aiden asked, looking at the women. "What about powers? Could we use ours before we were born?"

Becca picked up her coffee cup from the side table and cradled it in her hands as she answered. "Yes, you all were able to use your powers on a limited basis. Nothing big, just little things."

Aiden had done and seen so much in the last month that nothing should have surprised him. But the thought of unborn babies being able to control magic on any level was unbelievable. And here were Becca and Mia talking about it like it was nothing special; which to them, he supposed, it wasn't. "Would making the lights flicker be something a baby could do?"

"Yes, certainly. Why, is Lindsay's baby able to do that?" Mia asked.

"Yeah, plus a few other things." Aiden wasn't sure he wanted to know the answer to his next question but had to voice it anyway. "What all can we expect this baby to do?"

Becca's reply eased his apprehension somewhat. "Babies are pretty limited to what they can do before and right after they're born. They don't usually come into their *full* power for a couple of years."

Before Aiden could form another question, Becca continued.

"I imagine Lindsay will need someone to help her understand what the baby can do, since she doesn't have powers herself. Tell her if she has any questions, to please come to us. Between our four pregnancies, Mia and I have probably experienced everything she'll be going through. Even if the two of you have to leave, we're only a phone call away."

"Thank you, I'll let her know. I'm sure she'll be relieved. I know I am," Aiden smiled.

"Do you really think you'll have to leave?" Becca asked him.

"We'll see how she feels about it in the morning. I hope she decides to stay and let us all help her." Aiden ran his hand through his hair in frustration. "Hell, she'd rather I not be anywhere near her either, but after what the baby said, I'm not giving her any other choice."

"Just remember, son," Conner began, "she's been on her own for the last, what . . . five or six months?"

Aiden nodded his confirmation.

"You need to understand that even though she was at her wit's end and running out of options when she came to us, she's still a very strong and self-reliant woman."

"You think I don't know that?" Aiden demanded, not sure he was going to like where this was going.

"I'm sure you do, but there's something you need to keep in mind. When she approached you, she didn't fully understand what Carl was capable of. All she had to go by was the very little Steven had told her. In the last few hours, she's learned what an evil bastard he really is. You can't blame her for second-guessing her decision to ask for help. If he's done even half of what's rumored, what's to stop him from harming anyone helping her? Would you be so willing to take that chance, if you were in her position?"

Aiden sat and stared at his clasped hands. Everything his father said made sense and pretty much followed what Lindsay had said. But there was no way that he could let her go on alone, and he told his father as much.

"We wouldn't expect anything less," Conner said again.

"Assuming she does decide not to stay here, can you think of some place we can go? If a showdown with Carl is coming, I'd like it to be someplace remote. I wouldn't want anyone caught in the crossfire. Not to mention, if I have to use my powers, the fewer people around, the better."

"That makes sense," Conner agreed, looking over at his brother. At Ben's nod, he turned back to Aiden. "We'll give it some thought."

"Thanks."

Aiden sat and talked with his family for a while longer. They went over everything they could think of regarding Carl and

Margaret Donnelly. The consensus was that they didn't believe Margaret to be a threat.

"I think there's a chance she may help us when it comes right down to it," Ben said from behind the mini bar where he poured his wife another glass of water. "She may have already helped Steven to get away from his father."

"Yeah, but we don't know that for sure," Aiden replied as Ben handed the glass to Mia. "And I would hate to need her in a pinch, only to find out she's too afraid of her husband to do what needs to be done. I can't take that chance. There's too much at risk." Aiden gave it a few more moments of thought. "No, I'm going with the assumption that she's in this with him."

"I guess that's smart until we know for sure," Ben conceded as he resumed the seat next to his wife on the couch opposite Conner and Becca.

"If you do have to leave to face Carl on your own," Becca started, "are you going to feel comfortable using your powers to that extent? You can guarantee he's going to use his against you. Fast and dirty. And with lethal intent."

Aiden focused inside of himself for a moment, looking for the answer.

"I'll do whatever I have to do to keep them safe," Aiden said with conviction.

His mother studied him and then nodded.

Everyone's attention was drawn to Mia when she spoke. "We'll need to work with him on his spells. If he has to do this on his own, he'll need that, along with his other abilities."

Spells? Damn.

Aiden had a pretty good handle on his natural-born gifts, but writing and working spells were still giving him fits. It all came down to sentence structure and making sure the words were in the correct order. Kind of like English class in high school, except instead of just a bad grade, it could quite possibly result in catastrophe.

The amused look on Becca's face told Aiden she knew what he was thinking.

"Don't worry about it," she told him. "Everyone makes mistakes."

"Great," Aiden mumbled, but everyone caught it and laughed at his discomfort.

6

A short time later, he made his way back up the stairs to his room. As he stood outside the door, he glanced over at Lindsay's and thought briefly about looking in on her. Ultimately, he decided not to. She needed time to think.

When he entered his own room, his gaze was drawn to the closed door adjoining her room to his. He realized he'd forgotten to tell her he was right next door. He'd better take care of that in the morning, so she'd know he was close if she needed anything.

Aiden knew he was too wired to sleep anytime soon but went ahead and got ready for bed. If all else failed, he could read until his brain shut down.

He hadn't been in bed long when the door between his and Lindsay's room opened.

"Hi," Lindsay said as she stood in the doorway.

Aiden sat up against the headboard, conscious of his nakedness beneath the sheet. "Hi. Are you okay? Do you need anything?"

"You."

Lindsay started across the room towards him, unbuttoning her blouse as she approached.

Aiden couldn't take his eyes off her as she uncovered her glorious form, inch by inch.

She dropped her shirt to the floor as she reached the side of the bed. She stood naked before him.

"Lindsay . . ." he began.

"Shhh." Grasping the sheet, she pulled it away from him and tossed it aside. His arousal stood tall and proud.

Before Aiden could utter another word, Lindsay straddled his hips, took his face in both hands, and moved in for a kiss that shattered every thought in his mind.

Her full, swollen breasts were pressed against his chest, and her warm, wet core waited so close to his searching erection.

Aiden reached beneath her, guided the head of his shaft to the entrance of her body, and slowly thrust upward.

Her body gripped him tight and wrenched a groan from deep in his chest.

Aiden dropped back onto the bed and let Lindsay ride him.

He rolled the hardened points of her nipples between his fingers and was rewarded with her gasp of approval.

Lindsay's tempo picked up, and soon the only sounds in the room were that of flesh slapping against flesh and labored breaths as they both rushed toward completion.

Aiden felt her inner muscles tighten around him. He thrust upward one more time and held her close as she erupted in his arms.

Only when she was limp and sated did he concentrate on finding his own release.

Knocking on his door woke Aiden a split second before that final, crucial moment.

He sat straight up in bed with the mother of all hard-ons and was dismayed to find it had all been a dream.

Lindsay hadn't come into his room, and she hadn't made love to him.

"Fuck." Aiden ground his palms over his face, digging the heels of his hands into his eyes as he tried to get his libido under control. Lindsay was the last person he should be having wet dreams about.

For God's sake, she was pregnant.

Another knock on the door interrupted his thoughts, and before he could get up and throw some clothes on, the door slowly opened.

"Hi," Lindsay said as she stood in the doorway.

Aiden sat up against the headboard, conscious of the state of his body beneath the sheet. "Hi. Are you okay? Do you need anything?"

This was too much like the dream he'd just had. Was this still the dream? Oh shit, not again, Aiden thought as he watched her walk across the room.

"No, I'm fine. I wanted to talk to you."

Wait, that part's different. And her clothes are different this time, too.

Not a dream then, Aiden assured himself, trying to pull his brain back into reality. He needed to focus on the here and now. Forget that as far as his body was concerned, he'd just spent the last half hour buried balls-deep inside the woman standing before him.

He had to clear his throat before the words would come out. "What did you want to talk to me about?"

Lindsay sat on the side of the bed, facing him. "I know we said we'd talk about this in the morning, but I've made my decision. I can't stay here. I can't let your family get into the middle of this fight."

Aiden finally had a grip on his hormones and settled in to hear her out.

"I know the baby told you we wouldn't survive without you. And since I would really like us to come out of this alive, I guess until this thing comes to an end, it'll just be you, me, and baby. Are you okay with that?"

"Yeah, I'm fine with that. I have one request though." No sooner did his first comment relax her, than the second made her wary again. "Could we wait just a couple of days before we take off?"

Confusion was written on her face. "Why?"

"My family said they would try to think of somewhere secluded we could go. I don't want any innocent bystanders around who could get hurt. Plus, my mom is coming up here in a few days to meet Conner and Becca in person for the first time. I just can't leave her to do that alone. As for Carl, it'll probably take him a while to figure out where you went, so I think we have some time for you to rest and recharge before we take off again."

Aiden sat in silence as she thought it through. She was dressed for bed in boxers and an oversized man's T-shirt that hugged the rounded shape of her stomach. Even though she was almost full-term in her pregnancy, she was still fairly petite. He imagined that before she got pregnant, she couldn't have weighed much more than a hundred pounds.

Her pale blonde hair, stormy blue eyes, and slight build, even with the roundness of her pregnant belly, were deceptive. One would think she was fragile and had to be protected—taken care of. But now that he knew her a little better, he knew she was just the opposite. She was one of the strongest people he'd ever met. To go up against someone like Carl on her own to protect her unborn child, and Aiden's own family, was more than a lot of people would do. Her inner strength and determination were incredible.

He was amazed by her grace. The added weight and bulk of the baby didn't seem to affect the way she moved or how she carried herself. She didn't waddle like a lot of the pregnant women he'd seen.

Looking at her, he could see the obvious signs of pregnancy that all women wore. An overall fullness accentuated in the belly, maybe the face a little, and of course, the breasts. Those ripe, rounded mounds which would one day nourish the baby.

He'd always heard that pregnant woman glowed, but until

he'd met Lindsay he hadn't really believed it. She was radiant, even in her pajamas.

Watching her sit on the edge of his bed, he was overcome with feelings he hadn't expected—feelings that were completely inappropriate under the circumstances. What the hell was wrong with him? He'd just had an erotic dream about a woman eight months pregnant. One who still loved her deceased husband, and had more on her plate right now than anyone should have to deal with.

With a force of will, Aiden turned his thoughts away from dangerous territory and asked again, "Would you mind waiting a couple of days? I really do think we have some time before Carl or any of his guys figure out where you are."

Lindsay finally looked up at him. "I guess it'd be all right. When is your mom due to arrive?"

"The day after tomorrow. I'm kind of nervous for them to meet each other. I know Becca said that she doesn't mind sharing me with my mom, but I can't get over the feeling that someone is going to feel left out. Maybe I'm wrong. Maybe I'm just expecting the worst. Who knows?"

"I can kind of understand how your birth parents have felt all these years. I mean, just the thought of having my baby taken away from me is what made me take off. Luckily, you were found by what sounds like a very nice woman who raised and loved you. I know that if I were in Conner and Becca's shoes, I would be very appreciative of that woman. And I'm sure they all know this will be hard on you. This meeting will go great— you'll see. You've got three people who love you and want only what's best for you. I haven't met your adoptive mother yet, but your birth parents seem like very loving and generous people."

"Yeah, they are, and so is Joann. There are a lot of similarities between Becca and her. You're probably right, and I have nothing to worry about."

There was still something on her mind, so he waited for her

to get around to it.

"Um, I have one more question."

"What's that?"

"Is raiding the fridge allowed?" Lindsay smiled.

"You know, I'm pretty sure it is." Aiden smiled back. "They're not real formal around here."

"Will you go with me?" she pleaded. "I don't want to get lost and wander around until I die of starvation."

"Well, we can't have that, so yes, I'll go with you," he laughed. "Give me two minutes to throw some clothes on, and I'll meet you in the hall."

"I'm sure no one will mind if we do our raiding in our pajamas."

"I'm pretty sure they won't either, but I'm not wearing any pajamas at the moment."

Her eyes tracked to the sheet covering him from the waist down.

He saw the moment she realized where her gaze had fallen; her fair skin blushed bright pink, and she jerked her focus back up to his face.

"You're *naked* under there? Oh crap." Now she was looking at everything *but* him. "I didn't realize . . . I didn't think . . . I'm sorry, I'll go now." She hustled back to her bedroom.

"Hey." Aiden couldn't help but laugh at her reaction. "No big deal. Just meet me in the hall, and we'll go find some munchies."

"Yeah, okay." But she still wouldn't look at him as she shut the door behind her.

7

Lindsay awoke the next morning from a very restless sleep. Her mind had refused to quiet last night, and when she *had* finally dozed off dreams invaded her subconscious to torment her.

Dreams featuring none other than the man in the next room.

How could this happen? Her husband had only been gone six months! Steven should be the one to star in her dreams and fantasies, not some other man she barely knew.

The more she thought about it, the more she felt she'd betrayed her husband's memory. My God, she still carried his child, and she'd thought—she'd *dreamt*—about another man.

She loved Steven, and she needed to focus on him and the last piece of him she had. Their child.

Resolve strengthened, she got out of bed and got ready for the day.

Everyone was already seated when she entered the dining room a little while later. Aiden rose to greet her and show her to the sideboard where all the food was set out.

Once her plate was full, she sat in the chair Aiden had indicated next to his.

"How do you feel this morning?" he asked.

"I'm fine. It's very peaceful and quiet here," she returned.

"Aiden just told us you plan to leave," Becca said.

"Yes. But not for a few days," Lindsay assured her. "I know

Aiden's adoptive mother is on her way to meet all of you. He's fairly certain we have some time before Carl finds me again." Lindsay smiled. "And to tell you the truth, it'll be nice not to have to watch over my shoulder for a while."

Mia joined the conversation. "I hope you don't mind, but Aiden mentioned some of your concerns about carrying and having a magical baby. Why don't we take these next few days to discuss what you can expect from that little one?"

"That would be great." Mia's generous offer made Lindsay feel as if a weight were being lifted off her shoulders. "I do have some questions that only you two can answer."

"Well, that's settled then," Becca broke in. "When we're through here, we'll go somewhere we'll have some privacy."

The rest of the meal was spent on last-minute plans for Aiden's mother's visit. Lindsay watched and listened to how Aiden seemed to fit seamlessly back into this family.

After breakfast, Becca and Mia showed Lindsay to a pretty little sunroom overlooking the gardens off the back of the house. Like everywhere else in the sprawling manor, the furnishings were expensive but comfortable and inviting.

It reminded her of the little house she'd shared with Steven. They'd taken their time to find just the right pieces to decorate it. They'd shopped and browsed, waiting for something to grab their attention. What they'd spent furnishing their little house didn't remotely compare to this, but the overall feeling was much the same. Warm, safe, and welcoming.

The sunroom had been done in greens and yellows. The floral prints were meant to match the gardens outside the wall of windows. The overall effect was that the room appeared to be situated in the middle of those gardens. Whoever had decorated it had done an amazing job.

Lindsay chose to sit on the loveseat. It looked cozy, but still easy enough to get out of. Becca and Mia sat together on the couch facing her.

"Aiden told us some of what he's seen the baby do already," Mia began. "He said it was able to make the lights flicker, and that it was also able to speak to him by telepathy."

"Yes," Lindsay confirmed. "It can also move small objects nearby." She paused, thinking about the flower pot. "I guess not so small anymore." She filled them in on what had happened on the mainland. "Aiden said if that pot hadn't fallen when it did, he'd never have known where I'd gone. Carl's man had me almost out of sight."

She looked down at her belly and rubbed it lovingly before bringing her gaze back up to the women across from her. "I guess this one is looking out for me as much as I'm looking out for him or her."

"We're all thankful Aiden was able to get you both here safely." Becca smiled.

Lindsay thought about how to approach her next concern. "What it's able to do now—is that an indication of what it'll be able to do once it's born? Are those the powers it will have for the rest of its life?"

"Most of the time," Becca told her.

Okay, that's a little scary, Lindsay thought. "What do you mean 'most of the time'?"

"Well, in some cases, the baby can tap into the mother's powers, but that doesn't mean it'll have those powers after it's born," Becca explained. "But in your case, since you don't have any abilities, I would say that whatever it can do now, will be pretty much what it can do later."

"But keep in mind," Mia interrupted, "as the baby grows, so does its power."

Instead of putting her more at ease, this talk was beginning to make her feel even more overwhelmed. "How am I going to be able to raise and teach this child all it should know about magic, when I won't understand half of what it's going to go through?" Lindsay moaned.

"Just like you would teach it anything else," Mia stated. "How would you deal with a child who had a higher than average IQ? Or a child who excelled at sports?"

Lindsay thought it over and could see where Mia was headed with this. "I would learn as much as I could about whatever it was that my child could do, or was interested in, and help them as much as possible."

"Exactly. It's no different with this situation," Mia told her with a nod.

"It *is* different, though," Lindsay countered. "I can learn a sport. I can even learn math or science. But I can't learn to have powers."

"You already have the most important one."

Lindsay was shocked at what Mia said.

"What are you talking about? I'm not a witch."

Mia smiled at her. "The most effective power you have, and will ever have, is that of being a mother. If done right, that alone will ensure that this child grows to be a solid, well-adjusted adult, with or without hereditary magic."

Lindsay could only sit silently as tears ran down her face. What Mia had just done for her was beyond anything she could ever repay. Nothing anyone could ever say or do would make her feel as strong and confident about her ability to raise this child than the words Mia had just spoken.

"And if that little one does happen to get carried away with the magic," Becca added, grinning, "you now know a few people who have the same abilities and would be more than willing to rein him, or her, in for you."

Lindsay went from tears to laughter in a heartbeat, and Becca and Mia joined her.

She knew she could come to love these two remarkable women. And knowing that made her decision to leave here with Aiden easier to live with. It wouldn't be painless to leave this home, or these people, but she felt better knowing they would be safer without her around. She would miss them terribly when she and Aiden left, so she vowed here and now to enjoy these next few days with them.

"So, is there anything else you've been wondering about?" Becca asked her. "You can ask us anything, even if it seems personal. We want to help in any way we can."

"Thank you." Lindsay was sincerely grateful, and it showed in her voice. "There is something else I've been wondering about. Why is my baby able to talk to Aiden but not to me? There's no blood connection between them. You'd think I would be the one it talked to, seeing as how it's inside of me." She paused to gauge their expressions. "Is it because I don't have magic, and Aiden does?"

"That could be," Mia considered. "But when I was pregnant with Gideon, he spoke to his father. He didn't speak to me, and I have powers. Maybe Aiden was easier for the baby to reach out to. Or maybe it's just not strong enough yet to speak to you. There's also the possibility it may never be able to speak to you telepathically. That its powers won't be advanced enough for that."

Lindsay hoped that wasn't the case; she'd love to have that special connection with her child.

8

While Lindsay talked with Mia and Becca, Aiden sat on the second floor veranda that overlooked the gardens. He decided to make a call to his future cousin-in-law.

The phone was answered by a deep voice on the second ring. "Slade Investigations."

"Answering your own phones now, Jack? What'd she do, take off on you already?" Aiden teased.

"No, smartass." Aiden could hear the smile in Jack's voice. "She and my mother are running some errands for the wedding, which I gladly leave to them. What can I do for you?"

Aiden had grown up an only child, so he was still getting used to the fact that he had a bigger support system out there now. Where before it was just him and his mom, it now included seven new family members who were all witches, and one almost-family member who was a PI. Not a bad group of people to have behind you. And all of them ready to help with any problem he may have. Being part of a large family might not be so bad, Aiden thought, and continued his explanation.

"Something came up, and I need your professional help."

"My professional help, huh?" Jack asked. "That sounds intriguing. What's going on?"

"Do you remember the waitress from Charlie's—the pregnant one who seated us the last time we were all there?"

"Vaguely," Jack admitted. "Why?"

"Well, the day you and Marissa left, she tracked me down at the docks."

"A pregnant woman tracked you down, huh? Is there something you need to tell us?"

At Jack's deadpan question, Aiden busted out laughing. "God, what is it with this family? Have you been taking lessons from Amber, or is it the other way around? I'll tell you the same thing I told her. No, the baby isn't mine."

Jack got his own laughter under control and apologized. "Okay, sorry man, I couldn't resist. I grew up with two brothers. Getting a couple of digs in is second nature." Jack tried to get serious. "So, what's the pregnant waitress' problem?"

"It seems her husband's family—her *late* husband's family," Aiden amended, "is trying to take the baby away from her."

Aiden had seen firsthand how good Jack's instincts were, and they proved true one more time.

"I have a feeling there's more to it than that. Give it to me."

Aiden went on to explain everything he knew.

"Wow."

"Yeah, so that's why I need your help. I'd like you to look into Steven and Carl Donnelly's lives, and let me know if there's anything more I should be concerned about. The fewer surprises I have in this, the better I'll be able to protect Lindsay and the baby."

"Sure, not a problem. I'll see what I can find out, but are you sure you want to do this? I mean, you barely know this woman, and she's dumped her problems in your lap. Magical problems at that. Are you going to be able to deal with this Carl Donnelly?"

Everyone in the family knew he hadn't had the easiest time coming to terms with this new part of himself. And he didn't blame Jack for the doubt he heard in his voice. But he'd come a long way in a short time and had already accepted what he might have to do.

"I'll do *whatever* I have to do to protect Lindsay and the baby, and that includes using everything I have at my disposal."

"All right, I just hope you know what you're doing. I'll start looking into the Donnellys and let you know what I find."

"Thanks, Jack. I appreciate the help. Be sure to tell Marissa hello for me."

"I will. I'll talk to you soon."

Aiden hung up and stared out over the gardens, not really seeing them. He wondered how Lindsay's talk with his mother and aunt was going.

As if his thoughts had conjured her, she exited the house beneath him.

Not bothering to examine the reasons why, Aiden rose to follow her.

By the time he made it back through the house, down the stairs, and out the same door, he'd lost sight of her. The grounds were so vast, she could be anywhere. He set off to find her.

Just when he thought about calling out to her, she was suddenly there, seated on a stone bench amid a sea of vibrant flowers. He approached from behind and slightly to the side of her. She leaned back on her arms, her face turned away and tipped upward as she soaked in the warm rays of the sun.

The sight of her there, like that, stopped him in his tracks. God, she was beautiful. The passage of time meant nothing as he gazed down upon her.

When she turned and spotted him, he fought to get his emotions back under control. For some reason, that wasn't proving to be an easy undertaking.

"Hey, you. How are you feeling?"

"Wonderful." She smiled serenely. "This place is beautiful."

"Good, I'm glad you're getting some time to decompress." He sat on the bench next to her. "How was your talk with Becca and Mia?"

"Very nice, and very informative. They answered a lot of my

questions and explained a few things that I should expect from this little one here.”

“I’m glad they were able to put some of your fears to rest,” he said, admiring her profile.

Lindsay turned and looked up at him. “Were you looking for me for something?”

“Yes, I was. I ran into my father earlier. He and my uncle have come up with a place for us to hide out until we have to face Carl Donnelly.”

Lindsay sat up straight and gave him her full attention. “Where?”

“It seems my grandfather had a hunting lodge. It sits on close to forty acres, not far from Charlevoix. It’s been in the family for years, but no one’s used it in a long time. Neither my father, nor my uncle, is that into hunting. There are caretakers who keep the place up, so it’s still in pretty decent shape. They’re going to call Mr. and Mrs. Maloney and have them stock it for us. We can leave as soon as we’re ready to go.”

“I can’t tell you how much I appreciate this.” She looked down and rubbed her hands over her protruding stomach. When she brought her emotion-filled blue eyes back up to meet his, Aiden felt his heart take a direct hit. *Damn.*

To make things even more uncomfortable for him, Aiden swore the bench was getting smaller and smaller the longer they sat there, pushing them closer together. He needed to get up and move before he made a fool of himself. He grasped onto the first thing that popped into his head as he hastily stood. “What do you say I give you a tour?”

Lindsay appeared a little surprised by the quick change of subject. “Um, okay, that sounds good, but don’t you have stuff to do to get ready for your mom’s visit?”

“Everything is pretty much taken care of.” Aiden held his hand out to help her stand. “Besides, it’s a beautiful Sunday afternoon, and I can’t think of anything I’d rather do than spend it with a pretty woman. Even if she does waddle ever so slightly," Aiden teased.

Lindsay laughed and hit him in the arm. "I do *not* waddle. How could you say that, you jerk?"

Aiden smiled, hoping he had covered any awkward moments.

As they walked and talked, he was able to get back to being at ease with her and enjoy the day. Whatever had hit him earlier was gone now, and he was relieved.

~~~

At dinner that evening, Lindsay was able to catch a glimpse into her own future with a child who carried within it a power she herself couldn't understand.

She watched Aiden and Amber tease and goad each other. Amber would make Aiden's plate disappear and then bring it back, and Aiden would retaliate by making a frog appear in the middle of his sister's plate. Childish things really, but, as Amber had said, they had a lot of time to make up for.

Aiden had finally come clean and told her that he'd only come into his powers recently, and that he was still dealing with who and what he was now.

She'd been shocked at first to learn he'd spent his whole life not knowing he was a witch. The whole reason she'd decided to approach him in the first place was because he was part of this powerful family, and she'd figured he was the only one who could protect her from Carl. Now to learn that he was still mastering his abilities was kind of sobering.

They'd talked long and hard about their fears and worries. Aiden had been completely honest with her in how he felt about learning he carried this extraordinary heritage, and how he didn't know where this left the rest of his life. But with the help and love of his family, he was beginning to see that being a witch and having magic didn't really change who he
~~~

was inside.

The power didn't rule them; it was just a part of them. Parts like athletic ability or the ability to excel at math or science, she reminded herself.

She'd listened to everything Aiden had had to say and decided to stick by her decision. She still felt he was her best chance against Carl. The fact that he hadn't been raised as a witch was, in her mind, irrelevant after seeing all the love and guidance his birth family had given him since his powers had returned.

She hoped that she could raise this baby to be as well-adjusted as any in this family, and that her son or daughter didn't turn out like its grandfather.

Her attention was snapped back to the present when her own plate vanished. And if the choked laughter coming from the chair next to hers was any indication, she'd just been fired upon in the war between Aiden and his sister. She turned her head to glare at Aiden. "Oh, that's just not fair. That's like shooting an unarmed man."

No sooner had the words left her mouth, than Aiden's plate upended and landed in his lap.

Laughter erupted around the table as Aiden tried to figure out who had done it. "It seems you have someone to protect you after all." His gaze fell on everyone in turn. "All right, who did it?"

Everyone around the table held up their hands and shook their heads in denial. A chorus of, 'It wasn't me' made its way through everyone seated at the table.

Aiden and Lindsay came to the same conclusion at the same time, and both looked down at the baby she carried.

"Way to go, baby." She rubbed her hands over her tummy. "That's right. You protect your mama from the big bad magic man." The laughter she couldn't tamp down ruined the note of hurt she tried to instill in her voice.

"Hey, buddy, I thought you were on my side," Aiden directed at the baby.

Lindsay suddenly felt something peculiar. It was almost like the baby had the hiccups but not quite. She turned curious eyes to Aiden.

"Nice. Even the baby's laughing at me. I can hear it in my mind." Aiden said, causing another round of laughs to erupt at the table.

"Just remember that the next time you decide to pick on a defenseless woman," his mother told him.

"Defenseless woman? There's not a defenseless woman in this whole house," Aiden argued as he tried to clean the food off his lap. "You all have your little ways of getting even."

Between bouts of laughter, Lindsay added, "Don't we, though?"

Aiden looked to his father and uncle. "You two sure are a lot of help here."

"Hey, we learned a long time ago never to go up against a woman, especially a magical one," his father told him.

"Thanks a lot," Aiden mumbled.

"Oh, quit your whining," Amber told him. "You had it coming."

"What are you talking about? You started it."

"You started it," Amber mocked in a childlike voice. "Yeah, but I didn't turn on Lindsay for no reason. I kept my shots aimed at you."

"How did the baby even know it was me? It could have just as easily been you."

"Because that baby knows I would never do anything like that." Amber tried to sound put upon.

"Oh yeah, right." Aiden still sounded aggrieved, but the hint of humor Lindsay saw in his eyes gave him away. "The baby's probably a girl, and we already know how you all stick together."

"Hey now," Lindsay jumped in. "It could just as well be a boy who was only protecting his mother from an unfair fight."

"I still say it's a girl," Aiden muttered.

Becca, with a grin still on her face, put an end to the argument. "All right, children. Do I have to send you away from the table with no dessert? I'm sure I heard Peter say he was making German Chocolate Cake tonight."

"We'll behave" was heard simultaneously from Aiden and Amber.

It had been a long time since Lindsay had laughed like that. And it felt really good. No matter what happened in the near future, she would always be thankful for having met this wonderful family. It made being away from her own a little more bearable.

She missed them dearly. Aside from very brief phone calls, she hadn't seen her parents in more months than she wanted to think about.

Lindsay's first thought when Carl had threatened her had been to run straight to her father. But then she realized that would be the first place he would look for her. Instead, she had jumped in her car, picked a direction, and driven.

She'd waited two days before she'd felt safe enough to call and let them know she was okay. And, even then, she'd kept the conversation miserably short.

Over the next few weeks, she had moved every couple of days. Always on the move, always on the run.

The little house she'd shared with Steven was gone. Banks frowned on homeowners going multiple months without a payment. Her mom and dad hadn't been able to help. They just didn't have the extra money to make her house payments along with theirs. Thankfully, they'd gone in and packed up most of her belongings and were storing it for her.

She missed it. She'd loved that house. But without Steven, she didn't know if she would ever be able to go back to it. It held too many memories.

Lindsay shook off the thoughts of what she'd lost and enjoyed the company of the people she had found.

Half an hour later, Aiden walked her to her room. "You seem to be getting along with everyone pretty well," Lindsay commented.

"Yeah. They're pretty easy to like." Aiden smiled. "What's great is that they don't put any pressure on me to just jump in and be a part of the family again. They know it'll take some time before I feel like anything other than a visitor."

"It must have been almost like culture shock to be dropped into the middle of a large family like this."

"It is definitely different here," Aiden agreed with a shake of his head. "Growing up, it was always just me and my mom, so dinner was usually quiet. Not that we didn't talk and laugh and have a good time. But dinners here—man, there's at least three different discussions going on at once. And what's amazing is that everyone is following each other's conversations. It takes some getting used to."

"I know exactly what you mean; it was the same for us—just me and my parents. I guess unless you grow up with it, it can be a little overwhelming. The quiet of the cabin will be a shock after being here for a few days."

Aiden put a hand on her arm and stopped her outside her bedroom door. "I know I shouldn't ask this again, but are you really sure you want to leave here and do this ourselves?"

She turned and looked up at him. "Yes, I'm sure. It's bad enough I have to pull you into the middle of all this, but I won't take the chance of someone in your family getting hurt because of me."

"Okay, I just wanted to ask one last time. I won't bring it up again."

"Thank you." Lindsay hesitated, not sure if what she were about to ask was a very good idea, given what had happened last night and the talk she'd had with herself.

Well, she would just have to deal with it, because she didn't want to be alone. She blurted it out before she could change her mind. "It's still kind of early. Do you want to come in and watch TV with me for a while?"

"Yeah, I can do that."

They walked into her room, and she excused herself to change into lounging pants and her sleep t-shirt.

Aiden was opening the doors on the large armoire where the television was hidden when she came out of the bathroom.

She settled on the couch that faced the TV. When Aiden joined her, they scanned the channels at least twice before finally agreeing to watch an action/adventure movie that had just started.

Midway through, Lindsay got the munchies. "Do you think there's any popcorn down in the kitchen?"

"I don't know, but it doesn't really matter if there is or not."

She wasn't quite sure what he meant by that. "Why not?"

Before she could blink, a big bowl of hot buttered popcorn sat on his lap.

"Okay, now that's just cool." She couldn't help but smile at the goofy grin he had on his face. "You may be handy to have around after all."

"I do have my uses," he told her. "Do you want something to drink?"

"Sure. Soda?"

"I heard caffeine wasn't good for you when you're pregnant."

Lindsay knew he was only trying to look out for her, so she tried not to let his remark get under her skin. "I was thinking a lemon-lime soda. No caffeine."

"Oh, right. Sorry." He gave her a sheepish grin when he realized what he'd done.

"Not a problem."

"I know I wouldn't like it if someone kept second-guessing

my decisions, so I'll try not to do that anymore."

Lindsay had to fight back a laugh as she watched him make an X over the left side of his chest the way children do to seal their promises.

"Cross my heart," he finished.

She waited, but he didn't give the next lines. "What?" she teased. "No oath to stick a needle in your eye?"

"I never could understand why someone would promise to do that." He sounded so serious she had to bite the inside of her cheek to keep from grinning.

"It sounds way too painful to me, not to mention gross."

Lindsay lost the battle to stifle her giggles.

Once she had her breath back, she conceded to his common sense. "You're right. That *is* gross, and it most certainly would be painful. So just stick with crossing your heart. Now, how about those drinks?"

Aiden grinned at her. "Coming right up."

A tall glass of clear bubbling liquid appeared in her hand.

With munchies and drinks taken care of, they settled in to enjoy the rest of the movie.

9

As Aiden awoke, he couldn't figure out how his bed had gotten so damned uncomfortable. Or why he couldn't move the left side of his body.

As his brain started to function, he realized he couldn't move because there was something pinning him down. What the hell?

Prying his eyes open, he found himself looking at the top of a head. A head of pale blonde hair. He recognized that color, that flowery smell. Lindsay.

Memories of the night before came trickling back to him, and he realized they must have fallen asleep while watching TV. Which is where they still were.

Thank God for oversized furniture, or they wouldn't have fit. Lindsay's belly, which was even now tucked against his side, took up most of the room. They were lying so close he could feel the movement of the baby as it did slow rolls inside of her. Taking advantage of the opportunity, he just watched her sleep.

And that act alone was unusual for him. He had slept with his fair share of women but had never actually spent any time unconscious with one—however inadvertently this instance had come about. Now that his brain was fully operational, he found he liked the thought of holding this particular woman in his arms all night long.

Her body curled and molded against him, his shoulder acting as her pillow. He didn't even mind that his left arm was completely numb.

If that was the cost of keeping her close, he'd gladly pay it.

But as much as Aiden was starting to wish otherwise, the woman in his arms just wasn't available. She was grieving. And pregnant. And hunted.

Any one of those reasons was enough to define 'wrong place, wrong time.'

He felt her starting to stir. Knowing she'd probably be embarrassed by how close she was curled into his body, he closed his eyes and pretended to sleep, giving her an easy out if she wanted one.

Aiden knew when she became conscious of where she was by the way her whole body stiffened. The weight of her head slowly shifted on his shoulder as she looked up at his face.

He kept his eyes closed and his breathing deep and even.

Slowly she rolled away from him and slid off the side of the couch, carefully getting to her feet.

Aiden watched her through lowered lashes as she made her way to the bathroom. He saw when she turned to look at him one more time before slowly and quietly closing the door.

As soon as the solid wood panel stood between them, Aiden left the couch and crossed to the threshold of his room.

Before leaving, he glanced back and wished things could be different.

~~~

An hour later, Aiden was pouring himself another cup of coffee at the sideboard when he heard his mother and aunt greet Lindsay.

"Good morning," his mother called out from her seat at the table. "You look rested this morning. I'm glad you're feeling
~~~

comfortable here and making yourself at home."

"Thank you, I do feel better." Lindsay made her way toward where he stood. "I slept great last night. I haven't been able to for quite a while. Most of the time, I feel as if I have to keep one eye open."

With his back still to the room, Aiden let a secret smile curve his lips. He liked thinking *he* was the reason she'd rested so well last night, wrapped in his arms the way she'd been.

Aiden made sure to wipe any knowledge of how they'd spent the night from his face before he turned and greeted her.

"Good morning."

He'd never considered himself a very good poker player, but he must have succeeded. All he saw in her face was what could have been a touch of relief.

"Morning."

He was brought out of his thoughts by his mother's question. "When is Joann due in today?"

Glad to have something else to think about, Aiden took his coffee and returned to the table. "She's supposed to be on the noon ferry, but I thought I would go early. Meet her there, maybe take her to lunch, and then ride back together."

"I think that's a great idea," Becca agreed. "I know I wouldn't want to make that trip into the unknown by myself."

"I wouldn't either," Aiden nodded. "It's bad enough she had to drive all the way from Saginaw by herself. I don't want her to have to make that boat ride alone."

Lindsay took the seat next to his. "Do you think you could pick up a few things for me?"

"Sure. Just give me a list, and I'll get whatever you need while I'm on the mainland waiting for my mom."

~~~

Aiden waited until he was on the ferry to look at Lindsay's
~~~

list. And wouldn't you know it? Feminine hygiene products.

He wasn't completely clueless about pregnancies; his mother was a pediatric nurse after all, so he knew she wouldn't need this stuff until after the baby was born. She obviously wanted to be prepared for anything. She was so close to her due date that she may well have the baby before they'd dealt with Carl. God, he really didn't want to think about that yet.

What did he know about babies, let alone delivering one?

As he studied the items, he saw that she had been pretty specific about what she wanted. This would be embarrassing, but it wouldn't kill him. He could handle it.

He'd just exited the ferry dock when he heard someone calling his name. Aiden turned and was surprised to see his adoptive mother running towards him.

"Oh Aiden," she took him into her arms. "Thank God you're okay. I've been going out of my mind worrying about you."

"Mom, I've talked to you on the phone, more than once." He smiled down at the woman who had raised him. "You know I'm okay."

"I know, smartass, but actually seeing you and holding you is a lot more convincing."

"Well, let me know when you're completely sure that I'm alive and well, and I'll treat you to lunch."

"Just one more minute." Joann gave him another squeeze.

She hadn't changed much from when he'd first come to live with her when he was two.

Her auburn hair was shorter now. All while he'd grown up, she'd worn it shoulder-length, so she could pull it up into a ponytail for her work as a nurse. It was now a tousled cap of waves that bounced in the breeze off the water.

She always kidded that if God were going to give her such a tall child, he really should have made *her* taller.

He'd only been eleven or twelve when he'd caught her in height. From then on, she had always made him sit down when she'd needed to talk with him about something he'd done wrong.

Joann had been the best mother he could have imagined. Everything about her was a comfort to him—her voice, her smell, her love.

Before she could step away, he tightened his arms around her and whispered, "I've missed you."

"I've missed you too, baby." She wiped the tears from her eyes when he stepped back. "You mentioned something about food?"

"I did, and after that I have some errands to run before we head back to the island. You made better time than I thought you would. I was going to get my running around done before you got here, but no big deal. You can help me."

"I'd be glad to help. What kind of errands do you have?"

"Actually, they're for a friend who's staying with us. Which is another story, and I'll explain that later. Come on, I know this great little seafood place you're going to love. Do you feel like walking? It's only a few blocks."

"Yes, that's fine. I've been sitting in the car for the last couple of hours. Walking and stretching my legs will feel good."

They set off, arm in arm, down the sidewalk.

When they turned the corner and she got her first view of Charlie's Sea Shack, he saw the trepidation on her face and laughed.

"I had the same thoughts the first time I saw this place, too, but you're going to love it."

She gave him a look of utter disbelief.

"Trust me."

"Famous last words."

Charlie met them at the door. "Aiden, my boy." His booming voice carried throughout the restaurant. "And just who is this beautiful woman you've brought for me?"

Aiden laughed at the shocked look on his mother's face.

Charlie had that effect on people. "Charlie, this is my mom, Joann Covington. Mom, this old piece of leather is Charlie of Charlie's Sea Shack."

"Your mother!" Charlie exclaimed. "I'd heard you'd been taken in by another woman when you were lost, but there's no way she was old enough for that. You gotta be yanking my chain; this isn't your mother."

Enjoying her discomfort, Aiden played along. "She is pretty great, isn't she? You know, all my friends growing up told me they thought she was hot."

"I can see why they'd think so," Charlie added. "I bet everyone thinks she's your sister instead of your mother."

"Oh, give it a rest, you two." She'd obviously recovered from the shock of meeting Charlie. "You both are so full of shit, it's amazing you can still stand upright."

Charlie's laugh rang through the building. "Got some fire in her, too—I like that. It's no wonder you turned out as well as you did. Come on, I'll show you to a table and get your food going."

Once they were seated, Charlie made his way back to the kitchen.

"He's quite a character, isn't he?" Joann looked off in the direction Charlie had gone.

"He is certainly that," Aiden grinned. "He was friends with Sophia—Conner and Ben's mother—before they were even born. He's like an honorary uncle."

She leaned in close. "Does he know about the magic?"

Aiden was floored by her question. "How do *you* know about the magic? I was going to try explaining it to you while you were here." Aiden hesitated and tried to gauge her feelings on the subject. "Are you freaked?"

"No, I'm not freaked." She reached over and rested her hand on his. "You're my son. I love you, and I always will."

The relief he felt almost overwhelmed him. "How did you

find out?"

"I remembered a few things Jack and Marissa had said, and what they'd asked me when they were looking for you. Once I put it all together, I could guess at the rest."

This woman never ceased to amaze him. "What did they ask you?"

"If anything unexplained had ever happened when you were little, when I first got you. The more I thought about it, the more it all sort of fell into place, and I figured you had a little something extra you inherited from your birth parents. I'm hoping while I'm here we can talk, and you'll let me know more about what's happening with you now."

"Of course, Mom. You can ask me anything." Aiden recovered enough to realize his mother had taken this new development in stride. He should have known she would; she'd always been a very open-minded woman.

"And you can be sure I will," she continued. "So, what about Charlie—does he know?"

"Yeah, he's always known. It's no big deal to him, though. I guess having grown up with Sophia, not much fazes him. I think everyone around here knows there's something different about the Marquands, but only a few know exactly what it is."

"How do you feel about that? You're a part of that family now. There's something different about you, too."

"I know. I think I'm handling it as well as can be expected."

She studied his face for a few moments. "Okay. But just remember that I'll always be here for you. I may not completely understand what you're going through, but you can talk to me anytime."

"I do know that." Aiden smiled at her. "And thank you."

"How are you getting along with everyone else?"

"Pretty good," he told her honestly. "They've all been really great helping me adjust to this new side of myself. It helps that I'm not the only one going through it. Before Marissa and Jack left, it was almost like being back in school again. We'd have classes on how to control our powers and how to do different spells. Amber especially has made it easier. Between her tutoring and constant teasing, I haven't had too bad a time here."

"I'm glad." She reached across the table to hold his hand again. "I'm so glad you finally found your family, and that you're happy with them. I hated that I was never able to get anywhere in our searches."

"If it hadn't been for Marissa's visions, we may still not know anything, but there's something I don't ever want you to forget." Aiden squeezed her hand. "I may have been born into another family, but you were the one who raised me and cared for me. You will always be my mom. No one will ever take that place away from you."

"Thank you," Joann sniffled. "What about Becca? How is she handling it? This must be hard on her, too."

"I'm sure it is, but she understands. We've talked about it, and she knows that you will always be first with me. She said that they can just be Becca and Conner. They're not trying to take your place."

"They seemed so nice when I spoke to them on the phone, but I'm still nervous about meeting them in person."

"That's why I came to meet you, so you wouldn't have to make the trip by yourself."

"Thank you, and I love you."

"I love you, too."

Joann checked her watch. "I'm sure Charlie's a great guy, but he needs to hire some better help. No one's come to take our orders."

"Oh, I forgot to tell you," Aiden confessed. "Charlie works a little differently."

"How differently?"

"When it comes to friends and family, he doesn't take orders, he just brings what he feels you should have, and it always seems to be what you would have ordered anyway. No one's been able to figure out how he does it. He may have been friends with Sophia, but from what I understand, he's never had any special abilities."

"If what you say is true, then I would say that he *does* have some special abilities. They may not be magical like all of yours, but they're special nonetheless."

"You know what? You're right," Aiden admitted with a smile. "And speak of the devil . . ."

"You speaking ill of me, boy?" Charlie asked.

"Not a chance, Charlie," Aiden chuckled. "I was just telling my mom that you've been around here so long, you told God how to create dirt."

"Don't let him lie to you, Charlie," Joann interrupted. "He was singing your praises. So what did you bring us?"

"For the lady, I have a grilled shrimp Caesar salad." Charlie set the plate in front of her.

"Mmm, perfect. It smells wonderful."

"Do I get the surf and turf again?" Aiden was hopeful.

"Nope. Today you're having seafood salad on a grilled hoagie bun with a side of fries."

"No surf and turf? Are you sure?" Aiden practically begged.

When all he received in response was a baleful stare, he gave in with a sigh.

Charlie didn't even wait for Aiden to take his first bite before he turned to leave; for him, it was a foregone conclusion that everyone would be satisfied with their meal.

Aiden's first bite was tentative. "Can't say as I've ever had seafood salad before, but he was right again. This is amazing," Aiden admitted. "How's yours?"

"Delicious," she told him between bites. "So who's this friend you're running errands for? I'm assuming it's a girl-type friend?"

"What makes you say that?" He set his sandwich back down on the plate.

"The look on your face when you mentioned it."

Aiden wasn't sure he wanted to ask the next obvious question but did anyway. "What kind of look?"

"That exasperated, don't-know-if-you-should-kill-her-or-hug-her look that only a woman can bring to a man's face." He thought he caught a grin tugging at the corners of her mouth, but it flashed by so fast he couldn't be sure. "So, tell me about her."

"It's not what you think," Aiden replied. It was all he could think of to say.

Joann set her fork down and gave him her full attention. "Well, tell me what it is then."

"Her name is Lindsay, and she used to work here at Charlie's," he explained, knowing he couldn't hide anything from his mother. "She's having some trouble and came to me."

"You haven't been here all that long. How well do you know her?"

"Not that well," Aiden admitted. "I had only met her once, and the next time I saw her, she was asking me for help."

"I don't think I like the sound of this." She wiped her mouth with the napkin and laid it on the table next to her unfinished plate. "What kind of trouble is she in?"

"She's in the kind of trouble that only someone like *me* can deal with."

"Someone like you? What does that mean?"

"Someone magical."

Aiden watched his mother's face closely to judge how she took his statement.

"I see." She paused in thought. "Is she?"

"Magical? No, but her late husband was."

"Late husband? All right, I think you'd better tell me what's going on. Everything at once—no more piecemeal."

"Lindsay's husband was killed in a car accident a few months ago. Up until that point, she'd had no interaction with his family. He'd always told her they were evil and to stay away from them. Which she'd intended to do, until they found out she was pregnant. She always knew her husband had magical powers, and that they were hereditary, like ours. So that would mean the baby she carried had them also. Pretty much on the day she buried her husband, his family started badgering her to give them the baby, seeing as how it was their last link to their son. She said no, of course, but they haven't taken that as an answer. Now that she's so close to delivery, she's afraid they'll just kill her and take the baby."

Joann gasped.

"She's been on the run ever since. Until about a month ago, when she landed here. She'd been here long enough to hear things about the Marquands and, having already known something about magic, decided to come to me. Her words were that she wanted to try fighting fire with fire, magic against magic, since she knew she didn't stand a chance against them on her own."

Aiden watched the emotions come and go on his mother's face until only anger remained.

"Just who the hell does she think she is, getting you involved in this? Tell her to find someone else."

"It's not that simple, Mom." In for a penny, in for a pound, he thought. "Her baby told me that she wouldn't survive without me."

"Her baby told you? What do you mean, her baby told you? You just said that she's pregnant."

"She is. The baby has powers, too. One of its abilities is to speak telepathically, and it told me that neither of them would survive if I didn't help. Lindsay was thinking of running away, but the baby told me I couldn't let her do it. So I'm not."

"Oh, Lord." Joann slumped back into her chair and rubbed

her hand over her forehead. "Here I thought I was doing pretty well at accepting all this magic stuff, but sometimes it's just a lot to take. Babies that can communicate while still in utero. Amazing." She paused and looked at him. "I think I already know the answer, but I'll ask it anyway. What are you going to do?"

"She doesn't want to endanger anyone else, so she and I are going to head to a hunting cabin that my grandfather owned somewhere near here. If her father-in-law tracks her down there, we'll be able to confront him without any innocent bystanders nearby."

"She doesn't want to endanger anyone else, but she will *you*?" Joann sat forward in her seat again and pinned Aiden with a look he hadn't seen since she'd caught him skipping school in tenth grade. She was pissed.

"Mom, I have to do this. You were there when I needed someone all those years ago—now I have to be there for Lindsay and her child."

"Oh, sure. Turn it back around on me," Joann said in disgust. "You just got through one dangerous situation with that Roanik character. Can't you be selfish, just this once," she asked him hopefully, "and tell her no?"

"You know I can't." He gave her a small smile, "and you don't really want me to be selfish, or I wouldn't be the man you raised me to be."

Resigned, she asked him, "Are you sure you can handle this? You're still new to your abilities, and she wants you to go up against someone who she's been told was evil? I'm guessing Conner and Becca know about this?"

"Yes. They're assisting as much as they can by letting us use the cabin and working with me to perfect my powers as much as possible in the time we have. For the last few days, I've been getting a more in-depth lesson than when I first got my powers back. They'll make sure I'm prepared to go up against Carl if it comes to that."

"I have no doubt you'll be able to stand on your own against *anyone*. I just hate that you're in a position *again* where you could get hurt or killed."

"I'm doing everything I can to make this as safe as possible for everyone," Aiden assured her. "I can't let her face him alone, Mom. I have to help her."

She studied his face, though he wasn't sure what she was looking for.

Then, what looked like sadness came into her eyes. "Oh, Aiden. You have feelings for her."

He thought about brushing it off as ludicrous, but his mother knew him too well. He huffed out a deep breath.

"Honestly, I don't know what I'm feeling. Sometimes I look at her, and I'm just struck by how truly beautiful she is and how strong she is. I never knew a pregnant woman could be so sexy. Then my common sense kicks back in, and I tell myself that it's ridiculous—that she's still mourning the loss of her husband. She's been so busy just trying to stay alive that she hasn't been able to grieve properly. And why am I even worried about it? I've only known her a couple of days. Once her in-laws are taken care of, she'll go back to her life, and I'll go back to mine."

"You're probably right. And I'm sure you'll figure it all out. Just promise me you won't make any life-altering decisions until you know more."

"I won't," Aiden swore, though he felt like there was something he missed in his mother's words.

10

Errands finished, Aiden and his mom strolled back to the ferry dock. They waited in pensive silence for the boat that would take them to the island where his birth-parents waited.

Once aboard, Aiden guided her to some seats on the upper deck, but apparently she was too restless to sit. She wandered to the rail to watch the water.

Aiden followed and knew by the way she chewed on the inside of her lips and cheeks, that she was really apprehensive about this upcoming meeting.

"Stop worrying." Aiden wrapped his arm around her shoulder.

"I'm not," she said between bites.

"If you keep chewing on your lips, you won't have any left to speak with." Aiden grinned down at her. "Relax. They're good people."

"I know you're right, but sometimes my brain just jumps to the worst possible outcome," she tried to explain. "That's all it is."

When the boat finally bumped against the Beaver Island dock, Aiden took her hand. "Well, here we are. You ready?"

"Yeah," she nodded.

A short while later, he slowed and pulled into the driveway. Aiden watched his mother out of the corner of his eye to see what her reaction would be to seeing Marquand Manor.

"Oh my." She leaned forward in her seat to see as much of the house as possible. "You weren't kidding when you said it was like a castle. This is unbelievable."

She liked it. He felt some of the tension in his shoulders ease.

"Yeah, it still amazes me that I have run of the place."

"A little bigger than the house we have in Saginaw, huh?" she grinned at him.

"Just a bit." He returned her smile. "But you know what? It has the same feel to it—love and comfort. And that reflects the people who live here." He parked at the base of the stairs leading up to the front door and turned the car off. "Come on. Let's go inside."

Aiden guided her up the steps to the huge double doors. When they opened, he tried to see it through her eyes.

A grand central staircase was directly opposite, gleaming wood everywhere.

It was open and spacious and light. Decorated perfectly, comfortably, richly.

She still hadn't said anything.

"Pretty cool, huh?"

"Yes, it sure is." She smiled up at him, and he relaxed. Seeing how his birth parents lived wasn't hurting her or making her feel less than she should.

"They're probably in the parlor waiting. It's just this way." Aiden led her to a room just off the entryway.

Once through the doorway, he saw only his parents, seated and talking quietly.

When they noticed Aiden and his mother, they came to their feet and crossed to where they stood.

"Joann, it is so great to finally meet you." Becca enfolded her in a brief hug. "First, I want to say thank you for taking such good care of Aiden all these years. It puts a lot of my fears to rest that he found a loving and caring home, and that he had a mother to love him just as I would have. And we hope that you'll be willing to share him with us."

"Becca, honey," Conner interrupted before Joann could form a reply, "let the woman breathe."

"I am so sorry. I didn't mean to accost you as soon as you walked in the door." She gestured to the couches and chairs around the room. "Please, have a seat. Would you like something to drink? Eat? Aiden, get your mother something to drink."

"Becca, honey."

Aiden grinned at Conner's second attempt at reining in his wife. When he looked down at Joann, she was smiling also.

"I'm sorry," Becca repeated. "I did it again. I'm just so nervous."

"I know why *I'm* nervous," Joann told her. "But why are you?"

Becca took a deep breath. "Probably for the same reason you are. That you won't like us, and you'll take Aiden and disappear forever, never to be seen again. Does that about cover it?"

"Yeah," Joann admitted with a smile. "That covers it."

Aiden couldn't believe what he was hearing. "Um, hello? Grown man here. I'm not going to be scooped up and taken away from either of you. I think I might have something to say about that."

"Son," Conner interrupted. "This would be a fine example of the female logic. Don't try to understand it, and try not to get tangled up in it."

Aiden watched as both women brought their gaze around to Conner, indignation joining them against the hapless male.

"Uh oh," Conner muttered. "Aiden, why don't you and I leave these wonderful women to themselves?" Crossing to Joann, he shook her hand. "Very nice to finally meet you. We'll talk again later. Aiden?"

With that, both men left the room.

As soon as the door shut behind them, the women burst into laughter at Conner's expense.

Once he heard that on the opposite side of the door, Aiden began to relax a little. "Are you sure about that? Do you think they'll be okay in there?"

"They'll be fine," Conner assured him, "once they work through their nerves. And they should do that a little faster, now that they have something in common to commiserate about."

Aiden was confused. "And what would that be?"

"Men. And how insensitive we can be."

Understanding dawned and with it, a higher respect for this man who was his father. "You made that comment on purpose—the one about female logic—knowing the reaction it would get. That they'd come together against you. Brilliant."

"I thought so," Conner said, a little smug.

"Won't Becca hold it against you later, though?"

"Once she stops to think about it, she'll know I did it on purpose, and only to help. Come on. Let's go get a beer."

Aiden agreed wholeheartedly. "Yeah, I think I need one."

<div align="center">~~~</div>

Aiden was pacing the entryway when he saw Lindsay come down the stairs sometime later.

"What are you doing?" she asked when she stopped at the bottom.

"They've been in there over two hours." He pointed towards the doors to the parlor. "What could they possibly be talking about for that long?"

"You, I would imagine."

He tracked back and forth a couple more times.

"How long have you been out here doing this?"

"I don't know. I'm not sure." He paused and looked at the door again.

Just then, raucous laughter could be heard from inside.

"That's good, right?" Aiden turned back to Lindsay with a hopeful expression.

"Yes, that's good." Lindsay linked her arm through his. "Come on. Let's leave them to their talk. We'll go take a walk in the gardens. I'm sure they'll come find you when they're finished, but it sounds like it's going well."

Once they reached the gardens, Aiden felt the tension leave his body.

"Thank you for getting me out of there. I was making myself crazy. I don't know why, but I kept having this image of them having a cat-fight and pulling each other's hair out over who was going to get to keep me."

"Please tell me you're joking," Lindsay laughed.

"No, actually, I'm not." He knew how ridiculous he sounded, but like his mom had said earlier, sometimes your mind just jumps to the worst possibility.

"First of all," Lindsay pulled him to a stop on the path, "like that would ever happen. Second, they both love you and know that if they didn't get along, it would only hurt you. I can't see either of them taking that chance. And third, by the sounds coming out of that room, I would say they're building quite a friendship."

"I know, I know. It was stupid."

"Yeah, it really was," Lindsay laughed again.

Aiden looked down into her smiling face and was caught again by her luminous beauty. Without even thinking, his head was lowering towards hers.

The moment before his lips touched hers, her hand came up to rest on his mouth as she backed away.

"Aiden, I can't," she whispered, her smile now gone.

"I'm sorry, Lindsay." Aiden turned his back to her in an effort to gain some control. "I didn't mean . . . I didn't realize . . . I wasn't thinking. Don't worry, it won't happen again."

He stalked a few steps away.

"Aiden—"

"No, you don't have to say anything." Aiden ran his hands through his hair in frustration. He turned back to face her. "Could we just pretend that didn't happen?"

~~~

Lindsay saw how distressed he was about the almost-kiss. She wanted to do or say something that would make it easier for him but didn't know how. How could she make him feel better when she was just as mixed up? It was hard for her to reconcile that, deep down inside, she'd wanted it to happen. She'd wanted him to kiss her.

Fortunately, better judgment had prevailed before it had become too late. Maybe forgetting about it was for the best.

"Yeah, sure."

"How about we finish that walk then?" Aiden suggested.

Though they walked the rest of the way through the gardens, the conversation was stilted between them. The memory of what had almost transpired hung in the air.

Lindsay was relieved when she saw Joann and Becca coming toward them. "Well, it looks like they've finished their cat-fight," she teased, trying to lighten the mood. "They look pretty good, and they both still have all their hair."

"That is so not funny," Aiden complained. "I poured my heart out to you, and you go and use it against me. I see how you are."

"Poor baby," she cooed at him. "I'll go and let you spend some time with your mom." She turned to walk away.

"No, please wait." Aiden took hold of her arm. "I want to introduce you to her."

Before Lindsay could make her excuses, the other women had caught up with them.

Aiden's eyes turned to the two women as they came closer.

"We hoped to find you out here," Becca said as they
~~~

approached. "We didn't realize we had been talking so long."

"Is everything okay?" Aiden asked.

"Everything is great," Joann assured him. "Once we both got over our silly fears, we were able to sit down and talk. Conner even joined us again."

"So no one is going to whisk me away somewhere, never to be seen or heard from again?" Aiden teased the women. "Whew! That's a load off my mind."

Lindsay grinned when Joann reached up and thumped Aiden on the shoulder. "Smartass."

"Have you met everyone else yet?" Aiden prompted.

"Not yet. Are they here?" Joann asked.

"Yes," Becca nodded. "They didn't want to overwhelm you, so they've made themselves scarce until the time was right. They'll join us shortly."

"We've been talking a long time. Haven't they been wondering what's going on?"

"They know," Becca told her.

"How—Oh, yeah, right."

"Don't worry about it. Sometimes I still forget, too," Aiden admitted. "We might as well start the introductions right here. Mom, this is Lindsay, the woman I was telling you about."

Lindsay held her hand out to shake Joann's. "It's very nice to meet you. Aiden has talked about you a lot."

"It's nice meeting you. Aiden's told me some of what you're going through, and I just have to say that I don't appreciate the position you've put my son in."

"Mom!" Aiden interrupted, horrified.

11

"No, Aiden. It's fine," Lindsay halted his protest. "She's right. I have put you in the middle of a dangerous situation that's not your own." She turned her attention fully to Joann and tried to explain. "I want you to know that I didn't make this decision lightly. I know that whomever I bring into this has a chance of getting hurt, but I couldn't think of what else to do to ensure my baby's safety. I hate the idea that something could happen to Aiden. He's just found his family again, and here I am, putting all of that in jeopardy. I tried to back out. I was going to leave and hope for the best. But this baby put a stop to that by telling Aiden neither of us would survive without him.

"Everyone is doing all they can to make sure we're ready for whatever Carl throws at us. Coming here, you may have been afraid someone would take your child away from you, but you didn't fear they would kill you to do that. I truly am sorry I've had to put your son in this position." Lindsay dropped her hands down to caress the baby she carried. "But just as you're trying to protect your child, I am also trying to protect mine."

Joann's gaze followed her hands. "You're right." She looked up at her own son. "I *would* do anything to protect my child." Then she again pinned Lindsay with a glare. "But know this . . . if something happens to *my* child while you're trying to protect *yours*, I'll do whatever is necessary to make sure you regret it."

"I understand completely."

~~~

"Are you two done discussing me as if I'm not here?" Anger rolled off Aiden in waves.

"Yes, I think we are." Joann dismissed him and addressed Lindsay again. "Now, how are you feeling? I don't know if Aiden mentioned it, but I'm a nurse. He said you were getting close to your due date?"

Aiden was dumbfounded at how his mother and Lindsay could sound as if they hated each other one minute, and then talk like best friends the next.

Conner had been right. All you could do was try not to get tangled up in their moods and logic.

"Yes, only a few more weeks," Lindsay confirmed.

"Have you been seeing a doctor regularly?" Joann inquired.

With a little laugh, Lindsay turned to look at Aiden. "Now I see where you get it from." She returned her attention to Joann. "Yes, I see a doctor as often as I can. I carry my file with me so each one I see knows my history."

"I take it Aiden already asked you about this?"

"Yeah, and I bit his head off for it." Lindsay smiled up at him. "I'm just not used to people second-guessing me about this pregnancy. The last doctor I saw said everything looked right on schedule and that he thought it would be a couple of weeks yet."

Joann voiced one of Aiden's top concerns. "What happens if you go into labor before you settle things with the baby's grandfather?"

"I'm hoping that doesn't happen, but if it does, we'll just have to handle it. Becca's assured me that everything I might need will be at the cabin. If not, Aiden could probably get it. But I'm not going to dwell on it. The doctor said I had a couple more
~~~

weeks. This whole mess should be cleared up by then."

A look passed between Becca and Joann, and it made Aiden nervous. That look told him that they may know something that Lindsay didn't. He just hoped it wasn't serious.

Ben, Mia, and Amber joined the group then, and Aiden finished the introductions. They also brought news that dinner would be served in half an hour, so the group moved back inside and into the dining room.

~~~

The next couple of days passed too quickly for Aiden. Her visit, overall, had been a good one. All three of his parents had become fast friends, and that eased his mind a great deal. It was one less thing he would have to worry about while trying to take care of Lindsay.

His mother did pretty well adjusting to all the magic, too. The day of her departure, Joann requested to sit in on some of his tutoring.

Aiden had been working with his dad outside when Joann joined them.

"Do you mind if I watch?" she asked. "I'd like to learn more about this side of my son."

"No, not at all," Conner told her. "You can even help us out."

"Me? How?" She sounded surprised.

"We're working on conjuring," his father explained. "Aiden needs to be able to call up anything at a moment's notice."

"Okay. Tell me what to do."

Aiden caught the sheen of excitement in her eyes at the thought of being involved in his training, and he smiled at her eagerness.

"I want you to call out an item, anything you can think of, and Aiden will conjure it."

She gave it some thought and then turned her focus to
~~~

Aiden. "My grandmother's teapot that you broke when you were thirteen."

That was so not what Aiden had thought she'd say. "Really?"

"Yes, really. I loved that teapot."

Shaking his head, Aiden brought the image of it to his mind. He saw the light and dark green of the leaves that made up the background, and the many different colored flowers which overlaid it. When he had it right, he brought it back into existence.

As it appeared on his outstretched hand, he heard his mom gasp. For all her bravado, the world of magic was still inconceivable to her.

Stepping forward, he handed her what he'd made. Tears shimmered in her eyes as she took it. He remembered how she'd cried when he'd broken it, and now she cried again as he returned it to her whole.

She cradled it to her chest for a moment and then shook off the emotions, looked up at him, and grinned.

"A Bloody Mary with the works, please."

Aiden rolled with laughter and made what his mom deemed the best cocktail she'd ever had—topped with "the works," consisting of a wedge of pickle, a couple of huge green olives, a cube of pepper jack cheese, a thin stick of pepperoni, a spicy pepper, and of course, a stalk of celery.

Holding the teapot and sipping on her drink, she called out a few more things before Conner stepped in to switch Aiden's training to pyrokinesis.

"Pyro? As in *fire?*" she asked. "I don't think I'm going to like this."

"It'll be fine, Mom. I hardly ever set fire to anything on accident anymore," he joked.

She narrowed her eyes at him and took a bite out of the celery. "Smartass."

Joann sat silently through a game of witch's skeet, and she

watched closely as he made a two-foot piece of log burst into flame with just a thought. She chewed on an olive as he ignited and extinguished fire after fire.

When his father ended the training for the day, she walked up to Aiden and hugged him to her.

"I'm not crazy about this ability of yours to start fires," Joann admitted, "so please promise me you'll only use it as a last resort, and only when absolutely necessary."

Aiden wanted to laugh but knew better; he could tell by her expression she was being completely serious and honest.

With a nod and salute, he dutifully agreed. "Yes, ma'am."

He'd already known he'd been blessed with a great adoptive mother, but now he felt twice as fortunate for her having accepted the changes in him without batting an eye. A mother's love truly was unconditional.

Before he knew it, it was time to take his mom back to the mainland for her trip home. He hated to see her go, but Aiden dropped her off at her car with a promise to keep her updated on the situation with Donnelly, as well as Lindsay's pregnancy. He said his good-byes and headed back to the manor, ready to turn his attention to the confrontation to come.

The first order of business was to get him and Lindsay to the cabin undetected, and then to get prepared for whatever Steven's father had planned.

Aiden had been toying with an idea that might bring this to a head quickly but had yet to pass it by any of the others. It involved tracking Carl down and having a little chat man to man, witch to witch. He knew his family would try to talk him out of it, but if he could make it clear that Lindsay and the baby were under Marquand protection, maybe Carl would back off.

Until Aiden worked out more of the logistics of his plan, he'd keep it to himself. He'd focus on one step at a time, and the next step was getting to the cabin.

Surprisingly enough, it went off without a hitch.

They took one of the many boats the Marquands owned and docked farther down the coast from the main harbor in Charlevoix. This put them closer to the land the hunting lodge was situated on and away from prying eyes.

His parents had driven over previously and left a car packed with all their clothing and essentials near where they would dock. There'd be a short hike from the boat to the car, but it wasn't anything Lindsay couldn't handle.

Everything went smoothly, and soon they were pulling into the driveway of the Marquand hunting lodge.

~~~

Lindsay was shocked when she first saw where they would be staying. When Aiden had told her about it, she'd pictured a small, one-room shack in the woods—very rustic and very close confines. She hadn't wanted to think about them both living there, together, for however long it took.

How would she handle it if she bumped into him every time she turned around? The way her body reacted to his, she could very well get into trouble being in such close proximity to him for any length of time.

That thought alone had caused her some doubtful moments.

But she should have known better. Everything the Marquands owned was magnificent.

The lodge was a single-story structure which boasted at least four bedrooms. It had to be close to three thousand square feet. Bumping into each other wouldn't be a problem. Unless, of course, they *wanted* to bump into each other.

Shit, back up. Lindsay straightened her spine, hardening her resolve. There would be no bumping into each other. No bumping of any kind. Period.

"Wow, this is some place," Aiden echoed her initial thoughts. "Not quite what I had pictured in my mind."
~~~

"No, me neither. Though I should have considered the castle they live in."

"Yeah, there is that," he laughed.

After checking it out, Aiden suggested they take the rooms adjoined by a bathroom. That way, if she were to call out for any reason, he would be close enough to hear her.

"That's fine," Lindsay agreed.

Over the next hour, they unloaded the car and unpacked what they'd brought. Aiden was already in the kitchen when Lindsay got there. He was bent over with his head in a chest freezer. She hadn't realized she'd stopped in her tracks and was staring at his ass until the sound of his voice snapped her out of it.

"Hey, what do you feel like having for dinner?" Aiden called from inside the freezer. "We have chicken, steaks, and pork chops, just to start. When they said they were having this place stocked, they weren't kidding. There's enough food in here to feed the whole family for a month. So whatever you have a taste for, we probably have it."

She was glad he hadn't noticed and caught her. As it was, it took her a moment to gather herself enough to speak. "Anything is fine. Something quick and easy."

<div align="center">~~~</div>

Aiden fought to regain control of his body before turning to face her. He'd been aware of her as soon as she'd walked into the room. He'd literally felt her eyes on him. Everywhere her gaze had landed had become overly warm, especially his ass. She must have lingered on that particular part of his anatomy for a while.

He hadn't failed to notice the wall she'd put between them since the night she'd slept in his arms. He'd just been so preoccupied with his mother's visit, he hadn't done anything about it. But now that they were here alone, he would start to chip away at it.

If they planned to get through this alive, they needed to rely on each other completely. She couldn't hesitate to call for him if she were ever in trouble.

Besides that, he didn't like the idea of her distancing herself from him, and he wanted the barrier gone.

When Aiden finally swung around, his face was devoid of any sign of his thoughts. "I noticed some shaved ham in the refrigerator. How about grilled ham and cheese sandwiches?"

"That sounds great. Do you need any help?"

"Nope. I can handle tonight's dinner. You just sit back and relax."

"Are you sure?"

"Absolutely. Have a seat."

Lindsay sat at the table and watched while he worked. "How long do you think it'll take Carl to find us here?"

"Now that we're away from the safety of the manor, I doubt it will be long. A few days maybe." Aiden looked at her over his shoulder. "If he's as powerful as we think, he had to have known where you were, but just didn't want to take the chance of going up against my whole family. With it just being the two of us now, that will probably change."

"What then?"

"I guess we wait and see how he wants to handle it." Aiden brought the food to the table and set a plate in front of her before taking his own seat.

"What if . . ."

"Let's not make ourselves crazy with 'what ifs'." Aiden placed his hand over hers on the table. "I'm sure we'll know soon enough. Now eat. I'm sure the baby's hungry, even if you're not."

When the lights flickered, they both grinned and dug into their sandwiches.

12

Aiden awoke early the next morning and made his way into the adjoining bathroom for a shower. When he stepped out moments later, he knotted a towel around his hips and let his body air-dry. He stood in front of the mirror and prepared to shave the night's worth of dark stubble from his face.

He'd just lathered up and taken a couple of swipes with the razor when the door to the other bedroom opened. He glanced over, ready to make some teasing remark, but the look on Lindsay's face brought him up short.

She was devouring him with her eyes.

There was no other word for it, and he was helpless but to stand there and let her do it. He felt like he was trapped in some kind of spell, and that spell was Lindsay.

Damn! How was he going to make it through this and stay sane? Why did she have such an effect on him? He'd never been so quick off the mark with any other woman.

Still caught in her gaze, he watched as she slowly backed out of the bathroom and closed the door. Once it was firmly shut, he heard her voice call through it. "Let me know when you're finished."

"All right," he choked out. Aiden dropped the razor into the sink and grabbed the counter with both hands. He took a couple of deep breaths and hoped that would calm his heart enough to keep it from busting through the front of his chest.

Over the next few minutes, his breathing and pulse slowly returned to normal. But since his hands still had a slight tremor, he took great care as he finished shaving.

When he was done, he went to the door on his side, and even though it was cowardly, called out just before he closed it tight. "The bathroom's all yours."

<p style="text-align:center">~~~</p>

Lindsay didn't answer; she couldn't. Her mind and body reeled.

The sight of Aiden in nothing more than a low-slung towel had shaken out all the cobwebs still in her sleep-clogged head.

In the time it had taken her brain to tell her body to back out of the room and close the door, she'd gotten herself an eyeful of one Aiden Marquand.

Broad shoulders, muscled arms, and a flat, hard stomach. Her eyes had slid lower and followed the thin line of dark hair that led down, down, and finally out of sight under the edge of the towel to areas she was better off not thinking about.

Thick, muscular thighs were next, leading to calves that looked nothing but manly, and then well-shaped feet which completed the whole package of a man who not many women— not those in their right minds anyway—would turn away.

The emotions she'd been bombarded with when she'd seen Aiden had flattened her. Backing away, she'd only made it as far as the bed before collapsing onto the edge of it. And there she'd sat as she tried to sort through all she was feeling. Lindsay desperately ignored the heat pooling in her lower body. She was eight months pregnant with another man's baby, for God's sake. This couldn't be happening.

But it was, so she needed to put her big girl panties on and figure out what to do about it. She'd tried to ignore it, but it hadn't worked. Keeping her distance hadn't been very successful either.

Did she really have feelings for Aiden? She'd loved Steven dearly, but this . . . this was something altogether different.

With Steven, their love had been soft and sweet and romantic. A first love. A young love.

What she felt every time she was with Aiden was anything but sweet; it was a flash fire. A volcanic eruption. Hot and combustible. Consuming.

She still missed Steven; she probably always would. But had she, somewhere along the way, begun to deal with his death?

Shouldn't that take longer than six months?

Did that somehow indicate her feelings for Steven weren't as deep as she had thought them to be? *No.* She'd loved him with all she'd had for the time she'd had him. Maybe she only felt this way about Aiden, because they'd been thrown into this crisis together. She tried to tell herself that's all it was, but she knew she couldn't lie to herself. It felt real. Too real.

How am I going to deal with this?

Well, whatever she decided, it would take more time to think through than she could do sitting here.

She slowly stood and crossed to the bathroom again. Opening the door, she paused to make sure he was really gone. She'd have to remember to knock in the future, and she would be sure to tell him to do the same, so he didn't walk in on her while she was in the tub or something.

Shit. Just the thought of that possibility was getting her all flustered again. Lindsay banished those thoughts from her mind and closed the door behind her.

~~~

Aiden was setting the coffee pot back on the hot pad when Lindsay finally made an appearance. He'd decided he'd take his lead from her about what had happened that morning. If
~~~

she brought it up, they'd discuss it. And if she wanted to ignore it, then he'd do the same. He really wasn't ready to get into it yet either. His emotions still had some raw edges, and he wasn't ready to feel his way over them just yet.

"Mmm, that coffee smells great. I wish I could have a cup," Lindsay said after a brief hesitation.

Okay, we're ignoring it. I can do that. "Well, someone must've thought of you, because this is decaf. I'll pour you a cup; how do you like it?"

"Black is fine." She walked right past him on her way to the refrigerator, not meeting his gaze at all. "Since you made dinner last night, I'll do breakfast. What sounds good?"

"I'm not picky. What sounds good to you?" Aiden pulled another cup from the cupboard, poured, and left it on the counter for her before turning and walking to the table.

"Omelets okay?" she asked after a quick inventory of the refrigerator.

"Yeah." Aiden felt his mood deteriorate the longer he tried to pretend as if nothing had happened.

Breakfast was made in tension-filled silence. And Aiden only lasted halfway through the meal before he couldn't take it anymore.

"You know what? This is stupid. Is this the way it's going to be for the whole time we're here? Uncomfortable silences and conversations a couple of strangers could have? We're going to be here for God knows how long. We can't be walking on eggshells the entire time."

His outburst snapped her back from wherever her thoughts had been. "What?"

"So you walked in on me this morning—big fucking deal. I wasn't naked, and you know what? Nothing happened, and nothing is *going* to happen. Yes, I obviously think you're beautiful and sexy and would love nothing better than to kiss you senseless, among other things. But that's not going to happen, so you can relax. I'm not stupid. I know you're still grieving for your husband, and you've been going through some pretty traumatic shit for the last few months, so the last thing I'm going to do is put more pressure on you. I'm not some high school kid who's ruled by his hormones. I know there are some things I just can't have, and this is one of them. So let's go back to being friends and stop tiptoeing around each other."

Appetite gone, Aiden pushed his plate away and picked up his coffee. He couldn't tell what Lindsay was thinking; she had yet to meet his eyes.

"Yes, I am still grieving for my husband," she finally said. "And I have been under a lot of stress lately, but I can handle all that."

Lindsay pushed her uneaten eggs around her plate.

"What I can't seem to handle, is that I *want* you to kiss me senseless, among all those other things."

Aiden sat in shocked silence as Lindsay dropped her fork to her plate and stood.

She set her half-eaten breakfast on the counter before refilling her coffee. With her back still to him, she continued.

"What I'm having the hardest time with, is that my husband has only been gone a few months. Shouldn't it take longer than that to get over someone you've loved? Someone whose baby I'm still carrying? Why am I feeling this way about you? Is it because of the situation, or is it something else? Something more?" Finally she turned back to face him and pinned him with a look of such torment, he knew her feelings were genuinely conflicted.

"I just need time to figure it all out." She looked down into her coffee cup. "I just need some time."

Aiden was speechless. Talk about sucker-punched. That was the last thing he would have ever expected her to say. That she felt some of the same things he did, and so soon after Steven's death. Yeah, he could see where she might feel as though she'd betrayed his memory, and he didn't want to do anything that would make that worse.

"Lindsay . . ." He rose and started towards her.

"No." She raised her head and held up her hand to stop not only his words, but also his advance. "Don't say anything. Just give me some space to work through it. And I hope in the meantime, that we *can* get back to being at ease with each other. But there's just one more thing I need to get off my chest."

"What's that?" After what she'd already told him, he couldn't imagine what she would say next.

"You in that towel? Wow! Had a major meltdown there."

"Thanks, I think." Aiden slipped his hands into his front pockets. He wasn't sure how to feel—embarrassed or smug that she'd liked what she'd seen.

With some of the strain relieved, they were able to work together to wash the breakfast dishes. He'd just dried a plate she'd handed him when his cell phone rang. Setting the plate aside, Aiden reached into his pocket for the phone.

"Hello?"

"Hey, buddy. How's life on the run?"

"Hey, Jack. Not too bad so far." Aiden glanced over at Lindsay and smiled. "This place isn't exactly what you'd call roughing it. How are you guys?" Aiden resumed his seat at the table.

"We're good. Business is good; new clients coming in all the time. Marissa's badgered me into letting her get more involved in the business, and I have to admit she's been a lot of help. Her visions have aided in cracking some of the cases. But don't tell her I said that."

Aiden heard Marissa's voice in the background. "I heard that. It just burns your ass that I proved you wrong in the Lawrence case. If it hadn't been for me, you would have spent half the day on a wild goose chase."

"I'll show you a wild goose," Jack taunted. "Come here, you

little witch."

The next sounds that came through the phone were not that of Jack and Marissa talking.

"Hey! Hey, break it up. I'm not going to sit here and listen to you two making out."

No answer. "Oh, this is ridiculous," Aiden muttered and glanced at Lindsay, who stood against the counter smiling. She was apparently enjoying his predicament.

"Jack!" Aiden yelled. "Hey, are you guys about done?"

"No, not nearly. But the rest can wait. So, what did you need?" Jack asked him.

Aiden rolled his eyes. "*You* called *me*, dumbass. Did you have something for me on the Donnellys?"

"Oh yeah, right. Yeah, I did."

"Well, what did you find out?"

"It turns out that Steven broke off all ties with his father about six years ago. Up until that time, everything seemed to be fine. He never really got involved in his father's business, but he still lived at home, and they seemed to be a happy family. All of a sudden, Steven just up and left. No contact between them at all. I haven't been able to find anything on why the split happened, but I'm still looking. Maybe Lindsay knows something she doesn't realize."

Aiden absorbed what Jack had said. "What about his mother? Where does she fit into all of this? Could we count on her for any help?"

"I wouldn't," Jack told him. "From everything I've dug up, she's ruled by her husband. If she did help Steven to escape his father, I'd be surprised. I think Carl has beaten her down for so long, she probably doesn't go to the bathroom without asking him first."

That was as Aiden had guessed, but it would have been nice to have someone on the inside. "Okay, thanks. If you find anything else, let me know. I really appreciate this, Jack."

"No problem. That's what family's for."

After Aiden disconnected, he turned to Lindsay and filled her in on what Jack had discovered. He asked if she knew anything about the split between Steven and his father.

"He never gave any details as to what had happened; he didn't like to talk about it." Lindsay scrubbed the counter as she answered. "He only stressed that his family was evil, and he asked me to avoid them at all costs and never have anything to do with them. I tried to find out more, but the only thing Steven would ever say was that his father had gone too far."

It didn't take a genius to see Lindsay was telling the truth. "Okay. We'll just have to wait and see what Jack and Marissa turn up."

Lindsay draped the washcloth over the sink divider and turned to face him. "Why did you ask about Margaret?"

"My dad and uncle wondered if she would be of any help against Carl. I was doubtful but thought I should check the possibility."

"Jack doesn't think so?"

"No, he believes she's been under Carl's thumb for so long, she wouldn't dare risk doing anything against him. Did Steven ever talk about her?"

"Not really. I always assumed she was included in the evil he warned me against. You don't think she's in it with Carl?"

"I honestly don't know." Aiden was frustrated at all the unknowns. "My family said Margaret always seemed like a nice person before she married Carl, and that she's always just been in the background since then."

"I'd like to think someone in Steven's family was sane, but I just don't know." Lindsay rubbed her hands over her stomach, obviously worried about her baby. "I don't think I'd take a chance where she's concerned."

"No, and I don't either. Jack's right; she's probably so scared of Carl, she'd never consider crossing him."

13

The next couple of days passed by pretty uneventfully. They talked most of the time or watched movies from the extensive collection of DVDs.

Aiden still worked on his magic skills—he wanted to make sure he was ready when the time came. He felt more confident with the whole spell-casting side of it, too. Other than a few mishaps he wouldn't mention.

Lindsay was still troubled over what she was feeling, and he hated that she had to go through that. He'd done and said everything he could think of to ease her mind, but she had to work this out for herself. She'd started taking walks around the cabin in the afternoon to think and get some exercise.

He didn't really like it, so he made her promise to stay close. And he figured the baby would let him know if something were to happen, even though he hadn't heard from him or her since back at his parents' house.

When Lindsay came in from her walk on the afternoon of the third day, Aiden could see that something was different. Her demeanor had changed—lightened somehow.

Suddenly he knew. She'd made her decision.

She crossed the living room to stand in front of him. "Can we talk?"

"Yeah, sure." When Aiden sat down on the couch, she moved to the other side and joined him there.

"I'm sorry I haven't been the greatest roommate for the last few days."

"It's all right. I know you've had a lot on your mind."

"Well, I've come to the conclusion that I have to go on living. When I'm with you, I feel alive again. Since Steven died, I've been so busy running, that I've only just existed. I don't know what this thing is between us, or if it will even last, but I want to feel again. I'm sure Steven would want that for me. You have to know, though; I will always have a place in my heart for him. He's my baby's father, and I won't take that away from him, or our child. But I would also like to see where this goes with you."

"I was hoping you would say that." Aiden leaned in and kissed her, giving in to the temptation he'd denied himself for so long now.

Although the kiss was everything he thought it would be, he held back, not wanting to let it go too far or overwhelm her. She may have come to a decision to try and get over Steven, but he knew he had to take it slow.

Aiden wrapped her in his arms and just held her. Until he felt her stiffen.

"What's wrong? What is it?" Aiden looked down at her.

She didn't answer. Something over his shoulder had caught her attention. Slowly Aiden turned, unsure of what to expect. Had Carl found them? Had he gotten into the house somehow?

When he swiveled around, his fears were confirmed. A man stood in the middle of the living room, watching them.

Aiden and Lindsay jumped to their feet. He placed himself between her and the stranger. "Who the hell are you, and how did you get in here?"

The stranger held up his hands to show he meant no harm. "Relax, Cousin. I'm not here to harm either one of you."

Cousin? "Gideon?" Aiden was astonished, but now that he actually looked at the other man, he could see his striking resemblance to Marissa. The same light brown hair and green eyes that were just a shade off from hers. "What are you doing here?" Aiden narrowed his eyes. "Wait a minute, *are* you here?"

"Not really." Gideon laughed, then looked past Aiden and acknowledged Lindsay. "Hi, you must be Lindsay."

"Uh, yeah," Lindsay stammered.

"Linds, this is my cousin, Gideon. Marissa's brother," Aiden clarified.

"I thought he was still missing?" Lindsay asked.

"He is. Kind of," Aiden qualified.

"What do you mean 'kind of'?"

Aiden tried to explain. "The Marquands have a pretty extensive well of power to draw from, and usually we each have some combination of three."

"Like you having healing, conjuring, and fire, or Marissa's visions, air manipulation, and telekinesis."

"Exactly. But Gideon here got lucky enough to have been born with *all* of them. We found mention in the family journals of these rare witches, but no one can remember the last time one was born." He paused and let that sink in.

"My God," Lindsay said, stunned.

Gideon picked up the explanation. "Like my cousins, my powers were bound after the coven ordered Roanik's attack, and we were lost. But because my abilities are so varied, it's taking time for them all to re-emerge, and for me to get a grasp on how to control them."

"I knew about the attack, but what's the coven?" she asked.

"They were behind what happened thirty years ago. It's made up of seven people," Aiden told her, "one leader and six followers. No one knows who they are, or where they came from. But their ultimate goal is to possess Gideon's power."

Aiden's explanation was interrupted by Gideon. "Until I have full use and control of *all* my magic, I'm better off staying out of sight."

Lindsay seemed to be taking it all in as Aiden watched her closely.

"But you're here now. Aren't you afraid they'll find you?"

"Technically, I'm not here," Gideon grinned.

Lindsay turned to Aiden in confusion.

"One of Gideon's talents is astral projection," Aiden explained. "What we're seeing is just an image of him. He usually uses it to come to us, since we can't go to him." A thought clicked into Aiden's mind and caused his gaze to swing back to Gideon. "And he usually only shows up when there's trouble." He turned to fully face his cousin. "Something's going to happen. What is it?"

"I'm not sure," Gideon told him.

"What do you mean?" Lindsay must have felt his tension elevate. "What's going on?"

"I had a vision that you were in danger," Gideon explained. "Men were surrounding you, stalking you."

"What else did you see?" Aiden asked when no other information was offered.

"Nothing more than that. For some reason, they only seem to be watching," Gideon told them.

"It's got to be Carl's men," Aiden said, almost to himself as he paced the living room. "I wonder what they're waiting for."

"Probably for this baby to be born." Lindsay wrapped her arms around her stomach protectively.

"If that's the case, they'll be out there for a while," Aiden grinned. "I hope it starts to rain. Or snow. Can we make it snow? Hail maybe?" he asked Gideon.

"I'm sure we can." Gideon laughed, then sobered. "But you both need to be on your guard."

"Is he going to make a move?" Aiden asked, serious again.

"I haven't seen that yet," Gideon answered.

"If you do see anything else, please let us know. We'll need all the help we can get."

"You have everything you need already," Gideon said

cryptically, looking between Aiden and Lindsay. "But yes, I will let you know if I see or sense anything else. Be safe, Cousin." And with that, Gideon was gone.

"That was . . ." Lindsay started, but evidently didn't know how to finish the thought.

"Yeah," Aiden agreed as he contemplated Gideon's message.

"Does he do that often?"

"No. He only seems to pop up when things are getting bad. With his gifts, he knows just about everything. He showed up to help Jack when Marissa was kidnapped by Roanik, and maybe one other time before that. This is the first I've seen him, though."

"So, no one knows where he is or where he's been for the last thirty years?"

"Nope. But that's not stopping the family from trying to find him. They just have to do it discreetly. If the coven were to get to him first, there's no telling what would happen."

"Okay." She paused. "Wow."

"Yeah, it's a lot to take in. But that's a fight for another day. Right now, we have our own problems to deal with."

"The men your cousin saw surrounding us," Lindsay concluded.

"Yeah." Aiden wondered if this would be his chance to put his plan into motion.

"You're thinking of something. What is it?"

He'd have to be more careful if she could read him that easily. "Nothing really. Just running through some ideas. None of them are taking shape yet."

"You'll tell me when one of them does, right?"

He hesitated, not sure what to say to her. Until he could figure out how to confront Carl and still keep her safe, he couldn't take the chance of her catching on to his plan.

"I won't be kept in the dark, Aiden. I have to know what's happening," she demanded.

"I know. But until I can come up with something which will keep you and the baby out of harm's way, there's nothing to tell."

He could see in her eyes she wanted to argue, but she let it go instead. "All right. So what do we do with what we know?"

"I think our best bet is to just go on as we have been. They don't know *we* know they're out there. We keep an eye on them as they keep an eye on us. I think I'll start joining you on your walks every afternoon, just to be safe."

"Won't they know something is up with that?"

"No, because all they'll see are two people taking a leisurely stroll. I'm thinking we could even hold hands." Aiden advanced closer to her. "Maybe kiss a little." He wrapped his arms around her middle, conscious of what lay within. "Or maybe a lot." Aiden bent his head and took her mouth with his.

He'd meant to keep the kiss light, but as soon as he felt Lindsay respond, he was lost. Aiden knew he shouldn't take things so far so soon, but he was powerless to stop.

The feel of her in his arms was better than he had ever imagined. The way her tongue dueled with his was almost more than he could handle. His blood flowed hot and heavy through his veins. It rapidly left his brain for a location further south. One that hadn't ruled his actions since he was a teenager.

His hands traveled with no command from him. They went from the nape of her neck, over her shoulders, down her back, and over her nicely-rounded ass, stopping briefly to squeeze and fondle, before continuing up her sides to finally cup her breasts. Even through her shirt, he found the small pebbled peaks that gave away her arousal. Groaning, he surrounded the twin mounds with his hands and began to knead them.

Her gasp of discomfort stopped him as nothing else could have. The sound that came from her lips was as effective as a bucket of ice water being dumped over his head. "God, I'm sorry. I didn't mean for that to go so far. Did I hurt you?"

"No, you didn't hurt me," Lindsay assured him. "My breasts are just a little tender, that's all."

"Are you sure you're okay?"

"Yes, I'm okay." She reached up to touch the side of his face. "Everything was fine."

"Everything? No feelings of guilt popping up?" Aiden asked gently.

"I couldn't think, let alone feel, anything other than you," she told him truthfully.

"What about now? Are you okay with what's happened and where it could lead? Or will lead?" Aiden almost hated to hear her answer but prepared himself for whatever she might say.

"How about I make you a promise? If at any time I feel it's too much for me to handle, or I start to feel uncomfortable with how things are progressing, I'll tell you."

Aiden studied her face. He looked for any sign that she may be having a hard time with this. He didn't find any. "I guess that's all I can ask. Just promise me you won't hide what you're feeling, regardless of whether it's good or bad."

"I promise," she agreed. "Now, how about we make dinner and discuss some of our options regarding Carl and the men he has watching us?"

14

They threw around ideas for more than two hours and were no closer to finding answers than they were before.

Aiden refused to let Lindsay get anywhere near Carl or anyone associated with him. And Lindsay refused to let Aiden do anything without her. So they were at a standstill.

What Lindsay didn't know was that Aiden's plan to confront him had finally taken form. As he stood at the window in the living room, he thought over what obstacles were in his way. The biggest one he would have to work around was Lindsay herself. He would have to come up with some way to get out of the cabin without her knowledge, so he could have a chat with one of Carl's men in private.

He had a message to send—one that would either bring this whole thing to an end, or bring the fight straight to their door. He hoped for the former but would prepare for the latter.

Lindsay called his name. He could tell by the tone of her voice that she'd spoken to him more than once. "What?" he turned towards her.

"Where'd you go?" Lindsay asked.

"Not too far away. Just lost in thought," he hedged. "Did you need something?"

"I was asking what you wanted to do for the rest of the evening."

Aiden knew what he would like to do with her for the

foreseeable future. Live out all the fantasies that had constantly rampaged through his mind lately. A few would obviously have to wait until after the baby, but a lot of them could be achieved even in her current state.

The moment she started towards him, he knew his thoughts had been written all over his face.

She stopped right in front of him and reached up to bring his head down to meet hers.

The kiss blew him away, and he quickly lost control. He knew he needed to put a stop to this or at least slow it down.

Aiden called on reserves he didn't know he had and separated his mouth from hers. "Lindsay, we shouldn't . . ."

"Yes, we should."

Mindful of her belly, he lowered her down onto the living room floor and tried again to slow things down. "Linds, honey . . ."

"Aiden, shut up."

Aiden looked deep into her eyes just to assure himself she was really okay. What he saw put all doubts to rest. He gave in and lowered his head back down to hers. "Okay. Shutting up now."

"It's about damned time," she gave him a sexy grin.

Now that he actually had her in his arms, he wasn't quite sure where he wanted to begin. So many options, but what called to him most were her breasts. He'd always been a breast man, but he remembered what she'd said earlier about them being tender. Determined to keep control and be gentle with her, he broke away from her hot mouth to watch her blue eyes turn smoky as he aroused her.

Propped up on his right elbow, he ran his left hand down the valley between her breasts and back up again, around the outside of one and then the other, forming a figure eight around them. Slowly, and ever so gently, he cupped her breast in his hand and found her nipple through her shirt with his thumb and forefinger. He rolled it back and forth between his fingers, becoming increasingly aroused at her response.

She arched her back up off the floor as she searched and begged for more, but he kept his touch soft and slow.

Aiden needed to feel her silky skin beneath his hands. He reached down and found the hem of her shirt. He wanted it off; he needed it gone.

Its upward path was met with resistance. She grabbed hold of the hem and pulled it back down.

"Don't. Leave it on," she pleaded.

Surprised by her request, he brought his gaze back up to her face. "Why? What's wrong?" he asked tenderly.

She looked away before she spoke. "No one other than me and my doctor has seen me without my clothes since Steven died. I'm eight months pregnant and as big as a house. I have stretch marks that make my stomach look like a road map and . . ." She paused, placing her hands around her middle, "my belly button has started to poke out."

Aiden waited for her to look at him before he answered. "And you think that's going to bother me?"

"It would bother anyone. Don't get me wrong—I love being pregnant. I wouldn't change it for anything, but lately it's not so cute anymore."

"You don't think so, huh? Let's put it to the test." Aiden rolled to his feet. He reached down for her. "Come on, stand up."

He took the hand he still held and brought it to the front of his jeans where his obvious arousal was demanding freedom. He rubbed her hand up and down his fly, tracing the size of him. "Remember the feel of that." He removed her hand, reached for the hem of her shirt again, and lifted it over her head before she could react. "Okay, now the bra."

"What are you doing?" she asked, unsure.

"A little experiment. Trust me. Take off your bra."

She just stood and stared up at him. He hated that she felt

so self-conscious and embarrassed, but he had a point to prove.

The emotions and uncertainty in her eyes almost made him give in and let her keep her clothes, but he didn't want her to hide anything from him. Not her body, not her feelings, not anything. He strengthened his resolve and waited.

Slowly she removed her bra and dropped it to the floor.

God, she was beautiful.

Aiden felt his shaft jerk at the sight of her and harden even more.

He took her hand in his again and brought it back to the bulge in the front of his pants. "It's still there. I've seen you in all your glory, and it hasn't gone away. I know for a fact it's harder than it was before."

"So, you don't find me repulsive to look at?" she asked sheepishly.

"Far from it," he assured her with a smile. "Now, where were we? Ahhh, yes, I remember." Aiden ducked his head to lightly run his tongue around one of her nipples, which instantly puckered at his touch. He replaced his mouth with his hand as he slid is tongue to her other nipple, and by the time he withdrew, Lindsay's hesitancy was gone.

Aiden ran his hands over her ripe body, over her protruding stomach, up and down her back. When he slid his hands into the back of her jeans and over her butt, she groaned.

He followed the curve of the soft rounded mounds of her ass and pushed both her pants and panties down and over her hips where they fell to the floor.

And there she stood, totally naked before him.

Aiden knew his control wouldn't hold out much longer; he had to have her soon. He turned and grabbed the pillows from the couch and tossed them to the floor.

Once he had a soft nest built for her, he took her hand and lowered her onto it. Aiden laid down beside her and took her mouth in a fiery kiss. His tongue invaded, swept around the inside of her lips, and found the ridges along the edges of her teeth. He gave her a sample of what else he might do with his tongue.

He ran his hand down and over her stomach, and then lower to find the thatch of hair at the juncture of her thighs. Aiden found her hot and wet, just for him. "Oh God, baby," he moaned.

Lindsay went to work on the buttons of his shirt. She fumbled a few times because of what his hand was doing to her, but finally she got the buttons undone and her hands were on him.

Her mouth and hands on his body felt better than he could have imagined. He had dreamt of this so many times he'd lost count, but now that it was a reality, he couldn't believe how incredible she felt on him.

When her mouth found his nipple, he sucked in a breath. When her teeth grazed over it, he completely lost that breath, along with all the others in his lungs.

He was so turned on, it was almost painful in its intensity. His shaft throbbed, and a light sweat broke out all over his body.

"Touch me. Lindsay, I need your hands on me."

Slowly, ever so slowly, her hand slid down his body and found him. She learned the shape and feel of him through his pants, but soon that wasn't enough for either of them.

"Take them off," she demanded.

Aiden stood and quickly stripped out of the rest of his clothes. Before he could join her on the pillows again, Lindsay came up to her knees in front of him, took his shaft in her hands, and smiled up at him.

"You don't have to do that," he told her, but just the thought of that luscious mouth on him had him almost light-headed with anticipation.

"I want to." She leaned forward and ran her tongue from the base to tip, where she made a circle around the head, then across the top.

Aiden shuddered, then moaned in pleasure. This would kill him, he knew it. And if he somehow managed to survive it, he would never be the same again.

The things she was doing with her mouth and tongue had to be illegal. Her teeth scraped over the length of him, and he couldn't take anymore. Pulling away, he laid her down and bent to return the favor.

$\sim\sim\sim$

With the mound of her belly in the way, Lindsay couldn't see what he was doing, which made what she felt that much more intense. When the hot wetness of his tongue found her, she couldn't hold back the cat-like purr that rolled up her throat.

She was unprepared when the first orgasm erupted through her system hard and fast. "Oh. *Oh.*" She was a shaky, sweaty pile of mush, but he wasn't finished with her yet. With his hands and mouth, he drove her up again. This time, he kept her right on the brink. When he felt her climax was close, he would back off and let her calm, just a little, before taking her back up again. She didn't know how many times he did this. She just knew she was going crazy from wanting him. "Now. Now. Please Aiden, now," she panted.

He crawled back up her body before rolling with her until she was on top of him and straddling his hips. Lindsay reached behind her, took him in her hand, and guided him to the entrance of her body.

The head penetrated her soft folds, and she slowly slid down his shaft until she had taken him all the way to the base. She sat completely still for a moment and just enjoyed the fullness of having a man inside of her again. Slowly, she began to rotate her hips in small circles. The action ground their pelvises together, the stimulation sending shock-waves of pleasure throughout her body.

"You're killing me, honey," Aiden ground out.

"Shhh." Lindsay closed her eyes and let her head drop forward, which brought a cascade of her long blonde hair forward.

Leisurely, she moved her body up and down, setting a slow and torturous pace. It had been so long since she'd felt these sensations—having her body filled to stretching, the feeling of a man touching her, loving her. She wanted it to last forever.

Lindsay savored the slow ride until that just wasn't enough. Her movements became faster, her breathing shortened. That must have been the sign Aiden was waiting for, because he grabbed hold of her hips and took over their lovemaking. His thrusts were harder and deeper than hers had been. Before she knew it, her body was erupting in pleasure again.

Aiden thrust one final time and held her tightly to him. They were locked together so closely, she could feel the throbbing of his body as it emptied into hers.

Sated and replete, her head fell forward to rest on his chest.

Slowly, he eased her to the side, wrapped her in his arms, and tucked her head beneath his chin. As their breathing and heart rates returned to normal, Aiden was the first to speak. "Everything okay?"

"Mmm, everything is great," she purred. "Thank you."

"Definitely my pleasure."

15

When Aiden opened his eyes again, the room had grown darker. The sun was setting. They must have dozed off for a while.

He knew he needed to get them both off the floor, but he didn't want to lose the feeling of her naked body next to his.

The baby was awake; it rolled and bumped against the inside of its safe haven.

He rested his hand on her bare stomach to track the movements of the baby within and enjoyed the freedom to do so.

The baby grew more active, and the increased movements roused Lindsay. She dropped her hand to where the baby had given a pretty solid kick. "Come on, sweetie," she muttered, still half asleep. "Ease up a little. Not so hard."

Aiden watched as she came fully awake. He waited for her to remember where she was and with whom. When her eyes finally landed on his, he smiled. "Hi." His nerves settled when she grinned back up at him.

"Hi. Oh, man, did I fall asleep on you?"

"I think we both dozed off for a while." He leaned down and placed a soft kiss on her nose. "We should probably get off the floor though," Aiden suggested, "before neither one of us can move."

"Yeah, these pillows don't seem to be as soft as they were

before." She smiled up at him again, and his heart did a slow roll in his chest. "Or maybe I was just too distracted to notice," she teased.

Aiden lowered his head for another kiss, only this time he couldn't resist her mouth. He traced her lips with the tip of his tongue, and when her lips parted, he settled in to enjoy her.

He trailed kisses down her jaw and neck when she spoke.

"I think we both need some sustenance before we try this again. You know, build our resources back up. I don't know about yours, but mine have been severely depleted, and there's no way I could go another round with you without some fuel."

He pulled away and grinned into that beautiful face. "All right, I get it. You want some food. Come on, I'll help you up."

Over the last few days together, they had worked out their routine in the kitchen. He would take care of cooking the meat, and Lindsay would do the side dishes and salad. In no time at all, they had dinner on the table.

They spent the meal talking about likes and dislikes, their childhoods, and anything else that came to mind.

"Do you have any names picked out yet?"

Her mood dampened a little at his question, and she gave a sad little smile. "Not really. Steven and I had just started to talk about it. We thought we had time to figure all that out."

"What about since then? Surely you've tried out different names in your mind. What about growing up? Don't most girls have the names of all their future children picked out before they even have their first boyfriend?"

"Yeah, sometimes. I guess I just feel bad that Steven wasn't able to make that decision with me, so I've just put off thinking about it."

"Well, I think you need to start thinking about it; that baby will be here very soon. Calling it baby may be cute now, but I don't think I would want to be a sixteen year old boy called Baby."

As he'd hoped, she laughed. "Yeah, I can see where he might get beaten up over something like that."

"At least a daily pounding, if not two," he agreed, trying to sound serious.

"Well, we can't have that. I'll have to come up with something then."

"Let me know if you need any help choosing," he offered. "Being a guy myself, I can give you some insight as to which names will get a guy pounded on, and which ones won't. You're on your own with girl names, though. I wouldn't know anything about that. Though I have always been fond of the name Samantha, or Sami. Nice memories of that name."

Aiden made a point to stare off into space as if thinking about a time long ago.

Her eyes were bright and shined with amusement, and she laughed out loud at his antics. He hated to see her sad, so he tried to keep things light with her as often as possible.

"And why . . ." She could barely speak as she tried to hold back the laughter, ". . . have you always been fond of the name Samantha?"

Before he answered, he put a dreamy look on his face. "First grade, Mrs. Johnson's class, the seat right in front of mine. Samantha Ferris. I loved her as much as my six-year-old heart could." He paused and frowned as if he'd just recalled a bad memory. He knew he was laying it on thick, but he was enjoying this as much as she was. "Though now I think about it, she broke my heart that same year when she let a second grader, Brody Easton, which no kid of mine will *ever* be named, sit next to her at lunch." He turned his frown on her again. "You know what? Never mind. Samantha isn't a good name after all."

Lindsay lost the battle and busted out laughing. Aiden sat back and enjoyed the sound.

"Okay," she told him when she finally caught her breath.

"Samantha is off the list."

"So, what's on your list?" he tried to cajole. "Come on, give me something."

She hesitated for a moment before she finally admitted. "There was a name I always liked when I was a little girl."

"What? Tell me." He liked her like this, laughter in her eyes, cheeks flushed. She was happy at this moment in time, able to forget everything that was wrong in her life.

"I don't know if I should," she hedged.

"Come on, tell me." There was something in her expression he couldn't quite put his finger on.

"Oh, all right. Prudence."

"Prudence?" That was so not what he'd expected. Prudence? It was awful.

"Yeah, I always thought I could call her Prue, for short."

He didn't want to hurt her feelings, so he kept his real thoughts to himself. "That's a . . . nice name. Where did that come from?"

"I had a porcelain doll when I was about four years old, and that was her name. I always thought she was so pretty, I told myself when I grew up, I would name my daughter that to remind me of that doll."

"How . . . sweet." He tried so hard to be supportive. "You, ah, don't think she'd be teased over a name like that?"

"Definitely."

He was floored by her candid answer. "Then why would you name this baby that?"

"I wouldn't."

"But you just said you'd liked that name since you were a child." He was completely confused.

"No, I said I liked that name when I was four years old. I didn't say I liked it now. You asked me if there were any names I liked as a child, and I said there was," trying, unsuccessfully, to hold back her laughter.

"That was so not nice," he told her when he finally figured it out. "Here I was, trying to be nice when you said you'd name your daughter that horrific name, and you were teasing me the whole time. I'll remember that."

His speech only made her laugh harder.

When he saw she didn't buy his hurt feelings act, he laughed, too. "Just for that, you can do the dishes."

"The look on your face is well worth the punishment."

Aiden didn't leave her to do it alone, and by the time they had it all cleaned up it was quite late. But because they had both slept for the better part of the afternoon, neither was tired. They decided to watch some TV for a while.

They only made it about fifteen minutes before they started to kiss, then touch. When neither could take it anymore, they turned off the TV and made their way to Aiden's bedroom.

Lindsay fell into an exhausted sleep soon after they had made love again. Aiden waited until he was sure she was completely asleep before he left the bed.

Silently he picked up his discarded clothes and took them into the living room. Once he was dressed, he moved to stand close to the window.

Standing in the darkened room, Aiden opened his senses. He reached out with his magical abilities, searching for one of the assholes stalking Lindsay.

He pushed the boundaries of his power farther and farther, scanning, probing. *There*! Off to the left, about fifty yards in.

Remembering Gideon's warning about 'men' watching, Aiden continued his hunt. By the time he'd located all four, a light sweat had broken out over his body.

Noting their positions around the cabin, Aiden chose the one he thought he could get to without the others seeing.

Keeping a soft connection, Aiden slipped from the house and took off into the trees, tracking his prey.

Watching every step, Aiden advanced on the henchman. He

didn't come at him directly from the front, but went out wide to take him from the side. Once he had eyes on him, Aiden held up behind a large oak and watched.

Carl's man was sitting on the ground, back against a tree, not moving.

Was the fuckwad sleeping?

Unbelievable.

Aiden approached slowly.

Within reach, he grabbed the guy by the shirt with one hand and slammed the other over his mouth.

He came awake in a panic, but Aiden leaned in and used his body weight to hold him still.

When his captive recognized who had him, his eyes went cold with anger.

Aiden ignored the murderous look. "I have a message I want you to take to your boss. You let him know that Lindsay and her baby are now under the protection of the Marquand family, and if anything happens to either one of them, we'll destroy him. You got that straight?"

The goon only glared at him.

Aiden withdrew the hand holding the shirt, held it up right in front of the guy's face, and conjured a fireball. Holding it close enough so the bastard could feel the scorching heat.

He shrank away from it.

"I'll ask one more time." It wasn't hard to fill his voice with menace and hatred. "Do you understand my message, and will you take it to Carl?"

The man's eyes slowly tracked from the fireball to Aiden, and he gave a short, quick nod.

Aiden held him for a moment longer, then pushed off of him hard and left. As he made his way quickly back to the cabin, he hoped it would change Carl's mind, but he doubted it would be that easy.

When he let himself back into the lodge, all was still silent.

He eased back into the bedroom and slipped out of his clothes again. Lindsay only woke slightly when he crawled back into bed.

"Where did you go?" she mumbled.

"Bathroom," he told her.

"Oh, okay." She was asleep again almost as soon as she settled in next to him.

Aiden lay awake for some time and wondered how Carl would react to his warning.

16

Aiden found out the next day.

He and Lindsay had just come in from their afternoon walk when Lindsay suddenly grabbed her stomach and doubled over in pain. "Oh God. It's the baby. Something's wrong. Aiden, help me!"

Aiden picked her up, carried her to the couch, and laid her down, all the while fear clutching his heart. "What is it? Tell me what's happening!"

"I don't know. Something's wrong. Oh God, it hurts," Lindsay gasped. "Aiden, I don't want to lose this baby! Do something! Call 911! Call anyone, I don't care!"

Aiden was racing for his phone when someone called to him. *"Aiden."*

"Hold on, sweetheart. I'll get help."

"Aiden! I'm fine. Momma and I are both fine," the voice said. *"It's a trick."*

Aiden stopped in his tracks, mind whirling. "What?"

"Aiden, please hurry!" Lindsay pleaded as she panted through the pain.

"It's a trick?" Aiden asked. "Who's doing this?"

"Grandfather. He's making Momma think I'm in trouble. He's out there, waiting. He's close by."

Indecision warred within Aiden. Finally, he made his choice. "Okay, baby, I hope you're right about this." Aiden tamped down his own fear and returned to Lindsay. He knelt next to the couch and stroked a hand over her brow. "Linds, listen to me. You're okay, and the baby's fine. Fight it. The pain isn't real. Carl is making you *think* you're losing the baby, but you're not."

"What are you talking about?" Lindsay gasped out, her eyes filled with despair.

Her terror was killing him. Was he doing the right thing? "Listen to me." He brushed her hair back from her face. "The pain isn't real. Tell yourself that. Come on, you can do it."

"How do you know?" she cried.

"The baby told me. It said Carl was doing this, so you need to fight it. Just keep telling yourself the pain isn't real. Take a deep breath."

Lindsay took a deep, shuddering breath, and as she released it, repeated over and over that the pain wasn't real.

Aiden could see the tension leaving her body as she fought off the phantom pains. "Okay, sweetheart, one more deep breath."

Lindsay did as he asked and gingerly sat up.

"Aiden?"

"Shhh. It's okay, just give me one minute." Aiden shifted his focus to the baby Lindsay carried. "Where is he, sweetie? Do you know where your grandfather is?"

"Out on the road." Now that the panic of the situation was gone, Aiden felt anger and rage replace it.

"I'll be right back. You take care of your momma for a minute." Aiden moved to stand up.

"Aiden? What's going on?" Lindsay demanded.

"You sit right here until I get back. I've got to do this." Aiden left the cabin.

The drive to the cabin twisted and wound through the woods before it came out at the road. Aiden took off into the trees, a straight path to where he hoped to find his target. He ran until he thought he'd pass out, and then ran faster. As he came up to the road, he pulled up short, just inside the tree line.

Two cars were parked there. Aiden focused all his attention on the car closest to him, and within a matter of seconds, it exploded and went up in a ball of flames.

The smoke obscured his view of the second car. He couldn't get a shot at it, and by the time the air had cleared, they were gone. He just hoped the bastard had been in the car that blew up, but he wasn't betting on it.

He turned to head back to the cabin.

When he walked through the door, Lindsay was back to normal. "What the hell was that? It sounded like an explosion. Aiden, what's going on?"

"Donnelly and some of his men were out there. He's the one who made you think you were losing the baby. I blew up one of their cars, but I'm not holding my breath that I got him."

"*No, he got away,*" the baby's voice said.

"Well shit. Better luck next time, I guess," Aiden muttered.

"Why would he do this? Why now?"

Aiden wasn't going to feel guilty for what he'd done. He'd been protecting her and her baby. If she didn't like the way he did that, then that was just too bad.

With a little more belligerence than necessary, Aiden told her about the message he'd sent.

"You did *what?*" she asked in disbelief. With each word, her voice rose a little higher.

"You heard me just fine." Aiden turned and started for the kitchen.

Lindsay grabbed his arm before he'd taken a step. "Don't you dare walk away from me. You stand here and tell me why you did that. And why you felt you had to sneak around to do it."

The madder she got, the more his own temper boiled

"Why are you getting so angry about this?" He kept a tight rein on his temper. He had control of his powers, but sometimes when his emotions ran high, they would still slip his hold. "I was just doing what you asked me to do—protect you and the baby. I figured I would tell him that the Marquand family was behind you now, and that you're off-limits to him. I guess he didn't listen."

"Didn't listen?" Lindsay asked incredulously. *"Didn't listen?* I'd say he listened well enough for it to piss him off! That's the reason he did this to me, isn't it? Isn't it!" She shocked him by thumping him in the chest with her fist. "Why would you risk me and my baby that way? What were you thinking? After everything we've learned about him, what made you think a simple threat would be enough to make him back off? He doesn't let anything or anyone stand in his way when he wants something, and he *wants* this baby."

Her anguish broke through his anger as nothing else could have. He gently held her wrists, so she couldn't hit him again. "I thought if he were going to strike back, it would be at *me*, not at you."

"I told you—he's evil. If you didn't believe me, you should have believed your parents. They told you the same exact thing. He'll do whatever he thinks is necessary to get what he wants. Hell, he probably thought he could kill two birds with one stone. Punish us for the threat, and then wait for us to panic and make a run for the hospital. If he ever gets his hands on me, Aiden, I'm dead."

She was the one to turn away this time, pulling her hands free of his. "God, how could you take a chance like that?"

The devastation in her voice doused what was left of his temper. He pulled her into his arms and fit her back against his front. "I'm sorry, Lindsay. I thought if he knew that you weren't on your own anymore, that you had the magic of the Marquands behind you, that he would be forced to leave you alone, and this would all be over for you. And you're right— he *was* out there waiting, ready to make a move when we left here," he admitted. "I guess I should just leave the macho PI stuff to Jack. He's the one used to dealing with people like this." He burrowed his face into the side of her neck and inhaled her scent. "I'm sorry," he whispered.

She turned in his arms and looped hers around his neck. "I think you're doing fine with the macho stuff. If I didn't, I wouldn't have put the safety of my child in your hands. But if you ever try anything like this again without telling me, I'll rip that macho head of yours right off."

"Understood." He lowered his head to hers and took her mouth in a kiss that was meant to reinforce his apology. When he finally pulled back, he could still see the wariness in her eyes and the pain and terror she'd felt just a short while ago.

"Do you want to go to the hospital to get checked out? Make sure everything's okay?"

"No, you said the baby confirmed everything was fine and I wasn't having a miscarriage. I believe it now that the pain is gone, but at the time I couldn't get away from the thought of losing the baby." She paused briefly. "You know, I wasn't sure how I felt about the connection you seem to have with this little one, but now I'm glad it's there. If you hadn't had that link, we wouldn't be here now, safe. We'd be out there somewhere trying to make it to the hospital, and maybe even trapped by Carl."

Aiden gently followed the contours of her face with his hands. "I'm just glad you're both all right. You came to me to keep the two of you safe, and I almost blew it." One hand molded to the back of her head while the other slid around her waist to press her tightly against him. "I don't know what I would do if anything happened to either one of you. You both have become very important to me."

She leaned back just enough to look up into his face. "We're both fine, and we'll stay that way as long as no one takes any more unnecessary risks."

"Got it. No more grandstanding." He grinned at her, but his

expression sobered almost instantly. "We need to figure out our next step. Now that he knows we know he's out there, he'll be on us hard. We need to make a stand and find a way to get him out of your lives forever."

"I know. But how? I'm scared, Aiden. He's out there just waiting, playing with us," Lindsay admitted as she stepped away from him, walking towards the kitchen.

He followed her into the other room and tried to soothe some of her fears. "He will never get anywhere near you, Linds. I promise you that."

"He's never going to stop, you know. Not until one of us is dead."

Aiden didn't like the sound of defeat in her tone and gripped her arm to turn her towards him. "Well, if that's the case, then we'll just make damned sure it's him."

"Oh, Aiden. What have I done?" Lindsay dropped into one of the kitchen chairs and looked up at him. "Now you're talking about killing someone. You can't do that. You're not that kind of person. You're not like him—like Carl."

Aiden knelt in front of her and took her hands in his. "Lindsay, no one knows what they're truly capable of until they're faced with it. But I damned well *know* that if it came down to him or you, or him and this baby, Carl wouldn't make it out alive. Without a second thought or regrets afterward. Hopefully it won't come to that, but we need to be prepared."

"And how do you suggest we do that?" she asked him, her eyes bright with unshed tears.

"I don't know yet, but we'll think of something." Aiden stood, pulled her to her feet, and held her.

~~~

Later that evening in the living room, Lindsay told him that she needed to make a call to her parents to let them know she
~~~

was all right. "Would you rather I use my cell phone or the house phone?"

"Cell service seems to be a little hit and miss up here, so you might want to use the landline," he explained, rising from the sofa where he'd been sitting. "I'll just go in the other room and give you some privacy to talk."

Before he made it to the door, she called him back. "You can stay; I don't mind. Nothing I tell them is a big secret or anything. You already know everything that's been going on. I just wanted to fill them in so they wouldn't worry. Well, too much anyway." She smiled at him, but it didn't reach her eyes.

"Are you sure?"

"Positive."

Returning to his seat on the sofa, he picked up a book from the coffee table and pretended to read it while Lindsay placed the call.

He was curious about her, about every aspect of her life. He wanted to know everything there was to know about her, including what her relationship was like with her family. She had briefly spoken of them before, but he wanted to know more. He listened while she greeted them.

"Hi, Daddy." Aiden could hear the love she felt for her father in the tone of her voice and knew it must be killing her to be separated from them like this. His resolve to end this nightmare was strengthened that much more, just so she could return to them. "I'm fine and no, the baby hasn't come yet." Whatever her father had said made her laugh, a sound that was quickly becoming a necessity to his life. "I'll be sure to tell him you said that the very next time I see him . . . No, I won't forget. I promise."

Lindsay covered the mouthpiece of the phone with her hand and relayed the conversation. "My dad told me to tell Carl that he needs to find someone else to torment, because this is getting old, and my parents want me home where I belong.

And that if this goes on much longer, that my dad is going to kick his ass good for him." Her attention was pulled back to the other end of the line. "I was just telling Aiden what you said . . . Aiden is the man who's helping me . . . I told you the last time I called that I was thinking about finding someone like Steven and Carl to help me. Well I did, and his name is Aiden, and he's part of a very powerful family—a magical family, the Marquands . . . I know you've never heard of them, but then again, up until I met Steven, you didn't know magic existed either . . . I did check him out, Dad. I'm not totally naive, you know. The Marquands are highly respected in this area, and what's better is that they know Carl. They know what he's like, and what he's capable of . . . Dad, you don't need to do that . . . Dad . . . Dad, no . . ." She puffed out an aggravated breath. "All right, all right. I will." Lindsay held the phone out to him. "He wants to talk to you."

Aiden took the phone and put it to his ear. "Hello, sir."

The voice on the other end of the line was deep and smooth. If Aiden hadn't known the man he was speaking to was around the same age as his parents, he would have guessed he was talking to a much younger man.

"So you're the one helping our Lindsay, huh?"

"Yes, sir, I am."

"You have magic powers then, like Steven did?"

"Yes, sir, I do."

"Are you any good with them?"

"I think I've gotten pretty proficient, sir," Aiden told him honestly.

"What do you mean, you've *gotten* proficient?" Surprise was clear in Lindsay's father's voice.

Aiden felt he owed her parents the truth about his situation. "Well you see, sir, I haven't had them for all that long. They just came back, and I've been learning how to control them."

"What the hell do you mean, they just came back? How do

you expect to protect my daughter and grandchild if you don't even know how to use your own damned powers?"

"Well sir, I may not have had them for the last thirty years, but I *was* born with them, and it's ingrained in me how to use them. I've had more than enough training from my family to be able to protect your daughter and grandchild. And I haven't heard any complaints from either one so far."

"You may have my daughter's approval, but don't even try to tell me you know what that baby is thinking."

"Well, sir, I do sometimes know what the baby is thinking," Aiden told him.

"What, is that some kind of power you have or something?"

"Yes, it is a power—but it's not mine." He glanced at Lindsay to see if she took issue with what he was telling her father.

She wasn't making any 'stop' or 'shut up' motions, so he figured she was okay with it.

"What the hell is that supposed to mean?"

"It's the baby's power, sir. It can talk to me telepathically."

"It can . . . How is that possible? Lindsay just got done telling me that she hadn't had that baby yet. Do you expect me to believe that that baby is talking to you while still inside my daughter?"

"Yes, sir, that's exactly what I'm saying. It's spoken to me on several occasions, and has yet to voice any displeasure at the way I'm handling this. As a matter of fact, it told me that neither one of them would survive this if I weren't helping them."

He waited. He wasn't sure for what, but still he waited until what he had said sank in.

Lindsay's father was silent for the space of a few heartbeats. When he did speak, his voice was subdued. "The baby told you that they wouldn't live through this if you weren't there to help them?"

"Yes, sir, it did."

"How are you going to go about making sure they both survive this, then?"

"We haven't quite worked all that out yet, sir." Aiden met and held Lindsay's gaze before he spoke his next words, not only stating his vow to her father, but reinforcing the one he'd made to her. "But I can promise you that I will do everything in my power to see that Lindsay and this baby are safe and unharmed. I am fully prepared to do *whatever* it takes to make that happen."

Lindsay's father understood what he had implied. "Well, I can see why my daughter feels you're the right man for this. You keep me posted on what's going on there, and you let us know when that baby comes." There was a short pause. "I know I shouldn't ask this, but I will anyway. Since you've spoken to the baby, do you happen to know if it's a boy or a girl?"

Aiden smiled. "No, sir. When kids are little, they all kind of sound the same to me."

"Oh, well, you can't blame me for trying. Now look, Lindsay's mother is here pulling my arm off trying to get the phone out of my hand, so go ahead and put Lindsay back on. But I want you to know that I feel better knowing my daughter is with you right now."

"Thank you, sir. Here's Lindsay back." Aiden handed the phone over to her. "Your mother wants to talk to you now."

"What the hell was that all about, there at the end?" Lindsay asked Aiden.

"We can discuss it later. Right now, your mother wants to talk to you." He could hear her mother calling for her and motioned for her to put the phone to her ear.

Still watching him, Lindsay put the handset to her ear. "Hello, Mom . . . Yes, I'm fine."

17

Aiden walked over to the windows to give Lindsay some privacy, and to contemplate how he was going to keep the promises he'd made to her and her father.

He was vaguely aware of Lindsay's voice in the background while he thought over what needed to be done to eliminate the threat.

What they really needed to do, short of killing him, was find a way to ensure that Donnelly left them alone for the rest of their lives. If everything he'd heard about him were true, then there had to be something he didn't want known to the world.

He knew there were rumors aplenty floating around about Carl killing people who had gotten in his way, his parents included. Was there a way to find out if he had actually killed his parents? Someone somewhere had to know what had happened to them. Or maybe there was a law enforcement agency somewhere that would be more than happy to put an end to his reign. He had to have made plenty of enemies in his last fifty-something years.

He'd have to call Jack and ask him to dig deeper into Carl's past to see if there was some way to get something on him. Maybe they could hold it over his head to make him leave Lindsay alone. That could work if they found something big enough. He'd have to run it by Lindsay and see what she thought.

He was playing with a few more things in his mind when he suddenly became aware of the silence in the room behind him. Turning, he found Lindsay sitting on the couch watching him.

~~~

She'd initially watched Aiden at the window, wondering what he was thinking about, but was soon so engrossed in the conversation with her mom, she'd just about forgotten he was there.

They talked a little longer than they normally did. She figured since Carl already knew where they were, it couldn't hurt anything. Plus, it had been so long since she'd been able to do more than just say hello and that she was okay, that she wanted to take this time and enjoy it.

When she finally hung up and focused on Aiden again, she was amazed to see him juggling two little fireballs in his hand. She was so entranced by what he was doing, she didn't bother to let him know she'd disconnected the call. She watched him in awe.

He didn't seem to be aware of the burning orbs when he finally turned and spoke. "Finished talking to your mom?"

"Yeah, I am. What are *you* doing?" Lindsay asked him.

"Just thinking."

"Do you always do that while you think?" she asked him carefully.

"Do what?"

He was honestly oblivious of his own movements. She dropped her gaze to his hand. "That."

Astonishment flashed through his expression at the flames revolving in his hand. It had to have been a totally subconscious act.

"I didn't realize."

He made a motion as if to stop, but she told him to wait. She
~~~

was curious about these abilities that came so effortlessly, so she stood and walked towards him. As she neared him, she reached out her hand and held it over the top of his, amazed.

"It's real. They're hot." She looked up at him, mouth open. "Can *you* feel the heat? Does it burn?"

"Not really. I mean, I can feel it, but it's not burning me. There's some kind of barrier between the heat and my skin."

"What else can you do with them?"

Before her next breath, they disappeared. Then reappeared, dancing in his hand again.

"That is so cool."

"Watch this." He turned and threw one of the fireballs straight into the fireplace. It landed with a whoosh as it set the logs ablaze.

Her fascination with Aiden's power turned to apprehension. "Is that what you did to that car outside?"

~~~

"Yes."

The way her eyes clouded over told Aiden this may have just gotten too real for her. It was one thing to talk about fighting magic with magic, but to actually see it in action, to see its destructive force, was another thing entirely.

Whatever abilities Steven had had, along with the baby's cute tricks, hadn't prepared her for what magic could really do in the wrong hands. Aiden knew from personal experience it could be dark and sinister. The battle against Roanik had brought that lesson home in a big way.

Lindsay had to realize that the fight ahead could potentially get very nasty.

"I know you haven't really seen this side of magic before, but you need to keep in mind that it's not all flipping lights on and off, or conjuring up sodas and popcorn. It can be dangerous and
~~~

deadly when wielded by someone who doesn't abide by the first rule of Wicca, 'an it harm none'." Aiden lifted her chin so her eyes focused completely on his. "I'm hoping to come up with a way to deal with Carl without anyone getting hurt, but I want you to remember that this could get ugly."

"What way?" There was a glimmer of hope in her stormy blue eyes.

"I've been giving it some thought, and I'm sure there are any number of things he doesn't want known to the world." He led her back to the couch, and once they were settled he continued. "I'm thinking if we could find out a few of those things to use against him, we could share them with the right people—or in his case, the *wrong* people—and he might leave you both alone."

"What on earth could be big enough to make him back down?"

"Think back. Was there ever *anything* Steven may have mentioned about his father?"

"No. We didn't talk about them. He was so adamant I stay away, I didn't want to upset him by asking a lot of questions. We just didn't acknowledge that side," Lindsay told him. "I'm sorry. I just don't think this plan is going to work. Even if we could find proof of something Carl had done, what makes you think he would just leave someone out there who could bring him down? No one has ever been able to prove anything against him."

"There has to be someone," he stressed. "This man has done too much, to too many people, for there to be no evidence of his evil. I still think this might work. I'm going to call Jack and have him start digging deeper. Maybe we could find out what caused Steven to split from his family."

"I don't know if this will help, but I always kind of assumed it had something to do with his mother."

Aiden jumped on that right away. "Why would you think that?"

"Just the way Steven spoke of her the few times he would. I could tell he loved her very much, and it was obvious that it hurt him to not have contact with her. But because of whatever happened between him and his father, he wasn't able to do that. I think Steven felt it was his responsibility to protect his mother, and because of his dad, he wasn't able to."

Back to Margaret, Aiden thought. "She would be someone who knows everything he's done. I keep dismissing her, but I wonder if it would be worth it to pursue her help. We all thought she'd been so beaten down by Carl that she wouldn't do anything against him. But what if we can offer her protection from him? Would she help if we could guarantee she wouldn't have to live under his rule anymore?" Aiden looked down at Lindsay. "This is taking a big leap, but I think we need to try and contact her. See what she says."

"And just how do you plan on doing that?"

"I'm not sure yet. But if you're okay with the idea, it at least gives me a place to start." Now that he had an idea, he wanted to get it rolling. Rising from the couch, he walked over to the phone. "First I want to call Jack and get him started."

Before he could pick up the phone, Lindsay's words stopped him. "Aiden, it's almost midnight. Don't you think it's a little too late to be calling?"

"I think this is important enough to wake him up." He dialed quickly and then listened to the line on the other end ring once, twice, three times. "Come on, Jack. Pick up."

On the fifth ring, it was answered. The voice on the other end was deep and not at all pleased.

"This had better be life or death, or believe me, yours may depend on it."

"Did I wake you?"

"Aiden, man," Jack recognized his voice instantly, "no, but your timing sucks. Speaking of timing, why are you calling me at midnight? What's the matter? Can't you handle one pregnant woman on your own?"

"Damn, who's a grumpy bastard?"

"Let me assure you," Jack returned, "you'd be a grumpy bastard, too, if someone interrupted what you just did."

Aiden cringed. "Okay, way too much information. I won't keep you long. I just wanted to tell you I think we've come up with a plan to deal with Donnelly."

"Okay, you have my attention. Briefly," Jack emphasized.

"Understood. I need to know if you've found anything in your search we can use to hold over his head. Something big enough that he'll disappear for good."

"Blackmail, huh? That could work if we could find the right information. Everything I've found so far has been aboveboard. The face he shows to the world is that of a respected businessman. I've just started to dig past the persona. I'll let you know what I find as I get deeper into it. Now, I have better things to be doing with my time than talking to you, so I'm hanging up now."

Before he could say good-bye, the phone disconnected. "Okay, so I guess he was a little busy."

Lindsay laughed when he smiled at her after hanging up the phone.

"Not too happy to hear from you, I take it?" she asked, amused.

"Not so much. But he did give me a really good idea." Aiden held out his hand, and when she grasped it, he gently pulled her to her feet.

"Oh, and what was that?" She stepped into his arms.

He lowered his head to cover her mouth with his. "This."

"Mmm, very nice. That *is* a good idea."

"I thought so. I say we move this to somewhere more comfortable and see where it leads."

When Lindsay smiled up at him, his heart gave a little stutter.

18

She followed Aiden into his room, stopping beside his bed where he proceeded to divest both of them of their clothes.

Framing her face in his hands, he took her mouth in a kiss so hot and steamy it fogged her brain.

By the time he finished kissing her, she could barely stand, but he wasn't through with her yet. Lowering his head to her breasts, he gave each his undivided attention until both of her nipples were puckered into hard little pebbles.

She was breathless with desire and wanted him to feel the same.

Reaching her hand between them, she found his jutting erection and wrapped her hand around it, giving it a light squeeze.

Her action was rewarded by his sharp intake of breath. When she stroked from the base to the tip and back again, he growled deep in his chest and pulled her hand away.

Before she could voice her complaint, he turned her around, fitting her back to his front where his engorged shaft nestled in the valley of her bottom. Using both hands, he cupped her breasts and rolled her already-sensitive nipples between his very talented fingers and thumbs.

When her hips, of their own accord, started to grind back against his, Aiden brought one hand around to her back. He gently pushed her forward until her upper body was supported on the bed.

Sliding his hand down her back and over her butt, he found her wet, swollen entrance. Aiden removed his fingers and replaced them with the head of his shaft.

Moving both hands to her hips, he controlled the speed and depth of his invasion and entered her, inch by luxuriously slow inch.

Gripping the bed linens in both hands, she moaned, amazed at the new sensations Aiden was setting off in her body. Making love this way changed the angle of his thrust and touched places deep within her. She could feel every inch of his swollen shaft, so thick she was stretched almost to the limit.

~~~

Aiden pulled out just as slowly as he had gone in, enjoying the sensitivity of her inner walls pulling against his manhood, as if to never let him go.

Fuck, how he wanted to slam into her tight, hot, wet body until they were both sated and senseless, but he had enough brain cells left to control the depth of each thrust so he didn't hurt her.

"Aiden, please. Now. Now," she panted.

He knew she was begging for completion, but he held her on that glorious edge for several more strokes.

She started to push back with each of his forward thrusts, enhancing the pleasure for both of them. He felt her internal muscles begin to tighten around him, signaling her impending orgasm.

Reaching around to the front, he found the little nub hidden in the folds of her sex and ever so lightly slid his fingers over it back and forth.

Lindsay buried her face in the comforter and screamed as her inner muscles convulsed. Aiden let himself go, the walls of
~~~

her channel milking every last drop of fluid from him until he was drained and spent.

Leaning forward over her back, he planted kisses along her spine and across her shoulders.

"Are you okay?" Aiden asked her between kisses.

Her response was muffled, since her face was still buried in the comforter. "Linds? Are you all right?" Aiden repeated.

Turning her head, her eyes met his, and she smiled. "I'm perfect."

"You certainly are." With a final kiss on her shoulder, he gingerly separated their bodies. Sliding his arms beneath her knees and shoulders, he picked her up and set her in the middle of the bed.

After turning off the lights, he joined her under the covers, where he pulled her into his side so he could wrap his arms around her.

"Mmm. This is nice," Lindsay murmured.

Before he could agree, her breathing deepened, indicating she had already drifted off.

Aiden lay in the dark, wondering what he was going to do about her. He was pretty sure he loved her, and it scared the hell out of him. His emotions were tied up in knots, and they already seemed to be connected to hers. It made him happy if she were happy. If she were sad or upset, it ripped his heart out.

What would he do if she decided she didn't want to continue their relationship after Carl was out of their lives? What if she decided she still loved Steven too much for there to be any room in her heart for him?

Damn, he was making himself crazy worrying about it. Well, he just wouldn't give her a choice. That's all there was to it. He would push and shove until *he* held a place in her heart, too. He wasn't giving her up, or this baby. He already had a connection to it, and he would just use that to stay close to her until she loved him back.

There, problem solved.

He tightened his hold on her as if that alone would stop her from getting away from him.

With her body nestled so close to his, he noticed when her abdomen tightened.

He soothed her by rubbing small circles and making soft, hushed sounds. With his hand on her stomach, he felt when it softened and relaxed. "What the hell was that?" he whispered. Unsure of what had just happened or what to do, he kept his hand protectively over her belly.

A short while later, her stomach hardened again. This time it lasted a little longer, but he was able to sooth her through it.

After a third and fourth time, he had a pretty good idea of what was going on. He started to take note of the time in between the hardening of her stomach. About every fifteen to twenty minutes.

Lindsay was in labor.

He'd heard labor was really hard on women, so he figured she'd need as much sleep as she could get right now. The longer he could sooth her through them without her waking up, the better it would be for her.

He helped her through the next few contractions before they finally roused her from sleep.

"Aiden, what's going on?" she asked, disoriented.

"You, my dear, are in labor. The contractions are coming about every ten minutes now," he told her.

"Labor?" She was completely awake now. "It's too soon. The doctor said I had two more weeks."

"Yeah, and when was that?" he asked. "About two or three weeks ago?"

When she realized he was right, she put her head in her hands and groaned. "Oh God." She looked up at him. "Ten minutes apart? How long have they been going on?"

"About an hour and a half. Not long after you fell asleep."

"And I slept through that?" she asked, dismayed.

"They must not have been very strong ones. The only reason I felt them is because I had you plastered against me. I could feel your stomach contracting and releasing."

"And you started timing them?"

"Once I finally figured out what was happening, yes," he admitted with a grin. "I'd never been anywhere near a woman in labor before, so I didn't know what to expect. But once they started coming over and over, being the smart guy I am, I deduced that you were in labor."

"Well, since that's confirmed, what do we do now? We didn't really plan for this to happen while we were here. Do we make a run for the nearest hospital or what?"

"I think that would be our best bet," Aiden agreed, getting out of bed. "You stay there. I'll find you some clothes and help you get dressed."

"I think that's a good idea, especially since another contraction is coming."

Sitting on the edge of the bed, he started rubbing her stomach again. "Did you ever take any birthing classes? Did they show you how to breathe?"

"I never made it to any," she panted through the pain. "I was afraid Carl would find me if I signed up."

"Well, I'm sure you've watched enough women giving birth on television to get the basics. They'll show us the rest when we get to the hospital." At least he hoped so, because he knew next to nothing about labor, and even less about delivering a baby.

He could feel the contraction easing. He waited until she took a deep breath and relaxed against the pillows. "You okay?"

"Yeah, for another ten minutes or so." She smiled at him. "Let's get me dressed before another hits." She slid to the side of the bed and slowly stood as he made his way through the adjoining bathroom and into her bedroom. He'd no sooner picked up her clothes than he heard her scream.

"Aiden!"

Hearing the pain and fear in her voice, he dropped the clothes and bolted back through the bathroom. Before he cleared the doorway, he saw her standing next to the bed clutching her stomach. "What happened?"

"Something's . . . ohhh! It hurts. Aiden, help me."

As he got closer, he saw there was a puddle of blood forming on the floor between her feet.

Her panic escalated another notch when she glanced down to see what he was looking at. "Oh God. Oh God, there's blood. Something's wrong." Her eyes implored him to do something— only he was at a loss as to what to do.

Laying her back down made the most sense at the moment, so he helped her into bed and instructed her to lie back.

The pains were coming almost constantly now, only giving a moment's respite between contractions. The blood still flowed at an alarming rate.

He was close to panicking himself when he heard a little voice in his head. *"Aiden."*

"Please tell me what's happening, sweetie?" He was desperate for any help.

"I'm coming, but momma's going to need your help once I'm out. You'll have to heal her. Something ripped loose inside of her."

"Aiden, we have to call an ambulance," Lindsay panted between the pains, unaware of the conversation between him and the baby.

"There's no time. She needs you now," the baby's voice said.

"What do I do?" he asked, positioning himself between Lindsay's bent knees.

"Aiden, what are you doing? What's going on?" Lindsay demanded when he moved closer to her.

Bringing his gaze up to her face, he explained in as calm a

voice as he could manage, "Lindsay, we don't have time to wait for help. The baby's coming, but something's happened. You're losing too much blood. No one can get here in time. We have to do this here. Now."

"Aiden, I'm scared," Lindsay cried.

"I know you are, honey. So am I, but we're going to get through this. We have to."

He waited for her nod of agreement. "Now you have to listen to me. As soon as the baby's out, I'm going to do everything I can to heal whatever went wrong in there. But I need you to hang on. Don't give up. You fight for all you're worth, damn it!"

"Okay," she promised as another pain hit.

The next few minutes were fraught with tension. Each contraction brought the baby closer to birth, but it also brought Lindsay closer to death.

Aiden didn't know how they were going to get through this. He'd never been as scared as he was in this moment. He just hoped he had enough power to heal whatever had torn, because he knew he couldn't lose her.

"Be ready, Poppa. I'm coming, but you'll need to hurry to save Momma."

Aiden was so focused on what was happening with Lindsay, that he almost missed what the baby had called him. When it registered, he was stunned. "Poppa?" But before he could figure out how he felt about that, his attention was drawn back to Lindsay. The baby's head was crowning.

Lindsay was barely conscious. Thankfully, her body knew what needed to be done and took over delivering the baby.

"Stay with me, Linds! Don't you give up on me!"

He caught the baby as it finally made its appearance into the world. He quickly tied off the cord and separated the baby from Lindsay. It wouldn't be until much later that he would wonder how he knew what to do.

With a quick check to make sure the baby was okay, he laid

it on the bed and bundled the comforter up around it to keep it warm. He then turned his attention back to Lindsay and what he needed to do.

"*Hurry, Poppa.*"

"I will, baby, hold on. I'm not letting her go without a fight." He laid his hands on Lindsay's abdomen from his position between her legs, and concentrated on the healing heat of his power.

19

His focus was so complete, he could actually see where the placenta had pulled away from the wall of the uterus during labor, causing the hemorrhage.

Seeing the damage brought home the fact that he could lose her if he didn't do this right. He gathered himself and banished all doubts. He knew if any fear invaded his mind, it would cripple him.

He planned it out step by step. Stop the bleeding first, heal her ravaged uterus, and then hope that would be enough.

Once Lindsay's body had finally expelled the placenta, Aiden poured even more power through his hands and into her body to make sure every last rip and tear was healed.

When Aiden felt he had done all he could to save her, he sat back on his heels and his head dropped forward. He sat that way for a few moments, completely drained.

Knowing there was still work to be done, he wearily got to his feet.

As hard as it was for him to see Lindsay lying there pale and weak, he knew sleep was the best thing for her right now, the trauma of the last few hours having taken its toll on her body.

Turning to the baby, he watched as it lay sleeping on the bed next to Lindsay. Bending to gently lift the bundle, he spoke. "I've done all I can to fix your momma. Do you know if it was enough?"

At the sound of his voice, the tiny eyelids fluttered and opened. Deep blue eyes seemingly met his, but no answer was forthcoming.

"It's okay. We'll wait and see together. But in the meantime, I need to get you and your momma cleaned up.

"Now, where to put you, little one?" His first thought was a crib but decided that would be too big right now. He tried to think of something smaller, something more portable.

What about a cradle? That would be perfect. Aiden put everything he knew about cradles together in his mind and tried conjuring one. It took a few tries to get it right, but when he finally had it the way he wanted, he laid the baby, blanket and all, into it.

"Now, you just sit tight," he told the tiny human looking up at him. "As soon as I get your momma cleaned up, I'll come back and take care of you, okay?"

Turning his attention back to Lindsay, he walked to the side of the bed and stood there, watching her breathe.

He brushed her pale blonde hair from her face and then leaned down to place a feather-soft kiss on her cheek. Taking a deep breath, he turned and headed into the bathroom. Scrounging through the cabinets, he grabbed some of the supplies he'd bought the day his mother had come.

Once she was washed and dried, he pulled one of his clean T-shirts over her head. As far as the rest, he'd seen enough feminine hygiene commercials to know how to take care of her in that regard. After she was dressed, he gently picked her up and carried her into the other room. Tucking her into bed, he gave her another soft kiss before returning to finish the clean-up.

Blocking out the sight of the mess and what it meant, Aiden stripped the bed. Once the sheets were disposed of, he wondered what to do about the mattress. Lindsay's blood had soaked right into it.

Even if he could haul it out, what then? No. He needed to come up with another plan.

A quick call to Becca, and he had a spell in hand which would remove the stains. When it was clean, Aiden found fresh sheets and remade the bed.

Walking back into the adjoining bedroom, Aiden picked Lindsay up again and brought her back to the bed they'd shared. The bed where they had fought to bring her baby into the world.

When she was as comfortable as he could make her, he went back into the bathroom. He put the stopper in the sink, turned on the water, and adjusted it so it was nicely warm. Then he laid out towels on the counter. Before leaving the room, he grabbed one more towel, turned off the water, and dropped a washcloth into it.

Crossing to the cradle, Aiden looked down. "Okay, little one, now it's your turn." He gently unwrapped the baby and quickly transferred it to the clean towel, ensuring it stayed warm. "Now, I hope you're going to make this easy on me, since this will be the first time I've handled someone as small as you."

He carried the infant to the makeshift bathing station, laid it down, and opened the bit of fabric covering it.

"Well, what do you know? You're a little girl. I guess I was so worried about your momma, I didn't even stop to check. So, baby girl, what do you say? Are you ready for 'poppa' to give you your first bath?" She seemed to be listening intently to what he was saying, although he still didn't hear her answer.

He kept up the soft-toned conversation. "I had a few things on my mind at the time, but I do remember you calling me that," he leaned in to whisper. "I have to say, it threw me a little, but now that I've had some time to think about it, I kind of like the way it sounds. I hope that means I get to keep you both in my life, because I would really like to have that happen. I don't want to give up either one of you."

Aiden proceeded to clean her up, making sure to get in all the cracks and crevices which make up a baby's body. He also kept up the one-sided conversation throughout the whole process, hoping it would keep her calm so she wouldn't cry. He wasn't sure what he would do if she did.

He didn't know if the talking helped, or if she just took pity on him, but it went well. Once he had her clean and dry, he realized she would need some clothes and blankets to keep her warm. And diapers.

Aiden was trying to decide if he should just conjure it all himself or place another call to Becca when he felt a disturbance in the air. Wrapping the baby tightly against him, Aiden slowly walked back into the bedroom.

There was a large box with a big pink bow on top, sitting in the middle of the floor. The tag said, 'From Becca and Mia.'

"What do you think they sent us?" Aiden asked the tiny bundle in his arms.

Aiden untied the ribbon and removed the top. Inside were tiny white onesies, pale pink nightgowns, a couple of blankets, some diapers, bottles, a can of powered formula, and even a gallon of purified water.

"Well, it looks like they got it all covered."

After he'd gotten her diapered and dressed in a nightgown, he wrapped her in one of the blankets. Aiden was running on fumes now, and since it looked like Lindsay and the baby would be sleeping for a while, he laid her in the cradle.

Aiden positioned her next to the bed within easy reach before pulling up a chair for himself. He got as comfortable as he could, propped up his feet, and was asleep within seconds.

~~~

When Lindsay finally awoke, the sight which greeted her brought tears to her eyes. Aiden sat in a chair beside the bed,
~~~

holding her baby up against his shoulder, both sound asleep.

She didn't know how long she'd been out of it, but if the sun coming through the window was any indication, she'd been asleep all night and most of the morning.

As she lay there, memories of the night before came back to her. The blood, the pain, and most of all, the fear.

What she didn't remember was the birth of her child. She'd been so delirious by then, all she had were vague impressions of Aiden telling her not to give up, that she needed to hold on. She didn't even know if the baby was a boy or a girl, and she couldn't tell by the blanket Aiden had wrapped around it, since it was white.

Lindsay shifted on the bed to get more comfortable, and the mere rustling of fabric woke Aiden.

When his eyes opened, his gaze zeroed in on her. "Hi. How are you feeling?" he asked her, his voice laden with concern.

"Not too bad, all things considered. Tired, though I seem to have slept for quite a while."

He kept his voice low so as not to disturb the baby in his arms as he explained. "You lost a lot of blood last night. Sleep is the body's way of recovering from that."

"What happened? Why was there so much blood? I don't remember a whole lot."

"The placenta detached from your uterus while you were in labor, and that caused the hemorrhage. The baby warned me, so I would be ready to heal you as soon as she was out. It took me a while, but I stopped the bleeding and repaired all the damage."

"Thank you, Aiden." Lindsay paused as memory clicked. "The baby was right. If you hadn't been here, neither one of us would have made it last night. How can I ever repay you for that?"

"Thanks aren't necessary, and there's nothing to repay. I wasn't about to let you get away from me."

"Well, thank you anyway," she said in earnest. "Wait a minute. Did you say 'she'?"

"Yeah, she." Aiden smiled and started to stand with the baby. "You have a little girl." Placing her in her mother's waiting arms, Aiden sat on the edge of the bed.

Pulling the blanket down, Lindsay looked at her daughter for the first time.

"Oh, she's beautiful," she crooned, looking up at Aiden with tears trailing down her cheeks. Returning her attention to her daughter, Lindsay unwrapped her and gave her the once-over, assuring herself that everything was where it was supposed to be, and she had the correct numbers of everything. "She's perfect. And look, she has hair," she exclaimed. "I guess all that heartburn I had counted for something then."

Aiden divided his gaze between her and the little blonde head. "She gets her hair from her momma. It's the same pale blonde as yours, and it's just as soft. She's as beautiful as her momma, too."

She met his eyes and smiled. "Thank you."

She was caught in the love beaming from Aiden and felt something similar to it blossoming inside of her. She tucked it away for the moment and directed her thoughts elsewhere. "So, what have you two been doing while I've been sleeping?"

He watched her for another second before he answered. "We've just been getting acquainted. She allowed me to bathe her, and she didn't give me *too* hard of a time while I tried to put her diaper on. She also graciously let me dress her without a peep."

"It sounds like everything went pretty well."

"I think she was just taking pity on me, since I don't know the first thing about taking care of babies."

"It looks like you've done a great job," she assured him with a smile. "Where did you get the clothes?"

"My mom and aunt magically sent over a box with everything

she would need. We did have a few tense moments when she got hungry, though. Thankfully, the can of formula had directions on it. Becca had sent a note with it saying that even if you planned on breastfeeding, it would be okay for right now."

She could hear the pride in his voice at having taken care of her daughter's needs while she'd been recuperating. Yet another thing to be grateful for. "Thank you for taking such good care of her," Lindsay said, tears welling up again.

"Stop thanking me. I'm glad I was here to help. And taking care of that little girl there," Aiden ran his large hand over her tiny head, "was more enjoyable than I ever could have thought. She's incredible."

"So are you." She grinned up at him, not bothering to hide her feelings. "I'm glad I decided to let you stick around."

"Me, too." Aiden leaned in to kiss her, a soft and tender kiss that had her emotions rising again.

She'd only been awake for a few minutes, but Lindsay could already feel the fatigue weighing her down. Aiden must have noticed it, too. "Would you like for me to fix you something to eat before you go back to sleep?"

Even though she wasn't really hungry, she knew she needed the nourishment to help her body recover. "That sounds good. Just something light, though."

"Okay, I'll go see what we have. Will you be all right here with her for a few minutes?"

She smiled down at the baby in her arms. "We'll be fine. We'll use this time to get to know one another."

"I'll be right back then."

Lindsay waited until Aiden was out of the room and out of sight. When she returned her gaze to her child, deep blue eyes were silently regarding her. "Hello. We've had quite a time of it, haven't we, sweetie? I'm glad you're finally here. I've been waiting so long to meet you. Aiden is right; you definitely have my hair, but you have your daddy's nose. Did you know that?"

She took a deep, shuddering breath. "I'm sorry you weren't able to meet your daddy. He loved you and wanted you very much, but a car crash took him away from us. Whenever you have questions about him, you go ahead and ask, and I'll answer as best I can."

She ran the backs of her fingers over soft baby cheeks. "I'll promise you right now that I will do everything I can to protect you from your grandfather. And I think even though that man out there isn't your biological father, he would die before he let anything happen to you."

Lindsay lowered her voice to a whisper. "We got pretty lucky when we found him. I didn't think I would be able to have feelings for a man this soon after your daddy passed. But I guess meeting Aiden must be a part of our destiny, because as soon as I met him, it just felt right. Can you understand that?"

She laughed at herself. "Probably not. Not yet, anyway, but I don't ever want you to think that I didn't love your daddy, because I did—with all my heart. Your daddy will always hold a special place in my heart, because he was my first love, and he gave me you. And I promise to tell you all about him as soon as you're old enough. I want you to know what a good man he was—that he was nothing like his father. He would never hurt people the way Carl does. And I sincerely hope you never have to know what an awful man he really is."

20

Mother and daughter were still quietly talking when Aiden returned with a tray topped with chicken soup and crackers.

"Is she telling you how inept I am at taking care of her?" he asked as he set the tray on the bedside table.

"Nope. She's been singing your praises," Lindsay grinned tiredly.

"You look about done in, hon. How about I take her, and you see how much food you can get in before you fall asleep?"

At Lindsay's nod, he placed the tray over her lap and then lifted the baby out of her arms. "Come on, baby girl. You can sit with me while Momma eats," he told her as he resumed his position in the chair next to the bed.

He watched to make sure she was going to eat before he spoke. "Have you given any thought to what you're going to name her?"

"I was thinking maybe Rose, after my grandmother. But I don't know. It's kind of an old-fashioned name, and then there's the whole teasing thing we were talking about the other day." She smiled at the memory. "And I would really hate to have her called Rosie."

He watched her as she nibbled on a cracker.

"I guess I'll just have to come up with something else," she finally said.

Lindsay had eaten about half of the soup before she was too

tired for more. Seeing that she was done, he picked up the tray one-handed and set it back on the table.

"You could always use that as a middle name," he offered as she snuggled down under the blankets.

"Yeah, but I'll still need to come up with a first name." Her eyes grew heavier.

"Could I offer a suggestion?"

"For a name? It's not Samantha, is it?" Lindsay teased him, already half-asleep.

"No, it's not, smartass. And if you don't like it, it's no big deal. You can come up with something else." Looking down at the baby, he added, "I just thought it kind of fit her."

"What is it?" Lindsay asked, her curiosity overriding her exhaustion for the moment.

"Hannah."

"Hannah." Lindsay gave it some thought and then looked at him suspiciously. "It's not some old girlfriend's name, is it?"

"No." He hadn't realized how much her decision mattered to him, and now he felt a little self-conscious about it. "For some reason, as I sat here with her, waiting for you to wake up, it just popped into my head. I thought you might like it."

"Hannah Rose." He sat silently while Lindsay tried it out and thought it over. "I do like it, and you're right—it does fit her."

Lindsay fought to keep her eyes open to say one more thing. "The next time she gets hungry, wake me up. I'd like to try breastfeeding her."

"Are you sure?" She still had dark circles shadowing her eyes, and he didn't want her to over-exert herself. "You should probably concentrate on getting as much rest as you can."

"I'm sure. All the doctors I went to recommended I do it for her health, so I'd like to try."

He knew she must feel strongly about it to fight off sleep in order to make her point. "Okay, but if it looks like it's taking too much of a toll, you'll have to stop until you've recovered more."

"Okay," Lindsay mumbled.

"Go to sleep now and rest." His words fell on deaf ears. She was already out.

~~~

By the second day, Lindsay was going stir-crazy being confined to the bed. While Aiden was in the other room giving Hannah a bath, she tested her strength by scooting to the edge of the bed and placing her feet on the floor.

No dizziness. That was a good sign. Slowly she pushed to her feet. She got a little woozy when she was fully upright but fought through it until it passed. Breathing in deep, she took a couple of tentative steps.

"What the hell do you think you're doing?" Aiden demanded from the bathroom doorway where he held Hannah, wrapped in a big, fluffy towel.

Lindsay looked over at him and grinned. "Busted."

"Ya think? I'll ask again—what the hell do you think you're doing?"

"I'm tired of being in that bed; I need to get up and move. I have to regain my strength before Carl comes at us again." She cautiously took a couple more steps.

"Speaking of which, it's been awfully quiet the last few days. Why hasn't he made any moves?"

Aiden started across the room towards her. "I don't know. Damn it, Linds. You're making me nervous. It wasn't that long ago you nearly *died*. Why don't you sit back down on the side of the bed, or if you don't want that, then sit in the chair. Just sit *somewhere*. Please." He looked down at the baby in his arms. "Hannah, I think your momma just scared a good ten years off my life."
~~~

"Oh, stop being so overly dramatic," she laughed. "I'm fine. A little shaky at first, but it's passing now. Besides, I have to be mobile and ready whenever it comes time to put a plan into action."

He looked like he wanted to argue with her, but she cut him off. "You know I'm right, Aiden."

"All right," he finally gave in. "But just take it slow. I healed what I could, but now it's your body's turn. It needs to replenish the blood it lost, and that isn't going to happen overnight. It'll take some time, so don't push it."

"I won't, I promise."

"Come on. Let's get you and Hannah settled in the living room. I'll try to find out what Carl's been up to. It *has* been suspiciously quiet lately."

~~~

Once Lindsay and the baby were seated and comfortable on the couch, Aiden went into the kitchen to make breakfast and call Jack.

He gathered what he needed to make French toast while he dialed Jack's number. It was answered on the second ring. "Slade."

"Hey, Jack. It's Aiden."

"Hey, buddy, how goes it?"

"Not too bad, although we had some excitement the other night. Lindsay went into labor, and as if that weren't scary enough, she started hemorrhaging."

"Oh, shit, man. Is she okay? What about the baby?"

"They're both fine, thankfully," Aiden told him. "Hannah was able to tell me that something had gone wrong inside of Lindsay, and to be ready to act as soon as she was out."

"Hannah?"

"Yeah, man, it's a girl. Hannah Rose."
~~~

"Well, tell Lindsay I said congratulations. I take it you were able to heal her?"

"Yeah." Aiden looked back over his shoulder to assure himself that Lindsay was still in the living room. In a lower tone of voice, Aiden continued. "I gotta tell you, Jack—I've never been so scared in my entire life. I just thank whatever force was looking out for us that Hannah was able to connect with me to clue me in on what was happening. If she hadn't, Lindsay would have bled to death before I figured it out. As it was, she lost so much blood, she passed out before the baby was fully delivered."

"Damn, I can't imagine going through that all alone. If Rissa and I ever have kids, I'm sure I'll drive her *and* the doctors crazy being overprotective," Jack half-joked. "Lindsay's fine now, though, isn't she?"

"It'll take her a few more days before she's back to normal, but she's doing fine. She's up and moving around today. Trying to rebuild her strength for whatever comes next. Which is the other reason I called. We haven't heard anything from Carl in the last few days, and we're kind of concerned about it. What's he up to? This would have been the perfect time to hit us."

"I take it you haven't been watching the news lately."

"No. We've been a little busy. Why?"

"It would appear Carl has had his own problems to deal with recently. It seems the police received an anonymous tip regarding some of Carl's business dealings."

"What kind of tip?" He could picture Jack on the other end of the line, seated behind his desk and leaning back in his leather chair.

"Apparently, a concerned citizen witnessed something suspicious going on and told the police."

"Is that so? And just what did this concerned citizen witness?" He had to stifle a laugh at Jack's innocent act.

"Well, from what I understand, this person happened to

see a shipment of some kind being unloaded at a warehouse. And wouldn't you know it—the building belonged to one Carl Donnelly."

"Of course it did," he agreed, deadpan, flipping the French toast over on the griddle.

Jack continued. "Allegedly, he'd been driving by when he saw several men unloading what appeared to be guns and other weapons, in addition to something which looked suspiciously like a rocket launcher. He couldn't be one hundred percent positive about any of it, but he was so concerned, he felt it was his duty to alert the police right away. So naturally, law enforcement had to go check it out."

"You didn't?" He laughed, pausing with French toast hovering over the plate.

"What? With all the terrorist activity happening lately, people can't be too careful. So this particular concerned citizen felt he had no other choice but to report what he'd seen."

"You're unbelievable, Jack." Aiden was in awe of the master. "How much longer do you think he'll be otherwise occupied?"

"Only another day, two at the most. Why, do you have something planned?" Jack asked.

"Not a plan really, just an idea."

"What's the idea?"

He finished loading two plates, then reached into the cupboard and pulled down two glasses.

"This situation needs to get resolved. Once Carl finds out the baby's here, he's going to pull out all the stops to snatch her. If we go with my plan to get incriminating evidence on Carl, then I think we need someone on the inside. Margaret Donnelly would be our best source of information. I need to get to her—find out where she stands."

"What about Lindsay and the baby? Are you going to just leave them there to fend off Carl on their own?"

"Not a chance. They'll have to go with me. There's no way

I'm leaving them alone anywhere. Lindsay should be stronger yet by tomorrow. Maybe we can sneak out of here and make our way to Chicago while Carl's making his way back here."

"Do you think he knows the baby's arrived?"

"I don't think so. Like you said, he's had other things on his mind, and we haven't been outside, so his men wouldn't know anything to tell him. The only problem we might run into is how to get out of here without anyone seeing us."

Jack was silent for a moment. "You know what? Put a call into the family and tell them what you need. They should be able to cause some sort of distraction for you."

"That could work. I'll let you know what we decide."

"You do that," Jack told him. "And if you think you'll need any help in Chicago, let us know."

"I will."

They talked for a few more minutes and disconnected. He found a tray large enough to hold the two plates, two glasses of milk, and silverware before turning to carry it into the living room.

Lindsay had one breast bared and was feeding Hannah. She was so wrapped up watching her daughter, she didn't hear him come back into the room.

When she did finally look up, she smiled at him. "What did Jack have to say?"

"First, he said to tell you congratulations." He sat on the sofa next to her and set the loaded tray on the coffee table. Turning back, he couldn't resist running his hand over Hannah's soft head. He noticed she had finished eating and was fast asleep. "If little bit here is done with her breakfast, it's time for her momma to eat hers."

Rising, Aiden took the baby and laid her in the cradle he'd brought out of the bedroom earlier. Resuming his seat, he waited until Lindsay had readjusted her clothing before handing her a plate.

She looked at the mountain of food he'd piled onto it. "There's no way I'm going to be able to eat all this."

"Just do what you can," he told her, reaching for his own breakfast. "Right now, your body needs to regenerate, and you're also breastfeeding. You need plenty of food and rest."

Between bites, he filled her in on Jack's suggestion to use his family as a cover.

"How could they help?" she asked, breaking off a piece of bacon.

"I'm not sure, but they *are* all witches," he reminded her. "They should be able to come up with something." He paused, waiting for her to look at him. "If you still don't want to involve them, we won't. We'll figure out something on our own."

She sat silent as she thought about it. "Do you really think they could do this?"

"Honestly? Yes I do. I've seen them in action. I think they may be our best chance at getting out of here without being seen. But if we're going to act, it needs to be within the next day or two."

"Why?" Lindsay asked around a bite of French toast.

He was glad to see she'd made a good dent in the pile of food he'd given her. "You're going to love this," he grinned, relaying what Jack had done.

Lindsay just shook her head.

"So while I'm grateful for the reprieve, it's not going to last much longer. We need to decide if we're going to do this, and quickly. Carl will probably be on his way back by then and, if we're going, we need to be gone before he gets here."

Lindsay leaned forward and set her almost-empty plate back on the table. When she looked back at him, he knew she'd reached a decision. "Call your parents."

"Are you sure?" he asked, finishing off the last of his own food.

"You and Jack are right. We're going to need all the help we can get for this." She slowly stood and gathered the breakfast dishes. "You make the call, and I'll clean this up."

It didn't take any special powers for him to see she was worried about something. Promising himself he would get to the bottom of it, he went to get his phone.

Fifteen minutes later, he found Lindsay still in the kitchen.

"They're on their way," he told her from the doorway. "They should be here in a few hours."

"Okay," she said over her shoulder as she stood at the sink rinsing the last pan from breakfast. "I guess I'll need to go start packing."

It was obvious how tense she was by the rigidity of her body.

"That can wait for a minute." He rested his hand on her shoulder and gently turned her until she faced him. He gathered her into his arms, her head nestled below his chin. Her body was trembling.

"Hey. What's wrong?"

"Aiden, I'm so scared," she finally whispered.

He held her, wishing he could take away all her fears and worries. "I promised you I would never let anything happen to you or Hannah, and I mean to keep that promise."

"It's not just that," she said against his chest. "It's you and your family. I'm so afraid of something happening to one of you."

"We're a pretty tough bunch of people. With all the power running through this family, Carl doesn't stand a chance," he soothed. "And if someone does happen to get hurt, I know of this really cool guy who has the power to heal."

"Oh yeah?" she asked. "A cool guy, huh? And who might that be?"

He kissed the top of her blonde head and then leaned back enough to see her face. What he found there eased the knot in his stomach. There wasn't so much worry and fear in her eyes. "I think you know exactly who I'm talking about."

She gave him a tentative smile. "I do know, and you *are* a pretty cool guy." She reached up and cupped his face in her hand. "My daughter and I are very happy to have you in our lives."

"Not nearly as happy as I am to have the two of you." He trapped her hand beneath his. Turning his head, he kissed her palm.

"We have some time before the troops arrive. Why don't you go lie down and try to get some rest? You're going to need all your strength for the next leg of this journey."

"Okay, but be sure to wake me when they get here."

"I will. Now go. I'll watch over Hannah."

21

Later that afternoon, Aiden was redressing Hannah after a diaper change when there was a knock on the door. Placing her safely in the cradle out of sight, Aiden cautiously approached the sidelight window to ensure it was his parents.

After confirming their identity, he opened the door just enough to let them in, double-checking that any sign of the baby was hidden.

"I'm glad you could make it," he told them as he quickly shut the door behind them.

"We're just glad you called us," Conner told him. "We'll do whatever we can to help."

"Where's Amber? I would have thought she'd want to be right in the middle of all this."

"She was all set to come, but as we were leaving the house, she suddenly changed her mind," Conner explained.

"What happened?" Aiden asked.

"We don't know," his mother answered. "She's been acting very odd lately. I don't like it. Something's going on, but she won't talk about it. And that in itself is very out of character for her. A lot of her behavior lately has been peculiar, and it has me worried."

Aiden didn't like the way this was sounding. "If you find out she's in some kind of trouble, will you be sure to tell me?"

"We will." Becca set the large duffle bag she'd been carrying on the floor and reached out to give her son a hug and kiss. "How are you?"

"I'm doing okay," he smiled.

"How's Lindsay?" she asked.

"She's a lot better. She still needs to build up her strength, so she's resting right now."

Becca's attention was then drawn to the baby still nestled in the small bed. "So, this is Hannah Rose." Her hopeful eyes looked up into his. "Do you think she would mind if I held her?"

"I don't think she would mind at all. She's a very good baby. She hardly ever fusses." He gently lifted Hannah and transferred her into his mother's waiting arms. "And thank you for the box of baby stuff."

"You're welcome, honey. It was fun shopping for baby things again." Becca held Hannah close and looked into her deep blue eyes. "Hi, sweetheart. I'm Aiden's momma. You don't know me yet, but I hope we can become friends."

"Nana B." Aiden heard the faint little voice inside his head, and it made him grin. "I think you two are going to be closer than you think."

"What do you mean?" Becca asked him.

Before he could answer, Lindsay entered the living room from the hallway. "I thought you were going to wake me?"

"I was about to. They just got here and were getting to know Hannah."

Lindsay stopped next to him and smiled at Becca. "She's perfect, isn't she? And it's all thanks to Aiden. If he hadn't been here, I'd hate to think what would have happened to us."

"He was right where he was meant to be," Becca told her. "I believe that whole-heartedly."

Clearing her throat, Lindsay wiped the moisture from her eyes. "Well, why don't you all have a seat? I'll put on some coffee, and then we can put together a plan to sneak us out of here."

Aiden looked up when he heard Lindsay coming back. She was carrying a tray which held four cups and a carafe of hot coffee.

He jumped up and took the tray from her. "Why didn't you call me to carry this? You shouldn't be lifting anything heavier than Hannah. Now go sit down."

"Jeez, bossy much?" Lindsay muttered under her breath.

"Yes, if that's what it takes to keep you from hurting yourself."

Once everyone was seated and had a cup of coffee, they got down to the matter at hand.

Conner was the first to speak. "What is it you need us to do? What's the plan?"

Aiden laid it out for them. "Lindsay and I need to get to Chicago to see if Margaret can be of any help to us." He went on to explain his idea of blackmailing Carl to keep him away from Lindsay and Hannah.

"What makes you think she'll know anything that could be useful?" Conner asked.

"I don't," Aiden sighed as his father zeroed in on the biggest 'if' in this whole equation. "But if anyone were to know his secrets, it would have to be his wife. And she may be willing to share a few, if we can promise her our protection."

"Are you sure she wants to get away from him?" his father questioned. "She may be in it just as deep as he is."

"That could very well be," Aiden acknowledged. "But this is the best plan we could come up with. The possibility still exists that she helped Steven to escape his father. If that's the case, it gives me hope she'll want the same freedom for Lindsay and Hannah."

Before Conner could voice another argument, Becca interrupted.

"They have to do this, dear. They have to go. It's the next step in finding what they need to bring this to a conclusion."

A look passed between his parents, and Conner asked if she were sure.

"Yes," Becca confirmed. "This is the path they have to take right now."

He knew his mother had some pretty impressive powers of her own and wanted to know what she'd been shown. "Do you know what the conclusion will be?"

"No, I'm sorry," she told him regretfully. "I just know that at this point in time, this is what you need to do."

The discussion was put on hold when Hannah made it known that she was hungry.

Lindsay rose, took her daughter from Becca, and excused herself while she went back to the bedroom to care for Hannah's needs.

Aiden watched her until she was out of sight. When he turned his attention back to his parents, they had curious looks on their faces. "What?"

"You're falling in love with her." It wasn't a question from his mother but a statement.

"It's that obvious?" It must be, for them to have read him so easily.

They both nodded, but it was his mother who asked, "Does she know how you feel?"

"Not totally," he admitted. "We've talked about our relationship, and we're taking it one day at a time."

"What about Steven?" Becca probed. "And her feelings for him?"

"We've talked about that, too. I know she'll always love him, and he'll always have a special place in her heart because he's Hannah's father, but she also said he'd want her to go on living." He took a quick glance down the hallway to make sure Lindsay hadn't returned. "She didn't have an easy time coming to the decision to move on with her life. Steven hasn't been gone all that long, and at first she felt she was betraying him by having feelings for me. But she came to the conclusion that whatever this is, it feels right. And I have to agree with that. I've never felt this way about anyone before. It's a little unnerving."

Taking a deep breath, he continued on. "So we're taking it slow, working our way through. Though, I have it on good authority that she and I will be in each other's lives for quite some time."

"How do you know that?" Conner asked.

"I told you that right before Hannah was born, when everything was going to shit, she told me what was happening. But what I didn't tell you was that she called me 'Poppa'." He grinned so big, he thought his face would crack. "I took that to mean that this thing with Lindsay would grow into something more."

"What did Lindsay say about that?" Becca asked.

"I haven't told her about that part of it yet," he admitted. "I don't want her to feel pressured about us. I may tell her eventually, but not right now. She has too much on her mind."

Becca was about to ask him something else but stopped when they heard Lindsay coming back down the hall.

"Piglet here took a little longer than usual. Did we miss anything?" she asked the room in general.

Aiden was the first to respond. "Nope, I was just filling them in on what's been going on up until now."

Lindsay walked over to where his dad sat. "Would you like to hold her?"

"I would love to." Once the transfer was made, Conner looked Hannah over. "You forget how small they start out. Though I don't think Amber was ever this little."

"No, she was close to eight pounds at birth," Becca grinned.

Talk returned to the plan, and over the next hour they came up with and discarded a lot of ideas until finally, in frustration, Lindsay muttered, "Too bad I don't have a twin. She could stay here in my place."

"That's it!" Becca practically shouted. "God, why didn't I think of that before? It's so simple!"

"What is?" Aiden was surprised at his mother's outburst.

Smiling triumphantly, she answered, "A glamour spell."

"A what?" Lindsay's question reflected his own confusion. Out of all the spells he'd learned, glamour spells hadn't been one of them.

Becca explained. "A glamour spell is usually used to enhance someone's looks. If you're tired and have dark circles, you whisper a little spell and—voila—no more looking run down. You still feel the same, but you *look* rested and refreshed."

"How is that going to help us?" Lindsay asked.

"The more power you put into the spell, the bigger the glamour. Big enough to change your looks completely," Becca told her. "You guys will become us, and we'll become you. For all Carl and his goons will know, we came for a visit and left a few hours later, leaving you both here for them to report on."

This might actually work. "How long will it last?" Aiden asked anxiously.

"As long as we need it to," Becca told him. "I'll teach you the spell, and when you're far enough away, you can remove it. When you're finished in Chicago and headed back here, just call us and we can switch again for your arrival."

"It sounds so easy," Lindsay commented.

"It should be," Conner returned, still holding a sleeping infant. "Just let us know what your daily routine is so we can follow it, and no one will know any different."

"What about Hannah?" Aiden wondered, glancing down at the baby in his father's arms. "She has to go with us. How do we get her out without them knowing there was a baby in here? We want Carl to think Lindsay is still pregnant."

Everyone was silent while they tried to figure out how to deal with this obstacle.

"What's in the bag?" Lindsay pointed to the one Becca had

brought with her.

"I wasn't sure what we would need magic-wise, so I brought a little of everything with me. Why?"

"I think I have an idea." Lindsay rose and picked up the duffle bag.

She set it on the coffee table and proceeded to empty it out. "Why couldn't we put Hannah in this to carry her out?" Lindsay's question was for everyone there. "Becca came in with it, so it wouldn't raise any questions if she left with it."

"Would she be okay in there?" Aiden also thought it could work, but if it in any way was hazardous to Hannah, he would scrap it in an instant.

"She'll be fine. We can line it with blankets to hold her in place, and I'll just leave the top open so she gets fresh air," Lindsay assured him. "It's perfect."

"Okay, since we've got that figured out," Conner said, "let's go over your day-to-day routine. We wouldn't want anyone out there to get suspicious."

"Most of the day we're in the house, so that won't be a problem. What might be, is that up until Lindsay had the baby, we would take a walk around the cabin."

"That won't be a problem," Becca assured them. "I'll just re-do the spell as pregnant-Lindsay, and then we'll go for a walk."

"Are you guys sure you want to do this?" There was concern in Lindsay's voice. "We don't know how long we'll be gone, and you'll be stuck here all alone."

"Alone is the operative word here," Conner smiled slyly at his wife. "We'll just treat this as another honeymoon."

Aiden saw the look in his father's eyes shift from playful back to serious to assuage them. "We'll be fine—don't worry about us. Go and do what you have to do. Even if Carl tries to pull something, we are well-equipped to handle it."

He looked to Lindsay to confirm she was okay with moving forward. When he got her slight nod in response, he turned back to his parents.

"Okay, let's do this."

While Becca taught him the spell, Lindsay got to work lining the duffle bag with a thick blanket for Hannah to lie on.

Conner went and set a sleeping Hannah inside her cradle, and then joined the others gathered in the center of the living room once all the preparations were made.

After watching both his father and mother complete their transformations, Aiden took a deep breath as he readied himself to alter his appearance.

He didn't quite know what to expect when the change was made. What was it going to feel like to completely alter your looks? Watching his parents go through it, it seemed easy enough. Neither had screamed out in pain or anything, so it must not be too unpleasant.

Glancing down at Lindsay, he waited for his mother's nod before reciting the words which would induce his metamorphosis.

"Transform my body, transform my face

Transform me wholly in time and space

Let all who see me, see another

Let all who see me, see my father"

When the skin on his face and body began to tingle, he knew something was happening. Within moments, the sensation was gone.

Judging by Lindsay's reaction, he knew the spell had worked. Her brows were drawn inward as she studied him closely.

"What did it feel like?" she asked him.

"Kind of weird, actually," he told her. "It didn't hurt, just felt

. . . bizarre. Are you ready?"

At her assent, Aiden started the spell again with a few adjustments. When she started touching her face lightly, he figured she was feeling the same sensations, and he was glad to see it wasn't freaking her out.

One moment he was watching Lindsay, and in the next, Becca was standing in front of him.

Okay, that's beyond strange. He just hoped it fooled the men in the woods long enough for them to leave.

All that remained was to hide Hannah.

After giving Lindsay's hand a reassuring squeeze, he turned and picked Hannah up from the cradle and held her close. He needed to have a little chat with her first.

"Okay, baby girl. You're going to have to be very quiet for just a little while. We have to sneak past the bad men outside, and if they know you're not in your momma's belly anymore, we could all be in trouble. So let's get through this, and we'll get you out of that bag real soon. Is that a deal?"

"Okay, Poppa," the little voice whispered in his mind.

"That's my girl." He gave her a kiss and gently laid her on the makeshift bed inside the duffel bag. He rolled up two more blankets and put them along either side of her, then slowly pulled the zipper almost closed. Picking up the bag, he laid the strap over Lindsay's shoulder and gently lowered it until it hung at her side.

Turning to say good-bye to his parents, he was again taken aback and laughed. "Okay, it's just creepy saying good-bye to myself."

"It's not that bad for me," his father told him. "I'm used to looking at Ben and seeing myself. Though I didn't realize I was getting so many gray hairs," his father said, smiling. "Here, you'll need these." He handed over the car keys and a wad of bills. "And don't forget to pay for everything with this cash. No one will be able to track you that way."

Despite having never done it before, Aiden went with his gut, leaned in, and hugged his father. "Thank you."

"We're just glad we could do this for you. Be safe, son."

Aiden grasped Lindsay's hand, and together they walked to the door where they made a show of saying good-bye to each other. Conner and Becca went back into the house, while he and Lindsay made their way to his parents' car.

~~~

It was still hard for Lindsay to believe she looked like someone else when she didn't feel any differently. She kept waiting for someone to call out a warning that they were getting away, but none ever came.

All she had to do was glance over at Aiden to know the spell was working just as Becca had said it would. The world of magic still amazed her.

Reaching the car, Aiden opened the door for her. He waited until she was settled and the bag carrying Hannah secured before he closed them in. Rounding the front, he slid in behind the wheel.

She sensed the tension in him as he started the car and pulled away from the cabin. When they reached the main road, he let out a sigh of relief. "I halfway expected someone to come running out of the woods to stop us," Aiden breathed, echoing her earlier thoughts.

"Yeah, I was thinking the same thing," she agreed. "It's still hard to believe I don't look like me. This is so weird."

He took hold of her hand across the top of where Hannah lay, and for a while they rode in thoughtful silence.

When he thought they were far enough from the cottage, Aiden pulled into the parking lot of a small convenience store.

"Why are we stopping here?" Lindsay asked.

"We need to get Hannah into a car seat. The bag was fine to
~~~

get her out of the house, but it's not safe for an extended ride."

"I agree, but I don't think a corner store is going to carry something like that. Until it's safe to stop at a real store to buy one, the bag looks like our only option," she reminded him.

"We don't need to buy one." Aiden pulled out his phone and did a search for infant car seats. Once he had a pretty good idea of what he was aiming for, he turned to face the back of the car. Concentrating on the image in his mind, Aiden conjured an exact duplicate.

"What do you think?" He grinned at Lindsay.

She studied the pink and grey padded infant carrier. "I think it's perfect."

It didn't take long to get Hannah strapped in and settled.

"Would you mind if I sat in the back?" Lindsay asked. "With her having to face backwards, I would feel better if I were back there with her in case she needs something."

"Are you kidding? If the manufacturer of these cars would have had the consideration to put an extra steering wheel in the back, I'd be back there, too. But since they didn't, I'll have to settle for being chauffer for the two most beautiful women in the world."

He held the back door open and waited for her to get comfortable. As soon as he was behind the wheel again, he turned in the seat. "I want you to let me know if you need to stop for any reason—even if it's just to stretch your legs, okay?"

"Okay," she easily agreed.

22

They drove for close to an hour before they dared to stop and reverse the glamour. Aiden spotted a sign for a large chain department store just off the expressway. This was probably as good a place as any to undo the spell and get what they needed, since they'd only been able to bring the very minimum of what Hannah needed.

"I think our own faces would serve us better now," Aiden suggested. "Even though we've put some distance between us and the cabin, this store is still fairly close to Charlevoix. I'd hate to have someone who knows my parents want to stop and chat. Chances are slim, but I'd feel better being more anonymous."

"That's probably a good idea," Lindsay agreed.

Aiden exited the freeway and made his way into the parking lot.

He chose a space far enough away from the others that no one would see them when their faces changed, but also not so far from the building that it made people wonder what they were doing.

With a final look to make sure there was no one around, he recited the reversal spell.

As soon as they were themselves again, he turned to Lindsay. "I think you should stay here with Hannah while I run in and get what we need. A mad dash through the store might be too much for you. It was only a few days ago that I almost lost you."

"Yeah, you're probably right." She sounded frustrated, but the weariness in her voice was evident. "All I've done is ride in this car for the last hour, and I'm already wiped out."

He was relieved she wasn't going to argue. "Just sit here and relax. We'll stop for the night soon. You can eat, stretch out, and regain some of your strength before we need to be on the road again. I wish we could've stayed at the cabin for a couple more days, but this was the safest way of trying to get close to Margaret without Carl knowing."

"I know. I understand," Lindsay reassured him. "I'll be fine. I feel better every day."

"You still need to rest," he stressed as he smoothed the hair around her face.

"I know, and I will. I can snooze while you drive, but like you said, this trip was something we had to do right now." Lindsay gave him a tired smile.

He turned back to the front and searched the car for a pen and paper. He found them in the glove compartment and handed both to Lindsay. "Write down everything you can think of that you and Hannah will need for the next few days."

While she made out the list, he took several bills out of the bundle his father had given him and put them in his wallet.

By the time he slipped it back into his pocket, she was finished writing down what she needed.

He looked it over to make sure he was clear on what she wanted. Like the first list she'd made for him, this one was pretty specific too.

"All right, I'll be back as soon as I can." He gave her a quick kiss. "You just rest until I get here."

"I will."

He hated leaving them in the car by themselves. She looked so tired and pale. He gave the car one last look to reassure himself she was okay, and then he went through the double doors and into the store.

Once inside, he consulted the list again to come up with a plan of attack.

Luckily for him, most stores in this chain were set up the same way. He wouldn't have to search for everything.

First stop was the baby department, where the bulk of his purchases would be made.

The most important thing on the list was diapers. Shouldn't be too hard; she'd even written down the size for him.

As he came around the end of the first aisle, his feet became rooted to the spot.

"Son of a bitch."

He'd found the diapers easily enough. You couldn't really miss them. One whole aisle was loaded top to floor with countless brands and sizes.

He started walking and just gaped at all the different packages.

"How on earth can there be this many different types of diapers? They all have to do the same thing," he muttered to himself, wondering how he was ever going to choose the right one.

Before he could make any decisions, a woman pushing a cart came around the corner. Perched on top of the cart was an infant carrier, and inside it was a baby boy not much bigger than Hannah.

He pretended to peruse the other side of the aisle but watched the woman out of the corner of his eye until she chose which pack of diapers she needed. He waited until she left to grab two of the same kind and threw them into his own cart.

He glanced down at the list again. "Okay. One down, what's next? Soap and lotion. Let's hope that's easier than the diapers."

It wasn't.

As with just about everything he needed for Hannah, there were numerous brands and types of everything. Soothing-this, and Lavender-that. Oatmeal? Who bathed in oatmeal?

Even following Lindsay's instructions, by the time he left the infant department, he was getting a headache. It shouldn't have been that difficult.

Who knew there were so many different products out there for babies? Most of what he bought, he chose because it looked vaguely familiar from TV commercials. The marketing departments sure made their money off of him.

Next was the ladies' department, then finally the men's. By the time he made his way to the checkout lanes, his cart was towering.

Glancing down at his watch as the clerk rang up the last of his purchases, he noticed that forty-five minutes had passed. Not bad for everything he'd had to buy.

~~~

Lindsay saw him coming and was amazed that he could even see where he was going.

The cart was full of bags, and perched across the top was a huge box.

As he got closer, she could make out the picture on the carton. He'd bought a stroller. And if she weren't mistaken, it was similar to one she'd checked out online.

She'd looked at all the different products out there for babies and had made her wish list. She'd even dreamed about a stroller like this one. But until she was no longer running for her life, she'd accepted the fact that big purchases were an impossibility.

And Aiden had bought one for her. Tears welled in her eyes.

God, her hormones must really be all over the place if she was getting watery over a stroller.

She laughed at herself and wiped away the remaining moisture before he saw it and thought something was wrong.
~~~

Taking the keys out of the ignition, she met him at the rear of the car. The press of a button had the rear deck lid popping open.

While she sorted through the bags to determine what could go in the trunk and what needed to stay in the car with them, Aiden opened the box.

"Went a little overboard on that, didn't you?" She couldn't help the smile that curved her lips.

Aiden was so busy pulling everything out, he missed her grin and went on to explain his reason for buying it.

"I figured this would just be easier." He never looked up at her, his head buried in the parts. "You shouldn't be lifting much right now, and I thought if she were sleeping, instead of picking her up and maybe waking her, we could put the whole car seat into this. I even got the same brand as the seat I modeled hers after, so it should still fit perfectly."

She didn't bother trying to hide her amusement. "That's very good thinking."

He must have finally heard the mirth in her voice, because his head snapped up, and his eyes locked on hers.

He stood up slowly. "Are you laughing at me?"

"Of course not." But the grin she couldn't hold back told the real story.

"Okay, it's more than we need right now; I'll admit that." He gave in and smiled back at her. "But it was so cool, I couldn't pass it up. Look at everything it comes with."

By the time he was finished showing her all the features, she was choking on her giggles. She tried to be properly amazed by this fine piece of equipment, but she just couldn't pull it off.

"Oh, shut up and get in the car," he told her in mock disgust.

"I'm sorry," she told him. "You just sounded like you were describing a sports car instead of a stroller." She leaned in and gave him a soft kiss. "Thank you Aiden, for all you're doing for me and Hannah."

Wrapping his arms around her, he pulled her into him. "It is completely my pleasure."

He gave her a kiss that was so tender and loving her heart fluttered and tears fell down her cheeks. She let them fall this time, and when he raised his head and saw them, he gave her a questioning look.

"Hormones. Ignore it, and they'll go away," she laughed.

"Are you sure?"

"Yeah."

One more quick kiss, and he released her. "Okay, let's get this stuff put away and get back on the road."

Most of the bags ended up having to go inside the car, because the stroller took up so much room in the trunk. But they finally had everything where it needed to be and were ready to head out again.

23

When Lindsay opened her eyes, it was to find Aiden lying next to her, sound asleep. They were obviously in a motel room, but she didn't remember how she'd gotten there.

They'd left the cabin pretty late in the day, and after stopping at the store had chosen to eat on the road. That was the last thing Lindsay could remember.

She must have been exhausted last night for Aiden to have been able to carry her without her waking up. And by the looks of the light peeking through the crack in the curtains, it was probably late morning.

Hannah.

Where is she? Why hadn't she heard her cry? She must have woken up hungry during the night. How could she sleep through her own baby crying? Why hadn't Aiden woken her up? God, the poor baby must be starving by now.

Lindsay lifted her head, looking around for her daughter.

She found her right next to her side of the bed, lying in the new stroller. He'd laid the seat all the way flat and used it as a bassinet.

Rolling onto her side towards her baby, she reached in to check on her. She was sleeping peacefully.

"Is she awake again?"

The mumbled words from behind her startled her. She jerked her head around to look at Aiden.

"Again?" she asked. "When was she awake before?"

"A couple of hours ago, I think," Aiden mumbled into the pillow.

"Why didn't you wake me to feed her? She must be starving by now."

The censure in her voice must have penetrated his sleep-filled mind, because he opened his eyes and raised his head to look at her.

"I *tried*, but you were dead to the world. I figured you needed the sleep, so I heated up a bottle and fed her." It wasn't hard to see he was pissed as he swung his legs off the side of the bed to stand. "I also bathed her and changed her diaper. Was that overstepping my bounds, too?"

Those were the last words she heard before he slammed the bathroom door, which promptly woke Hannah. She started to whimper and then graduated into a full-blown, pissed-off cry.

"Great," Lindsay muttered to herself. "Now I've managed to piss both of you off, and I've only been awake for a whole three minutes. What a way to start the day."

Sitting up on the edge of the bed, she noticed she was dressed only in her shirt and panties. She'd slept through Aiden undressing her, too, evidently.

Sighing, she reached into Hannah's makeshift bed and lifted her out. Settling herself back against the headboard, she gave her daughter some breakfast.

She listened to the shower run while Hannah ate, wondering why she had jumped all over Aiden. Of course he would have taken care of the baby during the night if she weren't able to. He loved this little girl as much as she did.

Her only excuse was that her sleep-muddled brain had freaked a little when she didn't know where her daughter was.

A little flimsy, but it was all she had. Now she needed to apologize to Aiden.

Hannah must not have been all that hungry, because she

was sound asleep again by the time the shower turned off.

She gently disengaged Hannah's little mouth from her nipple and laid her back in the stroller.

Standing, she made her way to the bathroom door. Having lived with him for the last few weeks, she'd gotten to know his routine. She knew he'd be standing at the sink, black hair wet and slicked back, towel wrapped low around his hips, shaving.

Not bothering to knock, she opened the door and stood in the doorway. He was right where she expected him to be. And he took her breath away. He gave her a quick glance in the mirror and went back to shaving, not saying anything.

Okay, he was still mad. "I'm sorry for jumping all over you," she told him. "I know you love Hannah and would do anything for her. My only excuse is that when I woke up, I didn't know where she was, and when I realized I hadn't heard her cry in the night, I freaked out a little. I'm sorry."

He finished the last few swipes with the razor before he rinsed it out and turned to look at her. "I'm sorry, too."

She was a little surprised by his apology. "Why? I was the one who lit into you before your brain even had a chance to wake up. *You* didn't do anything to apologize for."

She could see the change in his face at the realization he hadn't actually done anything wrong this time. With a smirk, he grabbed a hand-towel off the rack and wiped off his face. He tossed it into the sink and turned more fully towards her. "I didn't, did I?"

Hiding her smile, she moved forward and slipped her arms around his bare waist just above the towel. She leaned into him.

"How will I ever make this up to you?" She nipped at his freshly-shaven chin, inhaling the scent of the soap he'd used. "I've treated you horribly this morning. What can I do to show you how sorry I am?"

"You *have* treated me badly, and I don't think there's

anything you *can* do," he told her with as much dignity as he could muster with the obvious bulge growing beneath the towel.

"I think I can… *come up* with something." She kept her eyes locked on his as she kissed her way down his chest. She saw the exact moment he realized she was serious.

"Linds, I was only joking around. I don't expect you to—"

"Shhh. I want to." She smiled up at him, drowning in the green depths of his eyes. "God, it's only been a week, and I miss you already. How do people make it the full six after having a baby?" She kissed his chest, concentrating on his flat nipples. "I guess they don't all have you there to heal them afterwards."

"Speaking of which, we need to get you and Hannah to a doctor's office to get checked out."

His voice didn't sound all that steady.

"We can discuss that later." She made quick work of the knot holding his towel. It hit the floor in front of him as her eyes traveled the length of him and then back up to his face. His mossy green eyes had darkened with arousal, and his body was tense and hard.

Slowly she lowered to her knees in front of him, letting the discarded towel act as a cushion.

Her focus shifted from his eyes to what was in front of her. His erection was full and rigid. Standing straight out, as if it were straining for her touch.

With this intimacy so new between them, she was still learning his body. She was fascinated by the shape and size and texture of it. She wanted to know what he liked and didn't like. She wanted to drive him beyond crazy.

Wrapping her hand tightly around the base of his erection, she looked up and grinned. "Now be sure to let me know what you like."

"I think whatever you do, I'll like it just fine," he ground out as he reached behind him to grip the edge of the sink with both hands.

She leaned forward so her hot breath blew over him as she spoke. "This is still new to us, so I want to make sure not to do something you don't like or doesn't feel good."

She flicked her tongue in the v on the underside of the head of his shaft.

"Shit," he gasped. "That feels real good."

She smiled up at him and repeated the move a few more times, listening to his breathing stutter.

She took the head into her mouth and ran her teeth back and forth over the ridge.

The minute thrusts of his hips told her he wanted her to take all of him. She deliberately waited until he told her what he wanted. And it didn't take long before he was telling her what to do next.

"Oh, God, Linds, you gotta take more," he groaned out.

She took more, but not all. She stopped about halfway and tormented him.

Lindsay was enjoying herself so much, she forgot to wait for him to issue his next instruction. She took him deep, and as she withdrew ran her tongue up the bottom, from the base to the head and over the top.

"Oh fuck," Aiden panted. One hand came off the sink to tangle in her hair. "Again," he grunted beyond control, "take it all."

Looking at the size of him, she wasn't sure she could do that, but she'd take as much as possible to give him the pleasure he sought.

She skimmed her mouth up and down his shaft, taking more with each movement.

Aiden's grip in her hair grew tighter. She could feel, ever so slightly, the push and pull of his hand, guiding her up and down his manhood.

Getting more used to the shape of him, she took even more.

She consciously relaxed and felt him slide deeper.

His sharp, indrawn breath let her know just how much he liked what she was doing. The pressure on the back of her head increased, silently begging her to keep going.

Lindsay wanted to take all of him. She loved that she had the power to make him lose control.

Rising a little higher on her knees, she glided her mouth slowly down his shaft until her lips were pressed against the dark curly hairs at the base.

Feeling the pull on her hair, she backed off a little then pushed forward again, letting him slip deep.

Suddenly Aiden swore, fisted his hand in her hair, and thrust.

~~~

He couldn't believe what had just happened. Not only had Lindsay been extraordinarily selfless, but the way she'd done it had blown his mind. He had never felt anything even close to that with any other woman.

With his hand still wrapped in her hair, he gently pulled her up level with him. "Come here, you." Using his grip on her, he angled her head to receive his kiss. His other hand slid down the front of her abdomen and into her panties.

"Aiden . . ." She tried to speak.

"Shhh," He said against her mouth as his fingers found the lips shielding her inner core. She was extremely wet, having become aroused herself while she played with him.

His fingers brushed over that most sensitive spot, and he was rewarded with her quick intake of breath. She shuddered in his arms and leaned into him. Releasing her hair, he wrapped his arm around the small of her back to help support her weight.

Her face was now buried in his neck, her breathing coming in short gasps as she strained towards her own release.
~~~

Alternately circling and squeezing her now-swollen nub, it wasn't long before he felt her come apart in his arms. He held her while the orgasm took her over.

24

Aiden held her tightly until they'd both recovered.

"Wow."

"Yeah." He grinned over the top of her head. "Right back at you."

"Okay. Well, I guess you're not mad at me anymore," she said into his chest.

"Nope. And it has nothing to do with what just happened. If we fight, we fight. I don't want you to *ever* think I expect that kind of thing."

Still wrapped in his arms, she tipped her head back and smiled at him. "I know you're not that type of person, and neither am I. I would never use sex to try to manipulate you. I know we started out joking around, but the more I thought about it," she nipped at his chin, "the more it was something I wanted to do, for both of us."

He kissed her once more before they stepped apart and walked back into the other room. He watched as she went to check on Hannah.

"Are you hungry?" he asked, pulling clothes out of the shopping bags. "I saw a little restaurant when we came in last night. It's right next door; we could go over there to eat or call in a take-out order and eat it here. Whichever you prefer."

"Here would be better," she told him. "That way we don't have to wake Hannah again, and that'll give me time to get dressed. When you get back, I'll be ready." Finding her own clothes, she added, "And as soon as we're done eating, we'll go find Margaret."

He knew she was apprehensive about the plan, since they didn't know how Margaret was going to react. Would she be receptive to helping them, or were they just walking into a trap? They were taking a big chance, but this would be their only opportunity to get to her without worrying that Carl would intercept them.

Pulling his shirt over his head, he crossed the room to where Lindsay stood holding her jeans.

"We don't have to do this if you're not sure. We'll come up with something else."

"No. We have to talk to her. If there's a chance she'll help us, I have to take it. This could be the one thing that brings this whole situation to an end. Forever." She reached up to kiss his chin. "I'll be fine. I'm not scared—just nervous."

"Are you sure?" He watched her eyes closely, looking for any sign of fear.

"Yes. We need this. We need her."

~~~

After a quick breakfast that neither of them really tasted, they were back on the road.

Aiden didn't have any trouble following Jack's directions to the Donnelly house. They lived in an upscale community, but, thankfully, it wasn't gated.

The houses were large but still nothing compared to Marquand Manor. Each property looked to consist of about four acres, putting plenty of space between homes. Each also had a spectacular view of Lake Michigan.

He drove past the first time, just to scope the layout, specifically checking for a fence or guards, or anything else
~~~

which might keep them from getting in to see Margaret.

"Well, what do you think?" Lindsay's words broke into his thoughts as he rounded the corner again.

"I think we should find a place to park within view of the house and watch for a while. See if anyone comes or goes."

"Lucky for us there's not a ten-foot high concrete fence surrounding the house. We should be able to get in to see Margaret pretty easily here," Lindsay said before adding, "I kind of expected something more along the lines of a compound, after what we've heard about Carl."

"I think he may be under the assumption that no one would dare cross him because of his reputation."

Aiden didn't circle the block too many times because, according to Jack, that might draw attention as easily as being parked out front. On the next pass, he looked for the best place from which to observe that wouldn't cause too much undue notice.

Surveying the immediate area, he noticed a large number of cars in front of a neighboring house, about a block down from the Donnellys'. Someone was having a party. That should provide the perfect cover. What was one more car in a group that size?

He drove past and pulled into the first available driveway to turn around, went to the end of the line of cars, and pulled up behind the last one. He inched forward until he had a clear view.

Satisfied with his positioning, he shut off the car and took off his seatbelt. "You may as well get comfortable."

He didn't take his eyes off the house but could see out of the corner of his eye that Lindsay was taking him at his word. She'd also taken off her seatbelt. Turning around in her seat, she leaned over the back and checked on Hannah.

"Still asleep?" he asked her.

"Yup."

Sliding back down into her seat, she curled her legs under her and sat sideways facing him. "So, what's our plan when we decide to go in? Do we just ring the doorbell, or do we sneak in?"

With a quick glance at her, he grinned. "I don't think there's much sneaking with an infant in tow."

"So, the front door it is then," Lindsay said with a nod.

"Actually . . ." He hadn't wanted to get into this with her before now, because he knew she would fight him on it. But it was almost go-time, and he didn't have any other choice. He brought his gaze around to meet hers. "I'd rather you and Hannah stay somewhere safe until I can get a feel for Margaret. Find out if she's friend or foe."

Her eyes narrowed, and he knew she was gearing up to argue.

"Let me explain," he interrupted. "If we all go traipsing up to the door and ring the bell, what happens if she's just as evil as Carl? We'll have handed them just what they want—*Hannah*. I'm not taking that chance with either of you. I think I should go in alone and judge the situation. When I feel everything is safe, then you and Hannah can come in, and we'll all sit and talk."

He gave her some time to think it over while he focused his attention back on the Donnelly house.

Catching movement behind them, he glanced up at the rearview mirror and recognized the two people in the car that had just pulled in behind them.

"You've got to be fucking kidding me."

Lindsay turned to look out the back window. "What? It's probably just more people for the party," she offered.

"No, it's definitely not more party-goers." He hit the button to unlock the doors.

"Aiden?"

He detected the note of tension in her voice. "It's fine." He laid his hand over the top of hers. "I know who they are, and I shouldn't be surprised they're here."

~~~

Before Lindsay could ask who he was talking about, both back doors opened, and the newcomers slid in on either side of Hannah's car seat. They gently shut the doors in deference to her, not wanting to wake her up.

She got her first clear view of the couple. The woman had shoulder-length light brown hair, a trim figure, and startling dark green eyes. This was Aiden's cousin Marissa, and the man was her fiancé, Jack.

She recognized them from when they'd come into Charlie's.

They'd obviously come down from Detroit with the intention of helping out. She knew Jack was a private investigator, and that he and Marissa worked together.

Lindsay's attention was brought back to Aiden.

"What the hell are you guys doing here?" Aiden turned to look at them in the back seat.

Jack looked at Marissa over Hannah's car seat. "I told you he wouldn't appreciate this."

"Oh, shut up," Marissa shot back, turning to Aiden. "I told Jack we needed to get down here and help."

She knew Marissa's powers included the gift of visions, and her statement caught not only her attention, but Aiden's as well.

Before she could find out what Marissa meant, Aiden asked, "Did you have a vision?"

"Not exactly," Marissa hedged, looking to Jack for help.

Jack grinned and sat back against the seat. He crossed his arms over his chest. "Don't look at me—this was your idea. I told you we shouldn't do this. We have more than enough work back at the office to keep us busy. *You* can tell him why we came all the way down here."
~~~

Lindsay could definitely see what had drawn Marissa to Jack. He was tall and rugged, and would have been right at home in the old west. Where he would, no doubt, have been a lawman.

His gray eyes were bright with amusement right now, but she had a feeling they could change in a heartbeat, going either dark with passion or steely with rage. His sun-streaked blonde hair brushed the tops of his shoulders. He reminded her of the actor from that show about the plane crash survivors on that crazy island. A very handsome man indeed.

But he did nothing for her.

Her gaze shifted to Aiden, and she could instantly feel her heartbeat quicken and her blood flow hot.

He had completely ruined her for all other men. But that was okay. She just hoped she'd done the same for him.

Her attention was brought back to the couple in the backseat when Marissa spoke.

"I was talking to my mother the other day about the wedding, and the conversation turned to what was going on with you two. Since she and Becca talk all the time, and because we're all family, she didn't see any harm in sharing what you guys had planned," Marissa said in a rush.

Lindsay looked over at Aiden and saw he wasn't satisfied with her answer.

"And what about all that made you want to follow us out here?" he prompted.

All eyes were on Marissa for the answer.

The silence in the car continued to grow until Jack finally answered, "She wanted to make sure Lindsay wasn't taking advantage of you."

"Jack!" Marissa hissed, conscious of the baby sleeping between them.

"What?" Jack asked innocently, apparently enjoying the fact Marissa was the one in the hot seat. "That's basically what brought us to Chicago, isn't it?"

Aiden trapped Marissa in his gaze. "So you didn't have any visions telling you something was going to happen here? You didn't get any feelings one way or the other?"

"No, I didn't," Marissa's defiant stare matched Aiden's.

Aiden continued to drill her with his mossy green eyes. Lindsay knew she wouldn't want to be on the receiving end of that look. And evidently, neither did Marissa, because she ended up looking away first.

"Okay, I admit it. I wanted to come here and meet Lindsay, and find out for myself if everything she was telling you was the truth."

Marissa's eyes tracked to her. "No offense to you; it's nothing personal."

Lindsay smiled at her. "No offense taken. I understand."

Aiden looked at her incredulously. "How can you smile at her and tell her you understand? She came here, dragging this idiot with her, to judge whether or not you're a liar."

Jack just grinned good-naturedly at Aiden's dig.

Lindsay held her own smile in check and tried to explain. "No, she didn't. She came here to protect you, and her family. Which I'm sure you would do if the situation were reversed."

She looked back at Marissa, who was already nodding in agreement.

"And he *did* do the same thing to me," Marissa told her.

"What? When?" Aiden asked, disbelieving.

"I seem to remember a certain morning you told me that, since my brother wasn't around, you felt you should be the one to look out for me where Jack was concerned," Marissa reminded him.

"Why is this the first I'm hearing about that?" Jack chimed in.

"You stay out of this," Aiden directed at him, and then turned back to Marissa. "And that was completely different."

"Why?" Marissa narrowed her eyes at him. "Because I'm just a woman and can be easily taken advantage of? And you're a big, strong manly-man who can't be?"

Lindsay struggled to hide her grin. Aiden was at a loss for words. He didn't know how to get out of the hole he'd dug for himself. His helpless gaze swung to Lindsay, but she only raised her eyebrows and said nothing.

Aiden focused on Jack for help.

"Don't look at me. You told 'this idiot' to 'stay out of it.' Plus, I know better than to step in it that deep."

"Shit," Aiden muttered to himself.

"Yup, that's the stuff," Jack offered, deadpan.

A laugh burst from Lindsay. She tried to cover it with a cough, but when Aiden gave her a menacing look she knew she hadn't been successful in hiding it.

Marissa was also trying to hide the grin threatening to break over her face.

Lindsay knew the moment Aiden had admitted to himself that this was a losing battle. He took a deep breath and let it out slowly. "All right, I'm sorry. I didn't mean to imply that you were any less capable of taking care of yourself, simply because you're a woman."

Everything was going great with Aiden's apology until the next set of words left his mouth.

Looking at Jack, Aiden added, "But you're still an idiot for letting her drag you all the way here when a phone call would have answered all her questions."

"Hey." Jack raised his hands in surrender. "There's no *letting* her do anything. I'm just along for the ride. In case you've forgotten, she's *literally* a force of nature. I'm not pissing her off."

Lindsay wasn't sure what Jack meant by that. "What?"

Aiden smiled and explained. "You know Marissa can control the elements. Well, since our powers are affected a great deal by our emotions, when she gets good and ticked off, she's been known to throw people around." Aiden tried to cover a chuckle. "Especially Jack here."

She looked to Marissa and was greeted with a smug smile.

"You actually picked him up and threw him?" Lindsay asked her.

Marissa smirked at Jack, some sort of silent message passing between them. "I never actually *threw* him, but I did lift him off the floor a couple of times. And once I pinned him against the wall."

"Wow, cool," Lindsay told her.

"Can we get back to the business at hand here?" Aiden asked, looking at his cousin. "Or would you rather go on questioning Lindsay?"

"Aiden, stop being an ass." Lindsay had had just about enough. "I'll answer any questions she has until she feels more comfortable with me and this whole situation."

Turning back to Marissa, she offered, "Is there anything in particular you wanted to know?"

Now Marissa blushed. "No. My mom and aunt filled me in on most of it. I just needed to see for myself."

"If you ever need to ask me anything, feel free," Lindsay told her. "I know I just showed up out of the blue and dragged Aiden into the middle of my problems. I understand how that might concern everyone."

"Thank you." Marissa smiled at her, and Lindsay knew they could become very good friends if everything worked out.

25

"So what's the plan?" Jack asked Aiden. "You *do* have a plan, don't you?"

"We were just discussing that when you two showed up," he told him. "We were trying to figure out if Carl has actually left the house, and if he has, find the best way to get in to see Margaret."

"Well, we can help you out with one. We know for a fact Carl is long gone and on his way back to the cabin," Jack told them. "We got here last night and had the pleasure of watching him, and most of his guards, leave for the airport."

"So Margaret's in there alone?" Lindsay asked Jack.

"Pretty much," he agreed. "I can't imagine Carl took *all* of his guards. Some of them would have had to stay behind to watch this place. We don't know how many, though."

"So that should be first on the agenda," Aiden suggested. "I think Jack and I should check that out. Linds, you and Marissa stay here with Hannah."

They'd come full-circle back to the conversation they'd been having when Jack and Marissa had first shown up. Lindsay was getting ready to argue her point when Marissa reached up and touched her arm.

She turned to see what Marissa wanted and was met with a blank stare.

Lindsay wasn't sure what was happening, but by Jack and

Aiden's expressions, neither of them seemed alarmed.

"What's going on?" she whispered.

"Marissa's having a vision," Aiden told her.

"From me?" She wasn't sure how she felt about that. And just what was Marissa seeing?

Before anyone could answer, Marissa was speaking in a rush.

"Aiden, you and Lindsay need to get into that house. Now! Go! Jack and I will stay with Hannah."

The urgency in Marissa's voice caused Lindsay's heart to beat double-time. "What's going on? What's happening?"

"Margaret's trying to kill herself," Marissa told them. "She's about to ingest some kind of poison. She's in what looks like a library or . . . a . . . a den. You have to get in there, now! Before it's too late!"

Lindsay looked at Aiden, and they both grabbed for the door handles at the same time. They were racing across the street and up the sidewalk within seconds.

Aiden didn't bother knocking or ringing the bell. He just grabbed the handle, barely getting it turned before ramming his shoulder against it to force it open.

Lindsay knew by the tension and urgency she saw in Aiden just how much faith he put into Marissa's visions.

Never having been around someone who could see things, Lindsay wasn't sure exactly how it worked. But if Aiden was reacting this way, it must be dire.

Once inside the house, they were met with a long hall with rooms on either side.

"You check everything on that side, and I'll do this one."

The first room was a sunny parlor, and there was no sign of Margaret. Lindsay backed out and hurried to check the next.

This one was what Marissa had described. And there was Margaret Donnelly, lying on the floor.

Lindsay screamed out Aiden's name, ran to the older woman,

and lifted her into her lap. She called out to him again.

She heard him thundering across the hall, following the sound of her voice.

"She still has a pulse," she told him when he burst through the doorway, "but it's getting weaker. Aiden, you have to do something," Lindsay begged.

"I intend to." He crossed the room in giant strides. "Lay her flat on the floor."

Lindsay gently laid her down and then slid back out of the way so he could work.

She wasn't sure if it were possible to heal someone who had taken poison, but she had seen what he was capable of and didn't doubt his ability.

He placed his hands on Margaret's stomach and chest and concentrated on calling up the healing power coursing through his body.

While Aiden was busy with Margaret, Lindsay wandered around the room, looking for something that would explain why she'd done this.

Rounding the desk, she found what she'd been looking for, sitting front and center.

Margaret's suicide note.

She picked it up and began to read.

Carl.

I can't do this anymore. My entire married life, I have sat back and allowed you to rule me to the extent that I have lost everything I've ever held dear. My son, just the latest on a very long list.

You once told me the only way I would escape you was when I died. Well now I'm dead and finally free of you.

I just hope God will forgive me and let me join the children you took from me.

I hope someday you meet up with someone who will do to you everything that you have done to others.

Then you will know hell.

Margaret

"Children?" Lindsay whispered. She couldn't believe what she'd just read. "Steven never mentioned any other children."

At the sound of Margaret's gasp, she dropped the note and rushed back to Aiden's side.

It wasn't long before Margaret's eyes fluttered open. When her gaze landed on Aiden, confusion turned to fear.

As weak as she was, Margaret tried to fight her way free of the stranger who had his hands on her.

"What? Who are you? How did you get into my house?"

"Relax. We're not here to hurt you." Aiden used the voice he usually reserved for Hannah. Soft and gentle. He was trying to get through Margaret's fear to calm her.

"Who are you?" she asked again, and then noticed Lindsay kneeling there also.

Recognition struck. "Lindsay? What are you doing here? You have to get away from here. He'll find you."

She was shocked Margaret actually knew who she was.

"How do you know who I am?"

The smile that came to Margaret's lips was one of love. "Steven sent me pictures of you. He was so proud of you. He loved you so much."

"I didn't know he'd kept in touch with you. He always told me never to contact you. That he had broken all ties with you both."

"It had to be kept from his father," she told them. "It was the only way."

Margaret tried to sit up. She and Aiden were right there to help her.

Whatever Aiden had done to heal Margaret must have worked. Other than being weak, she seemed to be fine now.

"I think this conversation should wait for a little while," Aiden told both of them. "Let's get Margaret some place she can rest. She's been through a lot."

"Oh God, I'm supposed to be dead," Margaret moaned, remembering. "What did you do?"

"He healed you, Margaret." Lindsay gently took the woman's hand. "We came here for your help and found you on the floor. Aiden has powers, and one of them is the gift of healing."

Having lived for so long with someone like Carl, someone who used their magic for evil purposes, Margaret was obviously afraid. Lindsay couldn't blame her, but she didn't want her to fear Aiden.

"He's good, Margaret; he's so good. Like Steven was. Nothing like Carl. There's not a mean bone in Aiden's body. He's helped me so much."

She held Margaret's gaze, letting her know she spoke the truth, and she was safe with them.

"How about we get you somewhere more comfortable than the floor?" Lindsay suggested with a smile.

Margaret allowed her and Aiden to assist her to her feet and over to the couch where they settled her in.

With a wary eye still on Aiden, Margaret asked her, "You're sure?"

Lindsay took a seat on the couch next to her. "I am very sure. Without him, I wouldn't be alive. And neither would Hannah."

That was the magic word. Margaret's gaze swung to her.

"Hannah?"

"Yes. Your granddaughter," Lindsay said softly.

"Oh dear," Margaret said with a watery smile. "A little girl. Steven's little girl."

The happiness left Margaret's eyes quickly. "Is she safe? Please tell me she's safe. Carl can never find her."

"Yes. She's safe for now," Lindsay answered. "But we need your help to make sure she stays that way."

"My help?" Margaret asked. "What can *I* do? I can't fight Carl. No one can."

"Well, we intend to," Aiden joined in the conversation. "And if we have your support, it might make all the difference."

"I don't know," Margaret hesitated. "I've tried fighting him for the last thirty-five years. All it ever got me was trapped. And alone."

~~~

This wasn't getting them anywhere. Aiden was about to press his point when he heard a little voice whisper through his mind.

"Poppa, I need to come in there now. Nana Maggie has to see me, and then she'll help."

He hated to bring Hannah into this house, but he also knew that little girl was tuned into the universe in a way the rest of them weren't.

Ignoring Lindsay's questioning gaze, he left the room and headed for the front door.

He pulled out his cell phone at the same time he yanked open the front door. Looking at Jack across the street, he dialed his number.

Jack answered on the first ring. "Yeah?"

"You and Marissa need to bring Hannah up to the house," Aiden told him.

"Are you sure that's smart?" Jack asked.

"Not really, but Margaret is waffling. Hannah thinks if Margaret sees her, she will help us."

"She what?" Jack sounded stunned.

"I'll explain later. Just bring her in here."

"All right. We're on our way."

Sliding his phone back into his pocket, Aiden watched Jack and Marissa exit the car with the baby.

When they reached the door where he was waiting, he lifted Hannah out of Marissa's arms and into his own.
~~~

"I hope you know what you're doing, baby girl," he said to Hannah, who was wide awake and looking at him with big blue eyes.

"I do, Poppa," he heard.

"Okay. Well, here we go." Taking a deep breath, he turned back into the house with Jack and Marissa on his heels.

As soon as he crossed the threshold of the library, Lindsay was on her feet coming towards him.

"Aiden, what are you doing?" she asked in a hushed voice. "Why did you bring her in here?"

He relayed Hannah's message.

"Nana Maggie, huh?" Lindsay asked, rubbing the blonde fuzz on her daughter's head.

"Yeah, I caught that, too." He paused. "Linds, she hasn't been wrong yet."

"I know. It just scares me to have her in here."

"Nothing will happen to her." He leaned down to kiss her softly on the mouth. "She has us and Jack and Marissa here to protect her."

He passed Hannah to Lindsay. She turned and approached Margaret, who was resting with her head tipped back against the couch, her eyes closed.

"Margaret?"

Margaret's eyes opened, and she lifted her head.

"Someone wants to meet you," Lindsay told her, sitting next to her on the couch.

Aiden crossed the room, too, and sat in the chair adjacent to Margaret. He wanted to be close enough to protect Lindsay and Hannah if needed.

Glancing up, he noticed Jack and Marissa had stayed in the doorway to watch the hall and front entrance, making sure no one interrupted this moment.

Focusing his attention back on Lindsay and Margaret, Aiden was surprised when Lindsay handed the baby over to her.

Margaret broke down sobbing as she gently stroked Hannah's cheeks. "Oh my God. Oh, Steven, I'm so sorry you're not here to see this."

Margaret turned her tear-filled eyes towards Lindsay. "She's beautiful. I see some of Steven, but mostly, she looks like you."

"She has more of Steven than you know," Lindsay told her.

"She has powers?" Margaret asked. "Already?"

"She had them in the womb, and that was a surprise, let me tell you." Lindsay tried to keep it light.

"She'll be strong, then. Steven didn't even have them in the womb." She looked adoringly down at Hannah, tears still streaming silently down her cheeks. "Carl can never know." Dabbing at her tears with a tissue she pulled from the box on the table, Margaret went on. "I am so sorry for everything you have gone through because of this family. No one deserves this. You deserve to be happy and to raise your child in peace."

26

Margaret paused thoughtfully, taking in every feature of the infant in her arms. Aiden saw her nod as if making some sort of internal decision. She sat up straight and brushed away the fallen tears.

"But no more. I will not let this innocent child be another pawn in my husband's game." Margaret cradled Hannah a little closer to her chest. "What do you need me to do?"

Lindsay turned and smiled at Aiden. There was relief in her eyes, and the hope that this just might work.

"It's not so much of what you can do. We just need you to talk to us." Aiden confided their plan to blackmail Carl.

"I'm sorry, but that won't work," Margaret told them in despair.

"Why?" Lindsay asked her desperately. "You said yourself you've lived with him for thirty-five years. You must know something that will make him leave us alone."

Lindsay paused, looked down at Hannah, and then spoke gently. "Margaret, I found your suicide note."

The older woman took a deep breath and braced herself, as if she knew what was coming next. Aiden hadn't seen the note—didn't even know there was one—so he waited for Lindsay to continue.

"In it, you said Carl had cost you your children. *Children,* Margaret. Steven never said anything about having siblings.

Is that the reason he broke off from the family? Did Carl do something to them?"

Aiden was shocked by this revelation. In all their investigations into Carl, no mention had ever been made of other kids. How could this have been hidden? There should have been birth certificates, medical records, *something*.

He glanced at Jack with a questioning look, but Jack only shrugged, letting him know his research hadn't turned up anything either.

Everyone in the room waited to hear what Margaret would say next.

With tears coursing down her face again, Margaret explained, "Just one. One other child. Lauren, my beautiful little Lauren." Margaret looked down at Hannah and rubbed her soft cheeks gently before returning her gaze to Lindsay. "She was only three when she died."

"What happened to her?" Lindsay urged gently.

"Steven had been so gifted in his powers. From an early age, we knew he'd inherited gifts which surpassed even his father's. Carl was so proud. He started working with him to hone his skill and control."

Margaret uttered a humorless laugh. "Oh, Carl kept his more evil side from Steven, but I could see he was training him to someday take over for him, and it killed me to know that one day my sweet baby boy would be just as bad, if not worse than, his father. I tried to counter whatever Carl was teaching him with lessons in humanity, love, and generosity, but I had to do it subtly. If Carl ever found out what I was doing, he would have taken Steven away or just killed me."

Lindsay touched her arm. "Whatever you did worked. Steven was the sweetest and most gentle person I had ever met."

"Thank you for that," Margaret told her. "He didn't turn out so bad, did he? I just wish we could have been closer in the last few years."

Aiden wanted to keep her on track. He didn't know how much longer they had. "Why did he leave six years ago?"

"He found out his father had killed his baby sister," Margaret revealed.

"What happened?" Aiden probed.

"When Steven was seven, I got pregnant again. We were so happy, though for very different reasons. Carl wanted another son to train and mold, and I was hoping for a little girl," she said, looking down at the sleeping baby in her arms.

"Well, I got my wish." She smiled. "Lauren was born, and I was so thrilled. She was so petite, a lot like little Hannah here. And she had red hair." Margaret brushed a hand over Hannah's soft blonde fuzz before looking up at Lindsay. "My great-grandmother had red hair, so that must have been where it came from.

"Well, needless to say, Carl wasn't so happy about having a daughter, but figured he could still train her in the same way he was training Steven. But by the time Lauren was two, she still wasn't showing signs of having any gifts. Carl was incensed. He blamed me for the fact that she didn't have any magical abilities. Screamed at me that if he'd married someone with power, his children would have been unstoppable. Instead, he was stuck with a useless daughter."

Margaret stopped.

Lindsay reached out to pat the older woman's hand. "Margaret, would you like some water or something?"

"Yes, please, if you don't mind." Margaret gestured to the cabinet under one of the bookcases. "There's a little refrigerator in that cupboard there."

Lindsay rose to get her a bottle.

Since Margaret was still cuddling Hannah, Lindsay unscrewed the cap before handing it to her and then resumed her seat.

After taking a few sips, Margaret went on. "He pretty much

concentrated on Steven then and left Lauren to me. Over the next few months, I started noticing she was able to do things. Get her favorite doll out of her crib while she sat on the floor across the room. I'd find her sitting there brushing that doll's hair, when I knew I had put it away. She could turn the lights on and off. Just little things at first, but I knew as she grew, so would her abilities. I made the decision to keep it from my husband. Since he didn't pay any attention to her anyway, I figured he wouldn't notice, and she would be safe from him."

"Until one day he came to me and said he was taking her out with him. That he wanted to get close to her again—that she was still his daughter after all."

"I had always warned Lauren not to do any of her magic in front of her father, but I told her one more time before he took her away that day. I'll never forget that last moment with her. She put her little arms around my neck and whispered to me. She said, 'Don't worry, Momma. Lulu don't show tricks. Our girl secret.'"

Aiden knew whatever she was about to tell them next was almost impossible for her to voice.

"That was the last time I saw her alive," Margaret whispered.

He let Lindsay guide her through the rest of the questions, her softer touch coaxing the devastating truth from the distraught woman. "How did she die?"

"He said she got away from him when they stopped by the side of a country road to look at some baby cows. He said he turned to take a phone call, and when he turned back, she was gone. He said she must have fallen into a deep ravine that was near where the cows were. By the time he found her, she was already dead from injuries sustained in the fall. She was only *three*," Margaret cried. "She wouldn't have wandered off. I know that, just as I've always known he killed her, because he considered her a failure.

"Oh God," she sobbed in anguish. "If I hadn't kept from him

the fact she had powers, he might not have hurt her. It's all my fault."

Aiden could do nothing but sit and watch as this woman fell apart over the loss of her child, at the hands of her demented husband.

Lindsay tried to console her, but he had a feeling she'd bottled these emotions up inside for far too long, and it was long past time for them to come out.

She was still crying, though not as hard, when she told them the rest.

"When Steven found out the truth, he was enraged at his father. All that time, he'd been told it was an awful accident. Then to find out his father had killed his baby sister, because he felt like she was nothing—it shattered Steven's whole world. He loved that little girl as much as I did."

"Why was there never any mention of another child?" Aiden had to know.

"Carl wiped out all evidence of her existence," Margaret told them. "It's like she was never even here. And that hurts almost as much as losing her."

"How did Steven find out?" Lindsay asked her.

"He walked in on a fight between his father and me. He was blaming me for Steven never growing to be as ruthless as he, and that he should just cut his losses and get rid of him like he had that other useless whelp.

"Steven burst through the door and confronted his father, and Carl was mean enough to tell him exactly what had happened to Lauren."

With a kiss to Hannah's forehead, Margaret handed her back to Lindsay and rose. Walking to the window, she paused before turning back to face the room. Wrapping her arms around her middle as if to hold herself together, she resumed her explanation.

"I always knew deep down what had happened, but when he

finally admitted he had thrown her into that ravine, something died inside of me. Before I knew what was happening, Steven had attacked his father.

"Carl fought back, of course, but Steven was stronger—a *lot* stronger, it turned out. But he didn't have the same cruel streak his father had, and he couldn't finish it. Steven told him he had gone too far, and that he was done with him and this family. He walked out and never came back."

Margaret went to the bookcases and took a framed photo of Steven off the shelf, tracing his face with her finger.

"A few months later, Steven got in touch with me to let me know he was okay, but he wouldn't tell me where he was. We would talk as often as we could, always keeping it from his father." Margaret looked up and smiled at Lindsay. "That's when he told me about you, and how much he loved you. He was so excited you were pregnant. He couldn't wait for the baby to come. We talked about once a month until he died. I'll never be able to prove it, but I think Carl may have orchestrated it." She placed the frame back on the shelf. "Then, somehow, Carl found out about the baby, and he was hell-bent on raising this one himself to make sure it turned out the way he wanted— evil and cruel, just like him."

"This is all we're asking for," Aiden pressed. "For you to tell us some of the things Carl has done. Things he wouldn't want the police or the government to know about."

Margaret shook her head. "You don't get it. I could tell you every single thing he's done in the last forty years, and it wouldn't do you any good."

"Why not?" Lindsay asked.

"Because he doesn't care," she said in defeat. "No one can touch him. Not the police, not the government, not even the mob."

"There has to be something we can do," Lindsay said in desperation. "I can't continue to live like this, looking over my shoulder all the time, waiting for him to come kill me and take my daughter away." She pulled Hannah in closer to her chest.

Now it was Margaret's turn to comfort Lindsay. Returning to the couch, she sat close and rubbed her hand up and down Lindsay's arm. "We'll think of something. I promise I'll do whatever I can to make sure this baby stays safe.

"Now, I think you all should go," Margaret told them reluctantly. "I told the few guards Carl left behind to make themselves scarce today—I didn't plan on going anywhere, and I didn't need them hanging around. I would hate to have them come back and find you here."

"All right, we'll go," Lindsay agreed. "But we want you to come with us. You can't stay here any longer. You tried to kill yourself to get away from him. We can protect you."

Margaret smiled at her as she caressed Hannah head. "I can't go with you today. If I'm not here, he'll know something is going on. Plus, I have something to live for now. My granddaughter."

Margaret rose from the couch and waited for them to do the same. "Give me a number where I can reach you in case something comes up."

"I don't like leaving you here, but I can understand your reasoning," Lindsay told her. "We'll figure some way out of this, and you'll never have to deal with Carl again."

"Thank you." Margaret leaned in to kiss Lindsay's cheek. "I'm so glad I finally got to meet you, and thank you for bringing Hannah to see me."

"We'll see you again soon," Lindsay promised. "Hannah is going to need her Nana Maggie as she grows up."

Tears filled Margaret's eyes again. "Nana Maggie? I think I like that. No one's called me Maggie since I was a child."

"It was Hannah's idea," Lindsay smiled.

They were almost to the front door when Margaret came to a stop. She didn't understand.

"She can speak telepathically to me," Aiden told her.

"She can . . . Oh boy," Margaret stuttered. "She's going to be something, isn't she?"

"Yeah, we're pretty sure she's going to keep us busy," Aiden told her with a smile. "But between you and my family, we should be able to handle her."

"Your family is magical, I take it?" she asked.

"Yes. Conner and Becca Marquand are my parents. And this," he motioned to Marissa and Jack, who had stayed silent throughout the whole exchange, "is my cousin Marissa, and her fiancé Jack. Her parents are Ben and Mia."

"Oh my," Margaret gasped. "I've known your parents for years but lost touch a long time ago. Please tell them hello for me." She turned to Lindsay. "How on earth did you ever meet up with one of the Marquands?"

Lindsay smiled. "I happened to be hiding out in the town close to where his family lives. When I heard he was there and had powers, I tracked him down, knowing I would need magical help."

Jack broke into the conversation for the first time. "I think Margaret was right when she said we need to go. You can all get together after this is over and discuss everything."

"He's right," Aiden agreed. "And we need to come up with another plan to stop Carl."

"I'm sorry I couldn't offer more help," Margaret apologized.

Lindsay took hold of her hand. "Don't worry about it. We'll come up with something."

Before opening the door, Margaret turned and hugged Lindsay and Hannah. "Be safe, and keep in touch."

"We will, and you be careful, too." Lindsay returned the hug.

Aiden and Jack kept watch up and down the street as they made their way back to the cars.

Once Hannah was buckled into her car seat, the four of them got in, Aiden and Lindsay in front and Jack and Marissa in the back as before.

Not bothering to start the car, Aiden sat and thought over everything he had learned in the last hour. He was stunned and knew the others felt the same way. Turning around in his seat, he glanced back at Jack and Marissa. "Can you believe the life that woman has had to endure?"

Lindsay had her head turned away, looking out the side window. "We have to get her out of there."

"We will. I promise." He reached across the seat and took hold of her hand.

"So what's our plan?" Marissa asked to everyone.

Aiden looked back at his cousin. "'Our?' So, I take it you guys are sticking around?"

"Well, yeah," Marissa told him. "I'm with Lindsay. We can't leave that woman to Carl's mercy any longer. She needs to be free of him."

"I completely agree," Aiden told Marissa. "But I'm at a total loss as to what to do next. Margaret blew my blackmail plan right out of the water." He turned to include Jack. "You got any ideas?"

"I might." Jack's PI brain was working. "Let's head back to the motel, and I'll fill you in. I don't want to stay here any longer than we have to."

Jack and Marissa stepped out, returning to their own car.

Aiden tightened his grip on Lindsay's hand. "Are you okay?" She had yet to look anywhere other than out the side window.

"Lindsay?"

The sadness he saw in her eyes when she turned to him ripped his heart out. "I'm okay, but I can't stop thinking about Steven's little sister. How could Carl have done that to an innocent baby? To his own child?"

"He's a sick, twisted bastard," Aiden told her, rubbing his hand over her hair. "And we won't let him get away with it. We will put a stop to his evil. We'll put a stop to him."

~~~

A short time later, Aiden pulled into the motel parking lot with the others right behind him.

Getting out, Aiden opened the back door. He'd just reached in to release Hannah's seat from the base when Jack called to him. "Hey, before you get everything undone in there, why don't we all load in and go get something to eat?"

Aiden looked across the top of the seat at Lindsay to get her opinion. Her mood had eased somewhat on the drive back to the motel.

"Yeah, that's fine. I could eat something."

They returned to their seats as Jack and Marissa climbed in back.

He looked at Jack in the rearview mirror. "I'm not too familiar with Chicago. Do you have someplace in mind?"

"I do know of a pretty good steakhouse about half an hour from here. It's right in downtown Chicago."
~~~

27

About halfway there, Aiden became aware of a car which seemed to be following them. He had a bad feeling they hadn't gotten away from the Donnelly house undetected.

Before he could get Jack's attention and clue him in, the car rammed them.

"Goddamn it!" Aiden swore as he fought to keep control of the car.

Lindsay gasped in the seat next to him. "What's going on?"

"I think Carl left more men at the house than we originally thought," Aiden ground out as they rammed him again. "What the hell do they think they're doing? They have to know there's a baby in the car."

Trying to avoid the next hit, he asked Marissa over his shoulder. "Can you do anything with those guys back there?"

"You bet." She turned in her seat.

Everyone was so focused on the car behind them, none of them saw the car heading straight for them in the oncoming lane until it was too late.

Aiden had a split second when he looked up and saw the sedan aimed directly at them—nowhere near enough time to avoid the collision, and barely enough time to tell everyone to hang on.

The oncoming car hit them with a glancing blow that sent theirs spinning. Aiden tried to correct the spin by turning into it, but they were out of control and going too fast.

When the tires caught the gravel on the shoulder of the road, it sent the car into a roll as they tumbled down into a steep ditch.

The sounds of metal tearing and glass breaking were ones Aiden knew he would remember until the day he died. Hopefully that wasn't today.

The car came to a shuddering stop back on its wheels. The silence was deafening after the horrific sounds of the crash.

He lay with his head resting on the door, the roof a lot closer than it used to be.

His last thought before he lost consciousness, was that he should have protected Lindsay and Hannah better. And that he was sorry Jack and Marissa had to go through this too.

~~~

A ringing he couldn't identify finally roused Aiden.

When he opened his eyes, the sight of the broken windshield and crumpled metal of the hood brought the crash back in sickening detail.

He turned his head to look for Lindsay. What he found made his heart stop.

She was lying on the seat next to him, her head nearly resting on his leg. There was blood covering her face and neck.

"Lindsay."

The guttural sound that escaped his mouth sounded nothing like his voice. Swallowing a couple of times, he tried again.

"Lindsay." He reached a hand out to brush the blood-soaked hair from her face, only to stop short. He was afraid to touch her. His hand shook as it hovered over her.

Curling his hand into a fist, he took a deep, steadying breath.

Bracing himself, he gently moved her pale blonde hair away from her face and placed trembling fingers against her throat.
~~~

"Oh, thank God." He felt such relief when he found her pulse pounding steady and strong.

Shifting around to lean over her was excruciating. The movement called attention to every part of his body beaten up by the accident.

Finally he was in position and could wipe away some of the blood. He found the wound above the hair line, near her temple. She must have hit her head against the side window when they went careening through the ditch.

He covered the gash with his hand and used what little energy he had left to heal her.

When the cut was gone, he slumped back against the seat and rested.

His phone started ringing, and he vaguely recalled having heard something similar while regaining consciousness. This must have been what it was.

Fumbling in his pocket, he found his cell.

"Hello."

The voice on the other end was that of his father. "Aiden. We've been trying to reach you for over an hour. Something's going on here. Carl's men pulled out, and they didn't try to hide the fact they were leaving. I think he's coming after you."

"Yeah, he already found us," he said wearily into the receiver.

"What? Are you guys okay? Is Hannah all right?" Conner was worried.

He'd been so worried about Lindsay, he hadn't even thought to check on anyone else.

Shifting around again, he saw that Jack was leaning against the back door, just starting to come around, too.

The back door on the passenger side was hanging open. Marissa was nowhere to be seen.

And Hannah was gone.

"Oh shit. He's got her," Aiden said in barely a whisper, forgetting he held the phone to his mouth.

The frantic words coming from the cell phone brought him back.

"Who's got who? Aiden, talk to me!" his father demanded.

"Carl's got Hannah. His men ran us off the road, and he took her. I've got to go."

"Damn it, Aiden! Are you and Lindsay okay?"

"Yeah, I think so."

"I want you to keep us informed. Tell us what we can do to help."

"I will as soon as I figure that out, but I have to go now." He shut the phone on whatever his father said next.

Lindsay and Jack were both starting to groan, so Aiden split his attention between them.

Lindsay was the first to open her eyes. She looked up at him. "What happened?"

"Carl's guys ran us off the road."

"Hannah!" Lindsay pushed herself up off the seat to get to her daughter.

"I'm sorry, Linds. They took her." The look of panic and terror etched across her face at the news nearly shattered him. "I just came to myself, and when I did she was already gone. I'm sorry. I promise—I'll do whatever it takes to get her back. And when we do, I'm going to make sure he fucking pays."

Lindsay sat speechless. He knew she just wanted her daughter back, safe in her arms. He felt ripped apart when she dropped her head into her hands and cried.

The sounds of movement behind him drew his attention. Jack was awake.

"Rissa?" Jack opened his eyes and looked around. "Where's Marissa?"

"I don't know," Aiden admitted. "We just woke up, and she and Hannah were both gone."

Jack slid across the back seat towards the open door.

He had only made it about halfway when he made a strangled

sound Aiden hoped to never hear again. One of such anguish and torment, it caused his breathing to stop.

Turning further around in his seat, he saw Jack launch himself out the door and drop down beside the car.

"Oh, Rissa," Jack moaned. "Come on, baby, it's time to wake up."

Aiden tried to get his door open to get to his cousin, but it wouldn't budge. The force of the accident had wedged it closed. Having no other choice, he slid over the front seat and into the back where he got his first glimpse of his cousin.

She was laying on the ground where Carl's men must have tossed her in their haste to get to Hannah. She was still unconscious, and her left arm was bent at an awkward angle beneath her. His eyes swept down her body, and he noticed her left ankle was also broken.

Jack looked up at him, not afraid to show the tears in his eyes. "Oh, man, Aiden. I'm afraid to touch her. I don't want to make this any worse. You have to help her."

"I will. Give me some room." He gingerly slid out of the car and knelt beside her. "While she's still out, help me straighten her arm and ankle."

While Jack lifted her upper body off the ground, Aiden gently straightened her arm enough so the bone was closer to being aligned. They did the same for her foot, and even in her unconscious state, Marissa whimpered when they moved her.

Aiden set about doing what he could for her. He briefly looked up at Jack and watched the fear for the woman he loved turn into an icy rage for the man who had done this to her.

Marissa still didn't come around when he finished healing her broken bones. Remembering Lindsay's head wound and the way his own head felt, he figured she probably had a concussion. Moving up, he lifted her head out of Jack's lap and motioned the other man to the side. Cupping her head gently in his hands, Aiden tapped into his gift once again.

He just hoped he had enough energy. Between his own injuries, Lindsay's wound, and fixing Marissa's broken bones, he just didn't know how much he still had left in him.

If he couldn't do this, they would have to get her to a hospital. Quickly.

He could hear cars up on the road, but they were too far over the edge of the ditch. The other drivers couldn't see them.

Aiden was just about to tell Jack to go up and flag someone down when Marissa finally showed signs of waking.

He knew Jack wanted to shove him out of the way to get to her, but he restrained himself and allowed Aiden to continue.

When he'd done all he could, he moved back out of the way, exhausted. Jack was right there to scoop her up in his arms and cradled her to him.

Aiden sat back, completely spent, while his cousin and her fiancé comforted each other.

He glanced up to see how Lindsay was doing and was surprised to find her sitting on the edge of the back seat in the open doorway.

"Is she going to be okay?" she asked, looking at Marissa.

Going to her, he knelt in front of her. "Yeah, I think so." Reaching past Lindsay and into the car, Aiden found the diaper wipes in Hannah's bag. Pulling a few out, he cleaned the dried blood off Lindsay's face. When he was done, he paused to look into her eyes.

"How are you feeling?" She wasn't crying anymore, but he couldn't tell what her state of mind was. Her expression was blank, revealing nothing. "I healed the cut on your head, but I didn't have a chance to check out the rest of you. Does anything else hurt?"

She touched her head where it was probably still a little tender. "*Everything* is sore, but nothing I can't live with."

She looked down at her hands clasped in her lap. "We've got to get her back, Aiden. Just the thought of that man having my baby, knowing what we know about him, scares me to death." Her tear-filled eyes searched his. "We don't even know for sure if she survived the crash," she whispered, almost afraid to utter the words.

Aiden threw the now-bloody cloth back into the car and took her trembling hands in his. "Don't say that. She was strapped securely in her car seat. Those things are built with the express purpose of protecting the baby if something like this were to happen."

The uncertainty in Lindsay's eyes was killing him. He didn't know how to make this bearable for her.

Before he could think of anything else to say, Marissa was speaking from behind them. He turned to see Jack holding her securely in his arms where they sat on the ground.

"Hannah was fine when we came to a stop. When we lost control, I threw my power out around her. I held her as still as I could, especially her head and neck. I remember her looking up at me with those big blue eyes, and then nothing. I guess I passed out after that."

Aiden turned back to Lindsay. "See, hon? She's okay. Between the harness, Marissa, and all the cushioning built into that seat, she probably felt almost nothing of the crash." Aiden reached up to brush away her tears. "Remember—Carl needs her alive and well. The fact they took her means she's fine."

Lindsay looked at him with the smallest spark of hope in her blue eyes. "Has she spoken to you at all?"

"No, I'm sorry, she hasn't," he hated to admit. He'd been trying to call out to her, but so far he hadn't heard anything back. "Maybe she's too far away already, or she could just be sleeping."

He held her troubled gaze and made a promise he knew he would keep, even if he died trying. "We'll get her back."

Lindsay brought her hands up to caress the sides of his face.

Running her hands back through his hair, she leaned in to kiss him.

When the fingers of her right hand brushed past his ear, he swore and jerked back. "Son of a bitch!"

Lindsay immediately pulled her hands away from his head, and when she did, they both saw the blood on her right hand.

"Aiden, you're bleeding," she gasped. "Why didn't you say something?"

He tested the area behind his left ear, trying to discern how deep the cut was. "To be honest, it didn't hurt much more than anything else on my body until you touched it. Besides, you and Marissa needed me. That's all I could think about."

He held still while Lindsay parted his hair to get a good look at the cut. "I don't suppose you can heal yourself?"

"What's wrong?" Marissa's voice came from behind him again.

Aiden sat on the ground as Lindsay and Marissa talked over his head.

"He's got a good-sized gash on the side of his head, right behind his ear," Lindsay told her.

Looking back at him, she repeated, "Can you heal yourself?"

"No."

"Well then, we're going to have to get you to a hospital, so you can get a few stitches." Lindsay looked up the embankment to the road they had been driven from. "We need to call the police; no one can see us down here."

"No. We don't have time for that." Aiden stilled her hand when she reached for her phone. "Carl already has a good head start on us. If we wait around for the cops and an ambulance, it'll be *hours* before they're through with us," he reasoned, backing out of her grasp to stand. His wound throbbed when he was fully upright, but it was manageable. Hell, his whole body was aching in some form or another. "We have to figure out where he took her."

Jack stood too, his jaw set and teeth clenched. "Let's get started then. I'm all for finding that mother fucker."

28

All eyes turned to Jack and his ice-cold rage. Aiden knew just what he was feeling. But he also knew he had to keep a somewhat cool head to get through this to find the little girl he already considered his daughter.

Before any further comments or plans could be made, a motor home pulled over up on the road. An elderly couple stuck their heads out the side door. The husband asked, "Do you folks need some help? We almost didn't see you down there—if we weren't sittin' so high in this rig, we wouldn't have. We got ourselves a cell phone in here if you need us to call the police."

From the deep southern accent, it was clear the couple was way north of where they'd originated.

"We're fine," Aiden told them. "Nothing much damaged but the car. Had to swerve to miss some kind of animal," he lied.

"Yeah, know what you mean," the elderly gentleman agreed. "Sometimes those little critters come out of nowhere. Do y'all need a lift somewhere?"

Lindsay stepped forward before Aiden could decline the offer. "If it wouldn't be too much bother, our motel is just back that way. Could you drop us off there?"

"That's not a problem, honey," the woman told her. "Just pile on in."

Once they were all seated inside, the woman swiveled her seat around to face them. "Now my name is Millicent, but y'all can just call me Milly. And this is my husband Wyatt." Wyatt lifted a hand in greeting as he pulled back onto the road. "We're from Tennessee. We're on a road trip," Milly smiled. "One day, my Wyatt comes to me and says he wants to go traveling, and that I can come with him or not, but he's not sittin' on his butt on the front porch waitin' to die. He was a doctor, you see, and retired just a little while ago and has been kind of out of sorts lately. We live in a small town, and he was the only doctor, so he stayed pretty busy. That was, until our youngest, Collin, took over the practice for him. Well anyway, he says now that he finally has some time, he wants to see some of this great country. Well, of course I couldn't let him go alone, seein' as how he hasn't cooked for himself in over fifty years. Why, he'd have starved to death in under a week if I hadn't come along. Are y'all married?"

"Milly, that's none of our business. These young people only asked for a ride, not to have their ears chewed off," Wyatt said, not at all affected by the quick change of subject.

"I was only askin'." Milly smiled at her husband and then turned that smile on them. "I'm sure they don't mind. Do you, dears?"

Marissa choked on a laugh. "No ma'am, we don't mind at all."

Milly gave her husband a look as if to say 'I told you so.'

"So are you married?"

"No ma'am," Marissa admitted. "Not yet, anyway. I'm Marissa, and this is my fiancé Jack. That's my cousin Aiden and his . . ." Marissa looked at him for the answer.

"Fiancé," Aiden added, looking straight at Lindsay. He saw the shock in her eyes and knew he'd have some explaining to do later.

"His fiancé, Lindsay," Marissa finished.

"Well, isn't that nice?" Milly beamed. "Ya'll being cousins and engaged at the same time. Is it going to be a double wedding?"

"We don't know yet," Aiden jumped in, trying to stop this line of conversation before it went much further.

"That's okay, y'all have time to figure it out. It's God's blessing that none of you were hurt in that crash." Milly shook her head.

"Actually, one of us was," Lindsay said, looking straight at him.

"Linds, it's fine," he assured her.

"No Aiden, it's not." Lindsay turned to look at Wyatt. "He has a gash on the side of his head that I think needs stitches."

"It's fine," Aiden tried again.

"Well, my Wyatt will just have to take a look at that for you when we get you back to your motel," Milly said, settling the debate.

The rest of the trip was spent listening to Milly give them her and Wyatt's life history. By the time they reached the motel, their ears were ringing.

Aiden was impressed with the ease in which Wyatt parked the big motor home. Before he knew it, Wyatt had it shut down and was turning in his seat.

"Well, let's take a look at you now." Aiden sat quietly while the elderly doctor inspected the wound.

"It could use a couple of sutures," Wyatt said. "But I think I can close it up with some butterfly bandages for now. Just be sure to get to a hospital and have them fix it up for you."

"Thank you," Lindsay told him. "And I'll make sure he takes care of that."

As Aiden stood to follow everyone out of the motor home, Wyatt whispered to him, "Sorry about that. Sometimes, she just doesn't know when to quit, but I was just so relieved it wasn't my ear she was chewing on." Wyatt grinned. "I always knew she could talk, but until we started this trip, I hadn't realized how much. I love her to death, but sometimes, I wish I had packed some damned earplugs."

Aiden couldn't help but smile. "Don't worry about it, and thank you for the bandaging and the ride."

Milly was the last out of the motor home. "Now you be sure to call the police and report that accident."

"Yes ma'am. We sure will." Even Jack had come out of his killing mood in the wake of Milly.

"Thanks again for the lift," Aiden repeated as Wyatt and Milly loaded back up into their home away from home.

The light mood brought on by the elderly couple only lasted as long as it took them to enter the room Aiden and Lindsay were sharing, where the sight of Hannah's things brought it all back.

"I think we need to call Margaret—warn her that Carl's back in town and that he took Hannah," Lindsay suggested, picking up her daughter's blanket and hugging it to her chest. "We can ask her if she knows of anywhere he might take her."

"That's a good idea," Aiden nodded as she turned to make the call. "Tell her to be very careful. Carl is sure to know we were at the house talking to her. We need to come up with some way to track him. Find out where he's going." He turned to Jack. "Did you bring any of the information on Carl you put together?"

"Yeah, it was in Marissa's bag. Hopefully it's still there." Jack crossed to where Marissa was standing and slid her oversized purse from her shoulder.

A second later, he pulled out a manila file folder stuffed with papers. "It's all still here."

Lindsay, still holding the phone to her ear, turned and interrupted the conversation. "There's no answer. I've let it ring about fifteen times."

"Shit," Jack swore, looking at Aiden. "He must have gone back to the house and grabbed Margaret while his goons were running us off the road."

"He couldn't take the chance of leaving her behind. She's

probably the only one who knows where he'd go." He took the file folder from Jack and spread the contents across the table. "These are our only leads right now, so let's each take some. We'll go over it again and again until something jumps out at us."

~~~

For the next few hours, they scoured over property records, business documents, and everything else Jack had been able to dig up on Carl Donnelly.

Lindsay couldn't concentrate on what she was reading. All she kept thinking about was her daughter. Was she hurt, was she hungry?

When she'd read the same page for the fifth time, she put it down and pushed away from the table, needing to move, needing to *do* something.

Opening the door, she stepped out onto the sidewalk. She closed her eyes and lifted her face up to catch the heat of the day's last rays of sunlight.

Aiden had followed her out. With her eyes still closed, she shared her thoughts. "This isn't working. We're wasting time."

Turning to look at him, she went on, "There has to be something else we can do."

"I might have an idea," Aiden told her. "But before we go there, I think we need to take a small break, get cleaned up, and eat something."

That was the last thing Lindsay wanted to do. "We need to keep looking. We have to find her, Aiden."

"And we will. But we, and you especially, need to keep our strength up. Look at us. We're still covered in blood from the crash. Let's take half an hour to deal with that and order some food. While we're eating, I'll explain my idea."

Lindsay wanted to argue. She was tired of delays, and she
~~~

needed to find her baby. But she also knew Aiden was right. If she let herself get run down, she would be no good to her daughter.

She nodded and let him guide her back into their room where Marissa and Jack still sat at the table, watching them.

"What's going on?" Jack asked.

"I may have thought of a way to find Hannah," Aiden told them. "But before we get into that, I've talked Lindsay into taking a little break. Just long enough to wash up and eat. We need to keep our energy up."

They settled on pizza; it was quick and could be delivered. While they waited for their food, everyone took turns in the bathroom freshening up as best they could.

Lindsay helped Aiden clean around the wound on his head, gently washing the dried blood from his hair. Once he was clean and dry, she applied more bandages, pulling them tight to close the cut.

She knew he wouldn't take the time to get the stitches he needed, so she did the best she could.

When the pizza arrived, they cleared away all the papers concerning Carl and sat down.

Lindsay was so anxious to find Hannah, she wasn't sure how much she could force herself to eat. However, once she'd swallowed a few bites, she discovered that she was starving, and before she knew it, had eaten two full slices.

Aiden must have been satisfied with that, because halfway through her second piece, he began to explain his idea.

"A locator spell," Aiden told them. "It was one of the spells our parents taught us right after we came back. Do you remember, Marissa?"

"Yes. But for the kind of spell you're talking about, it's going to take a lot of power. It's not like we're looking for a set of misplaced keys."

"I know," Aiden admitted. "That's why I didn't use one at the cabin."

"Why would you have done a locator spell at the cabin?" Marissa asked him.

Lindsay sat back and waited for Aiden to explain to his cousin what he'd done.

"I wanted to find one of Carl's men, so he could pass along a message to Carl for me," he told them.

"Yeah," Lindsay teased, "and we both know how well that turned out."

"Oh, shut up," Aiden said good-naturedly. "I already told you—from now on, I'm leaving the PI stuff to Jack."

Jack looked at both of them before asking, "Do we even want to know what you're talking about?"

As Aiden recounted the events following his attempt to threaten Carl, Lindsay recoiled. The physical pain she'd endured, thinking she was losing her baby, couldn't possibly compare to the emotional agony of truly having her daughter taken from her.

"Lindsay was right," Marissa scolded. "That wasn't the smartest thing you could have done."

"Yeah, I know," Aiden agreed. "But everything ended up fine. Now, can we get back to this discussion? I was thinking we could call the family and find out how to boost our powers enough for a spell of this magnitude."

"How is that even possible? To boost powers?" She knew next to nothing about magic, but Aiden and Marissa had both had a crash course in it. She just hoped they knew what they were doing. Her daughter's well-being depended on it.

"I think I remember something about being able to draw power from others," Marissa told her. "We've learned so much in the last couple of months, sometimes my brain feels like it will explode, but something about that sounds familiar . . . being able to tap in or borrow powers from other witches."

Marissa smiled. "This might actually work. Aiden, go ahead

and make the call and find out what we need to do."

Lindsay watched as Aiden stood and pulled his phone from his pocket, dialing as he crossed the room. She had seen magic do some incredible things, but gather power? She was almost afraid to hope. If this worked, they would know where her baby was.

It seemed like an eternity, but Aiden finally hung up the phone.

"Okay. I have everything we need. Becca gave me a spell which should call and amass enough power for us to do this." Aiden looked over at Lindsay. "We're going to need your help too."

"*My* help?" She was stunned. "I'm not magical—I can't do spells."

"No, but you're Hannah's mother, and love is the strongest kind of magic there is. Becca said it would help," Aiden explained.

"Okay." She didn't hesitate. She'd do whatever it took to help find her daughter. Nervous, she rubbed her sweaty hands down the legs of her pants. "What do I need to do?"

29

Aiden relayed what his mother had said. "Lindsay, Marissa, and I will form a circle, holding hands. We recite the gathering spell, and then once that's done, the locating spell."

It sounded easy enough to her. But she also knew she was about to be intimately involved in something which would change her life forever. And she didn't even care.

She wiped her clammy palms down her legs once more. "Okay. Let's do this."

She and Marissa looked over both spells, committed them to memory, and then joined hands with Aiden.

Aiden started the gathering spell, and they recited together in unison:

"Power from far and near

Come and settle here

Borrowed briefly to aid our need

Swiftly returned at our heed."

Lindsay didn't think she would feel anything, since she herself wasn't a witch, but as soon as the words had left her mouth, she was filled with such a sense of power that it took her breath away.

The air around them shimmered with the magic they'd called. She looked across at Marissa and Aiden and could swear they were almost glowing. Lindsay wondered if she were, too.

The air was heavy with a static charge dancing all around them. She jumped slightly when the bulb in the bedside lamp burst in a shower of sparks.

Aiden smiled at her. "You okay?"

She could only nod.

"It's kind of a rush, huh?" he asked.

"Kind of a rush? Are you kidding me? I've never felt anything like this before. It's like there's electricity running under my skin. Is this how it feels to have powers?"

Marissa laughed. "It's not usually this intense. We're borrowing a lot of magic right now. So let's put it to some good use, shall we?"

They began the next spell.

"Hear our words

Hear our plea

Show us so that we may see

Hannah as she is to thee."

In the middle of their circle, the air began to swirl and move. Soon a ball of—fog was the only thing Lindsay could describe it as—started to grow.

When it reached about two feet in diameter, it changed again.

The center of the ball became clear, like a window they all could see into, and through the window was Hannah.

"Oh God," Lindsay gasped.

"Holy shit," Jack muttered, jumping to his feet to stand behind Marissa.

"Everyone take in details. We have to figure out where this is," Aiden told them. "Jack, you researched Carl. You know all of his properties. Look around, see if anything jumps out at you that will identify where this is." He paused. "And you can close your mouth anytime now," Aiden teased him.

"Screw you," Jack shot back before closing his mouth.

It was impossible for her to look at anything other than her daughter. She was being held in the arms of Margaret Donnelly.

They were seated on what looked like a small couch. Margaret was feeding Hannah a bottle and talking to her. She couldn't hear what was being said.

She couldn't tear her eyes away from the sight of her daughter, safe in the arms of her grandmother. At least someone was with her who would protect her.

Long before she was ready, the image started to waiver and fade.

"No, no, no," Lindsay moaned. "Just a few more minutes. Please."

The ball faded away until it disappeared completely.

"Oh, God, Aiden." She dropped to her knees, all her strength gone. He was right there to catch her. "I want my baby."

"I know. We'll get her back." Aiden held her in his arms. "Margaret is with her. She'll keep her safe. And remember—Carl wants her alive, so he won't hurt her."

Lindsay called on reserves she didn't know even existed to pull herself together, and then looked up at Aiden and the others.

"I'm sorry. I couldn't look at anything but Hannah," she admitted. "Did any of you see anything that would help us find her?"

"I may have," Jack said. "I can't be sure, but I think I saw something through the window just off to the left of the scene we were shown."

Jack ran his hands through his hair. "Shit. I wish that thing had instant replay. If I run with this, and I'm wrong about what I saw, we've wasted more time chasing nothing."

Lindsay walked over to Jack and took his hands in hers. "What was it? Please tell us. It's all we have."

"I think what I saw was a train," Jack told her, squeezing her hands in reassurance.

"How do you know it was a train?" She released Jack and turned in time to see Aiden take a seat in one of the dining chairs. He started shuffling through the papers again.

"You know how it looks when you're sitting at a railroad crossing at night, and lights from the oncoming traffic flash in between the cars?"

Jack waited for them all to nod.

"That's what I saw out the window. It was faint, though, like maybe it was only moonlight shining through."

She and the others were silent as Aiden found what he was looking for. "I count five of Carl's properties that are situated near railroad tracks."

"Five?" Lindsay held her fear at bay. "How are we going to figure out which one it is?"

"If we can't narrow it down somehow, we'll just have to check each one," Aiden said.

"Okay. How do we narrow it down? What do we need to do first?" She refused to let her panic overwhelm her. She would hold herself together until she had her baby back in her arms. She had to stay strong.

"We go through what we have on each property," Jack told her, "and we compare that to what we saw. Something is bound to match up."

Hours later, the table littered with coffee cups and soda cans, they finally had the most likely location.

As exhausted as all of them were, Lindsay wouldn't be talked into waiting until morning.

"No. She's not staying with that monster one moment longer than she has to," she decreed. "We go now."

"Linds." Aiden wrapped her hand in his. "We all agreed this is our best bet, but we may still be wrong. It could be one of the others."

"I know that," she told him. "But the faster we eliminate where she isn't, the faster we discover where she *is*."

"Okay," Aiden gave in. "Let's go."

Within half an hour, they were loaded into Jack's car and speeding through the deserted night-darkened streets.

Lindsay stared out the side window, barely hanging onto her last shred of sanity. Knowing that evil bastard had her daughter was killing her. If Hannah wasn't there, she didn't know what she'd do. Aiden had assured her they would check every property if they had to, but would there be enough time? The longer Hannah was gone, the farther away Carl could take her.

The pressure of a hand covering hers pulled her out of her thoughts. She turned and looked over at Aiden.

"We'll find her," he vowed.

She only nodded, not sure her voice would make it past the knot of terror in her throat.

It took about forty-five minutes to reach the house where they thought Hannah was, but to Lindsay, three eternities could have passed for all she knew.

When Jack slowed and pulled to a stop, Lindsay leaned forward in her seat.

"Which one?" she asked.

"There." Jack pointed to a white single-story house. "Someone's home—the lights are on."

Lindsay grabbed for the door handle, ready to march right up to the door. Aiden took hold of her hand to stop her.

"We have to follow Jack's lead here," he cautioned her.

She nodded that she understood, every second of delay like a knife through her heart.

Jack turned in his seat to address them all. "I want you three to wait here while I go do some recon. I need to see who's in there and how many we'll have to deal with."

She and Aiden both started to voice their objections, but Jack cut them off. "I know you want to be in there to get her, and you will be. Just let me have a look first. I'm the only one here trained to handle this."

Lindsay knew he was right. "Okay, we'll wait. But hurry."

Jack exited the car and was across the street when the darkness swallowed him.

Lindsay could do nothing but pray. She desperately wanted to curl into Aiden's lap for comfort, but she was afraid she might break down and never recover. So she sat still and straight, watching the spot where she'd last seen Jack.

He'd been gone roughly twenty minutes when suddenly the front door opened, and a tall figure stood silhouetted against the light from inside.

"That's Jack," Marissa announced.

She was the first taking off across the street, but Lindsay and Aiden were close behind her.

When they reached the porch, Jack stood back to let them enter.

Lindsay stopped and stared in shock. Two men were kneeling on the floor with their arms bound behind them. Each showed evidence of a fight, and when she looked back at Jack, she saw he wasn't looking any better than they were.

"What happened?" Marissa asked him.

"I'm sorry, Lindsay." She heard the guilt and defeat in Jack apology. "Hannah's not here. We chose wrong."

She'd prayed so hard that Hannah would be here. Lindsay felt the walls she'd built around her heart starting to crack while the conversation went on around her.

"Who are these two?" Aiden asked.

"They were the only ones here," Jack answered. "I figured while we had them immobilized, these two might be willing to provide us with some information."

"And you took them both on yourself?" Marissa asked, looking over Jack's split lip and bloody nose.

"Yeah," he said, giving her a quick kiss. "I was motivated."

In a daze, Lindsay walked up to the first man, only vaguely aware that everyone behind her had gone on alert the closer she got to him.

"Where is my daughter?" The words dragged on her dry throat. "Where is Carl hiding her?"

The two men looked at each other before bringing their gazes back to her, but neither said a word.

Lindsay took a step closer and repeated her question. Still, neither man spoke.

She felt the tight rein holding back her anger and fear start to slip. Without even realizing what she was doing, Lindsay doubled up her fist and punched one of the men with such force, it snapped his head around.

When he recovered his balance and looked up at her again, he sneered at her.

And that's when every tool she'd used to contain her emotions over the loss of her daughter suddenly gave way. All her fear, sadness, and hatred overwhelmed her at once. She lashed out over and over, landing blows and screaming for him to give her answers.

Time faded away until strong arms grabbed her from behind, and Lindsay hazily heard Jack tell Aiden to get her out of there.

When the cool night air hit her face, she sank to her knees and sobbed over the devastation in her heart. The world went spinning when Aiden lifted her from the ground and up against his chest.

30

By the time Aiden had carried Lindsay back to the car, the worst of the storm had passed, and now she just quietly cried. He didn't know what else to do, so he held her close and let her get it all out. He'd watched her closely since Hannah had been taken, and aside from when they'd first realized her baby was gone, she hadn't let herself cry. She had stood alone against the pain, not letting him offer any comfort.

When this house had proven to be the wrong one, Lindsay hadn't been able to cope with that loss anymore.

To see her lose control like that shredded his soul, but he knew nothing would end her pain until she was reunited with her child.

He gently settled into the back seat of Jack's car with Lindsay still in his embrace. Her face was buried against his neck, her tears soaking his collar.

Soothing her as best he could, he hoped she would cry herself to sleep. And by the time Marissa and Jack came back an hour later, she'd done exactly that.

Marissa sent him a questioning look when she slid into the front seat, but Aiden just shook his head.

He'd wait until later to find out if they'd had any luck with the men in the house.

Aiden raised one of her hands to see what damage she'd done. Her knuckles were red and swollen, and one was split, blood trailing down between her fingers.

Laying his palm over her injuries, Aiden concentrated on healing. He only wished he could mend her heart as easily.

Once back at the motel, Aiden gently stripped Lindsay and put her to bed. The emotional hailstorm she'd been through had taken everything she'd had.

Leaving her to sleep, he locked the door and quietly closed it behind him. Seconds later, he was knocking on Jack and Marissa's door.

Marissa let him in. "How is she?"

"Still sleeping," Aiden told her. "I think that's the best thing for her right now."

"How are *you* doing?" she asked gently.

"I don't know," he admitted, dropping down onto the edge of the bed. He ran his hands over his face and up through his hair before returning his focus to Marissa. "I knew she was bottling it all up. I wanted to comfort her, to cry with her, but she just shut me out. It was only a matter of time before it was all too much for her, but I never thought . . . I'll never get that image out of my head. The wildness of her attack and the strangled sounds she was making . . ."

Marissa came and sat next to him, taking his cold hands in hers. "She's lost so much to this man—first her husband, and now her daughter. We all saw the look in that bastard's eyes; he was mocking her pain. It's no wonder she wanted to kill him with her bare hands."

"We have to get Hannah back." Aiden didn't bother to hide the moisture gathering in his eyes.

Marissa took him in her arms and hugged him tight. "We will. We won't stop until we do."

Aiden absorbed some of Marissa's strength before releasing her and looking over at Jack. "I don't want to leave her alone too long. Were you able to get either of those men to talk?"

"No," Jack replied somberly. "Neither uttered a word, so

we're back to square one. We'll have to go through the rest of the properties, but not until we get some sleep. Go be with Lindsay and try to get some rest. Make sure she knows we're not giving up."

Aiden stood warily. "I will." He was almost to the door when he turned back. "Thank you both for coming to help."

"We're family," Jack reminded him.

Aiden's steps were dragging when he unlocked the door and opened it. Lindsay hadn't moved, but he could see fresh tear trails on her face. Stripping out of his clothes, Aiden crawled into bed and pulled her in tight against him.

$\sim\sim\sim$

When Lindsay awoke her head hurt, and her heart ached as memories of the night before came back. They'd chosen the wrong house and were no closer to finding her baby.

She became aware of the weight of Aiden's arms wrapped around her and the warmth of his skin beneath her cheek.

"We'll find her." Aiden's whispered words startled her; she hadn't realized he was awake.

"Will we?" She hated the defeat in her voice, but that's all she could feel right now. How were they going to find her before Carl disappeared with her completely?

Aiden suddenly rolled her onto her back and pinned her with a fierce gaze.

The determination she saw in his green eyes made them almost glow.

"*Yes*. And until we do, you can't lock yourself down like you did before." The intensity was gone now, replaced by tenderness. "We're all here for you—*I'm* here for you. Let us help you. Cry and scream at me, or *with* me, because I love her, too. Just don't shut me out again."

"I was afraid if I let go, I'd go crazy." Tears rolled from the corners of her eyes and down into her hair. "I'm so scared, Aiden. I can't lose her."

"You won't," he vowed. "We'll never stop until we find her."

He laid a soft kiss on her temple, capturing some of the moisture as it fell, and hugged her to him.

A little while later, he spoke. "We need to start our search again. Why don't you go take a shower, and I'll call Jack and Marissa?"

Her head still felt fuzzy from last night's meltdown. A shower and a couple of ibuprofen would probably go a long way toward fixing that.

Aiden was already dialing when she closed the bathroom door behind her.

She was standing under the spray, letting the hot, steamy water soak into her bones when she heard the door open.

"They'll be here in a little while," Aiden called through the curtain. "They just rolled out of bed, too. I asked if they'd bring some food, though it'll probably be sandwiches or something simple, since we slept most of the day."

Before she could answer, he pulled the shower curtain aside and stepped in.

She smiled tiredly when he reached out and took her into his arms. "What are you doing?"

"I'm taking care of you."

Setting words to action, Aiden stepped back and took the shampoo off the shelf. Squirting some in his hand, he proceeded to gently wash her hair.

No one had ever done anything like this for her before, and she didn't know how to react. But soon the massaging motion of his hands and fingers, and maybe a little bit extra that was Aiden's magic, did what the hot shower still hadn't—ease some of the tension she'd carried since Hannah had been taken.

She closed her eyes and let his ministrations calm her.

Once her hair was rinsed, he did the same with the

conditioner. Lathering up some body wash, he used his hands to spread it all over, washing her.

Naked, there was nothing to hide what this was doing to him. His arousal was full and strong, but his face never showed it. His complete focus was on attending to her, his own body be damned.

"Aiden." Something in her voice must have given away what she was thinking.

"This is for you. I'm fine."

"I'm not," she told him, stepping in close.

"Lindsay—"

"Shhh." She ran her hands up his chest, over his shoulders, and up into his hair, careful of the still-healing wound. Slowly, she pulled his head down to meet hers and placed gentle kisses along the seam of his lips, waiting for him to respond.

When he finally did, he took her breath away. Mouths fused, Aiden slid his hands down over her butt to the backs of her thighs. In one smooth motion, he had her legs up and wrapped around his waist. Turning his back to the shower spray, he pressed her against the wall.

The bathroom steamed around them as they kissed and touched. She could feel his manhood seeking her core, but he made no move to join them.

"Aiden."

This time, he shushed her. "I've got you." Aiden guided himself into her and thrust.

They moved in rhythm, each lost in sensation, both pushing away the heartache, if only for just a moment.

Spent, he slowly eased her feet down but still held her close. Backing up, he immersed them in the warm spray again.

Using one hand, he brushed the wet hair out of her face. "Are you okay?"

"No," Lindsay told him honestly. "But I'm better than I was."

"I guess that's all I can hope for right now." Aiden kissed her and then reached down to shut off the faucet. "We'd better get dressed before Jack and Marissa get here."

Half an hour later, Lindsay was brushing out her long blonde hair when Aiden let the others in, carrying take-out bags.

"Found a sub shop about a block up." Marissa pulled four sandwiches out of the bag. "I hope turkey's okay?"

Lindsay sat at the table. "That's fine. Thank you." She paused before looking up at Jack and Marissa. "I want to apologize for last night."

Marissa turned a chair and sat down facing her. She reached out and took Lindsay's hands in hers.

"There is absolutely nothing to be sorry for." Marissa stressed her point by squeezing her fingers. "We all saw the way he looked at you, and every one of us wanted to do exactly what you did."

Lindsay could see the truth in three sets of eyes. "Were you able to get anything out of them after I left? Did they tell you where Hannah is?"

"No," Jack told her. "Neither said a word."

"So we're back to where we started," Lindsay said, looking at the papers spread out on the table. "We can't afford another miss; we need to figure out a better way of narrowing down the possibilities."

"I think I can help with that."

Everyone jumped at the sound of a new voice in the room. No one had seen him enter.

"Damn it, Gideon," Jack ground out, relaxing the hand that had reached for his pistol. "Why can't you give a little warning before you do that?"

"Why?" Gideon smiled smugly. "It's so amusing to watch you start for your gun, only to realize it won't do you any good. And besides, I thought you might be glad to see me since I came to help."

Lindsay didn't care how he got there. If he helped them to

find Hannah, he could come and go as he damned well pleased.

"Do you know where Hannah is?" She sounded desperate, even to her own ears.

Gideon looked directly at Aiden. "No, but Aiden does."

"What?" Aiden was as shocked as the rest of them. "Do you think if I knew where she was, we'd be sitting here right now?"

"She speaks to you, right?" Gideon asked him. "Telepathically?"

"Yes."

"That's your connection," Gideon explained. "That's how you make contact with her."

Lindsay saw the frustration in Aiden's clenched jaw.

"Don't you think I've tried that, damn it?"

Lindsay was surprised at his admission. "You're still trying to make contact?"

"Yes. About every half-hour, I call out to her. She never answers."

"You don't have to call out to her," Gideon continued. "Just concentrate on the connection the two of you have, 'Poppa,' and you'll find her."

"How did you . . . ?" Aiden started to ask, only to cast a quick glance at Lindsay.

Something was going on she didn't know about. "What does he mean by that, Aiden? Why did he call you 'Poppa'?"

"He wasn't really calling me that," Aiden admitted. "He was letting me know, that *he* knows, that Hannah does."

"Hannah calls you 'Poppa'? Since when?" She was so taken aback by this news, all she could manage was a whisper when she asked, "Why didn't you tell me?"

She caught the scorching look Aiden shot at Gideon before he turned to her.

"The first time was the night she was born," he explained. "And I didn't tell you, because I didn't want that to sway your decision about you and me, one way or the other. I had hoped her calling me that meant both of you would be staying in my life, but I wanted you to make that choice on your own, instead of choosing it because you thought you had to."

"Oh." She didn't know what she was feeling. She and Aiden had been moving towards something, but they really hadn't had the time to talk it over. And there was still that fiancé thing to discuss.

She knew she loved him, and Hannah obviously felt strongly for him if she were calling him 'Poppa.'

Unless she was just confused and didn't realize that Aiden wasn't her father. He'd been there from the beginning of her life. Maybe she thought he was.

"She's just confused and thinks you're her father," Lindsay reasoned.

"No, hon. She knows exactly who her biological father is," Aiden told her gently, reaching for her hands. "And we won't ever let her forget him. But she's accepted me as a part of her new family, and I'm hoping you will, too."

"'Poppa,' huh?" She realized this felt right. "Well, who am I to argue with my very smart daughter?"

She cupped his face in her hands and kissed him softly on the mouth. "Now, find our little girl, so we can bring her home."

"I'm not sure I know how," Aiden told her, admitting his fear.

"I have every faith that you do," she reassured him. "Just do like Gideon said—concentrate on your connection to her. It saved her life before; I know you can do it again."

They turned back to Gideon for more answers, but in the time they had been talking, he'd disappeared.

"Okay. I guess it's just me then."

~~~

Aiden sat on the end of the bed, took a deep breath, and closed his eyes. He sat in silence, waiting for something, *anything*, to
~~~

happen. But nothing did.

He could feel the growing anticipation of everyone in the room, Lindsay's especially. They all wanted to find Hannah as quickly as possible, but the longer nothing happened, the more those expectations weighed on him.

Opening his eyes, Aiden looked up and met Lindsay's stormy blue gaze. "I don't think I can do this," he told her honestly.

Lindsay came to kneel in front of him. She took his hands in hers and held them tight.

"Yes, you can. I know you can," she told him, looking him straight in the eye. "Find our baby girl."

No one else existed for Aiden in that moment except Lindsay. He lost himself in her eyes, in the absolute confidence she had in him that he would find Hannah and bring her home safely.

Taking that confidence into himself, Aiden closed his eyes again and reached deep inside, searching for the true root of his power. He saw a bright, shining light and followed it to its source. It was his heart. All the magic he carried originated here. The love he felt for Lindsay and Hannah made it beat stronger and glow brighter.

He concentrated on what he'd felt for this tiny human from the moment she'd slid from her mother's body and into his waiting hands.

Aiden used every bit of that love to bridge the connection between them.

And then he was floating, rising up off the bed to hover above his body for a moment.

Before he could figure out what he was supposed to do next, he felt himself being tugged up and through the motel room ceiling. And then he was flying over a canopy of buildings.

Keeping thoughts of Hannah uppermost in his mind, he also tried to track where he was going. Not familiar with the Chicago area, he noted buildings and landmarks which would tell them how to get back to wherever it was he was headed.

In the distance, he saw a house and somehow knew that's where she was.

It was very generic—a plain ranch-style home with ordinary beige siding. Nothing about it stood out.

Focusing, he noticed there didn't seem to be any numbers on the outside, so Aiden made sure to memorize the street name and where it was situated.

He floated down through the roof and into the room they all had seen with the aid of the locator spell.

Margaret was asleep with Hannah still in her arms. Hannah's eyes were open, but she lay silent.

He advanced farther into the room to get a better look and was surprised when he heard her voice in his head.

"Hi, Poppa."

"Hi, sweetie. Are you okay?"

"Yeah, Nana Maggie is taking care of me. And Uncle G told me you would be coming soon."

"Gideon was here?"

"Not really. Just his voice inside my head."

Next time he saw Marissa's brother, he'd be sure to thank him for reassuring his daughter. "Were you hurt in the accident?"

"No, Poppa. Aunt Rissy protected me. I'm fine."

"Your grandfather hasn't hurt you, has he?"

"No. He just leaves me with Nana Maggie."

"That's good."

Aiden was relieved to know Hannah was fine and seemed to be none the worse for wear.

"I want you to listen to me now, Hannah. I don't know how long I can stay here like this, but I want you to know that your momma and I are coming for you real soon. We'll be here before you know it. Okay?"

"Okay, Poppa."

"Hannah, do you know where Carl is? Is he here?"

"No. He went away."

"Okay, that's good. Hannah, I want you to remember something for me. I want you to remember that no matter what happens, your momma and I love you very much."

"I know, Poppa. I love you, too."

He began to feel the pull to leave. "Hannah, baby—I have to go now, but I need you to be brave for just a little longer. Okay?"

"I'll be fine, Poppa."

The trip back to his body was a lot faster than the one to find Hannah. Within seconds, he was back.

When he opened his eyes, everyone was still staring at him.

"I found her." He looked up at Lindsay. "She's okay." He wanted to say more to reassure her, but a wave of dizziness was taking him under.

He heard Lindsay shout his name as if from a great distance, and then a strong hand was pushing his head down between his knees.

"Take it easy and just breathe," Jack told him, still holding the back of his head. "You must have gone on some ride. You were in a trance or something for close to half an hour."

The stars bursting behind Aiden's eyes were starting to dim, and his mind was starting to clear. "I think I'm good."

When Jack released his hold, Aiden carefully sat up. "Can I get some water?"

Marissa reached to grab him one as he turned to Lindsay.

"I saw her. I talked to her."

Lindsay sat on the bed next to him. "She's okay? You're sure?"

There was fear in her voice, so he took her into his arms. "She's fine. She said Nana Maggie is taking good care of her. And that Uncle G spoke inside her head, and told her I'd be coming soon."

"How are *you*?" She cupped the side of his face with her hand. "You scared me. What happened?"

"I don't know. I guess it took more energy than I'm used to."
Aiden kissed her forehead, ignoring the slight ache in his own.
"I'm fine now."

Lindsay buried her face in his chest and held on to him. He
wrapped his arms around her.

"Uncle G?" Marissa asked.

"That must be what she's going to call Gideon," Aiden told
them.

"Where is she?" Jack asked.

Still holding onto Lindsay, he filled them in on what he'd
seen and what Hannah had told him.

Jack, ever the professional, suggested, "I think we should
move on this now. Hannah said Carl was gone, but we don't
know how long that will be. Aiden, are you okay to look through
what we have on the rest of the properties and find the one you
saw."

"Yeah, I'm good."

Aiden sorted through the files and used the landmarks he
remembered from his flight to find the house he'd visited. Then
a quick plan was put together while they ate the sandwiches
Jack and Marissa had brought earlier.

While the others talked around him, Aiden thought about
what was coming and hoped to God everything worked out the
way they were planning to get Hannah and Margaret out. But
in case it all went to shit, he resigned himself to the fact that
this could be the day he and Carl came to blows, magical or
otherwise. Aiden vowed here and now that he would be the one
to come out alive.

There was too much at risk to let Carl get the better of him.

31

Finding the street, Jack bypassed the house a few times to see what they were up against.

Aiden thought it looked empty and said so.

"Carl wouldn't want to draw attention, so he can't very well have men patrolling," Jack warned. "If he has guards, they'll be inside."

Jack turned left at the end of the street and then left again, pulling to a stop in front of the house that sat directly behind Donnelly's. After looking at the layout of the neighborhood, Jack decided the best way to approach would be from the back.

He shut the car off before turning in his seat. "I think I should go in alone." Aiden hadn't even formed a reply to that when Jack continued, "The more people we have traipsing around in there, the bigger chance we have of getting caught. I can get in, get to Margaret and Hannah, and get them out."

"No," Aiden protested. "I gave Hannah my word that *I* would be coming to get her. I'm not going to break the first promise I've ever made to her. I'm going."

This wasn't something he could be swayed on. He refused to start out his life as Hannah's 'poppa' by lying to her. She was counting on him.

Jack must have read the resolve in his eyes, because he finally nodded. "Okay. But I still think the fewer people, the better. Marissa and Lindsay will need to stay here then."

"She's *my* baby," Lindsay asserted from the back seat. "I have to be there for her."

Aiden knew exactly what she was feeling but also knew Jack had a point. Turning in his seat to look directly into her eyes, he added, "And you will be. I'll bring her back to you. I promise."

"Lindsay, I think Jack is right," Marissa admitted, reaching out to grasp Lindsay's hand. "He knows what he's doing. They'll bring Hannah back to you."

Lindsay turned her head to look out the window in the direction of the house where Hannah was. Aiden waited silently, giving her time to make a decision.

Finally, her eyes tormented but dry, she nodded. "I want her back in my arms, Aiden."

"And you'll have her," Aiden promised. Taking a deep breath and shifting his focus to Jack, he asked, "You ready?"

With a final look at the women they both loved, they exited the car and started across the grass.

The rain that had started to fall lightly during the drive over now pounded down on them until they were cold and miserable. By the time they approached the rear of the target house, they were soaked completely through.

Aiden took Jack's lead and flattened himself against the wall beside the door. Jack cautiously tried the knob. A quick shake of his head told Aiden it was locked.

Jack pulled a small black zippered pouch from his back pocket. Aiden saw the tools he withdrew from it, revealing it to be a lock pick set. Jack knelt and went to work.

Within minutes, he was rising back up to his feet. He tucked the pouch back into his pocket, and this time when his hand emerged there was a pistol gripped tightly in it. He reached out with his free hand and turned the handle unhindered.

The rain Aiden had cursed not five minutes before was now working in their favor. The drumbeat sound of it on the roof covered any noise Jack or the door made.

The door slowly swung open, inch by inch, to reveal what looked like the kitchen. Aiden could see from his position that one of Carl's men had his head buried in the refrigerator, oblivious.

He pointed him out to Jack, and before Aiden knew what he intended, he was across the room, slamming the butt of his pistol into the back of the guy's head.

Jack helped him slide soundlessly to the floor and took whatever weapons he carried.

Turning, Jack whispered to Aiden, "Find something to tie him up with."

Aiden conjured a long piece of rope, just as Jack came back with a towel he used as a gag. Once the thug was securely bound, they moved on, conscious of the fact there would be more.

At the kitchen doorway, they stopped. Aiden could see a hallway to the right with three closed doors, and to the left was the living room where two of Carl's men were visible. They were both seated on the couch, deeply involved in the game on the television mounted on the opposite wall.

Jack pointed down the hall, then placed his finger over his lips, indicating the need for absolute silence. It was a wasted motion; Aiden knew if they were caught, they'd be as good as dead. He nodded his acknowledgement anyway.

The first two rooms were empty. Had they been taken away already? Were they too late? Had he lost Hannah? It would kill him if he had to go back to Lindsay empty-handed.

He and Jack turned to the last door. It too was closed, but when Jack tried to open it, it was locked.

Once more the pick set was put to work, and soon Aiden heard the telltale click which told him the tumblers had released.

Jack turned and silently mouthed to stay put until he ascertained what, or who, was inside.

Watching Jack in full PI-mode made Aiden appreciate him

and Marissa coming down to help out. He was sure he and Lindsay could've handled it, but having someone here who actually knew what he was doing was a relief.

Jack drew his gun again, and after a quick look to make sure the hall was still clear, slowly opened the door. There was only the barest of cracks when Aiden saw him smile and lower the pistol to his thigh as he pushed the door inward.

Walking into the room, a wave of relief washed through Aiden. Hannah was safe, asleep in a makeshift crib, Margaret standing protectively over her.

Aiden saw she was about to speak but quickly put his finger to his lips to keep her quiet. Stepping forward and leaning in to whisper, he filled her in on their situation.

Jack caught their attention and motioned that they all needed to move out. Quickly.

Aiden picked Hannah up into his arms, holding her close.

Jack took lead, Aiden waved Margaret out next, and he followed behind. They made their way back down the hall, intending to exit the same way they'd come in.

They were just about to make the turn into the kitchen when a voice called out to them from the living room.

"Unless you want these two ladies we found sitting out back hurt, I suggest you step out where we can see you."

The quick flash of fear in Margaret's eyes told Aiden all he needed to know. Carl Donnelly was in the house, and he had Lindsay and Marissa.

Fuck. What did they do now? He looked to Jack for the answer, but before any plans could be made, Carl was speaking again.

"I have no problem causing them pain," he taunted, making the decision for them.

Jack and Aiden emerged from the hall to find Carl seated in a large chair on the far side of the living room.

Carl was a brute of a man. Aiden figured he had to be six

feet tall and could easily weigh in around two hundred and fifty pounds, none of which was fat. For a man in his fifties, he was built like a professional wrestler.

No wonder Margaret had been so willing to die just to get away from him. The man was huge and every inch evil.

"Margaret," Carl said in a voice which brooked no argument, "bring the child and the gun to me."

Aiden saw the fear and apology in Margaret's eyes as she took Hannah from his arms. She turned to Jack and grasped the pistol he held out to her before going to stand behind her husband's chair and setting the gun on the mantle behind her.

Aiden swept his gaze across the room to where Lindsay and Marissa were restrained and held at gunpoint.

Aiden expected Lindsay to be distraught over what was happening, and maybe inside she was, but all that showed was her hatred for the man who'd made the last few months of her life a living hell.

She fought against the hold Carl's man had on her. "Give me my daughter!"

"No." All eyes turned to Carl as he rose slowly from his seat and crossed to where his henchman was holding Lindsay.

Carl reached up and wrapped his massive hand around the back of Lindsay's neck, squeezing hard. When she winced and drew in a quick breath, Aiden's temper boiled, and his hands balled into fists.

He started to take a step toward them when Jack's hand caught his arm and held him in place.

He wanted so badly to rip that bastard's head off, but he had to keep his anger under control. He couldn't let his magic strike out at Carl and risk hurting Lindsay in the crossfire.

"Let her go," Aiden demanded through clenched teeth.

Carl's head swung around at his words. "Oh, I don't think so, Mr. Marquand," he said before returning his attention back to Lindsay. "She and I have a few legal matters to discuss—

namely custody of the child. She's going to sign it over to me. All nice and binding. If not," he shrugged, "she'll die." Lindsay grimaced when Carl's grip tightened to make his point.

"You *will* do this. I won't be crossed by you, or anyone else. Ever." His evil leer landed on Margaret. "Isn't that right, my dear?"

Margaret gasped in agony. One hand flew to her head, while the other firmly held Hannah close. "Yes, yes," she pleaded.

Aiden remembered how Carl had caused Lindsay to think she was in pain. He was obviously doing the same to Margaret now.

"Stop!" Lindsay shouted. "Stop hurting her. She's done nothing wrong!"

"She's done *plenty*, but I'll take care of that another time," he promised forebodingly, his focus still on his wife.

They had to stop him. Aiden knew if he were allowed to leave here, Margaret's life would most likely end at his hands.

When Carl finally turned away, Margaret sank to the floor, released from the excruciating hold he'd had on her.

Carl's attention focused completely on Lindsay again. "It's up to you. We can do this the legal way, or I can just take you and your family out of the picture altogether."

"I would think," Jack mocked, "that you've had your fill of legalities lately. From what I've heard, you've gotten up close and personal with it recently. Something to do with one of your warehouses?"

Carl released Lindsay and slowly came around to face Jack. "You instigated that?" he said as he started forward. "Oh, I will take great pleasure in returning the headaches you have caused me with that stunt."

Beside Aiden, Jack suddenly grasped his head in both hands and crumpled to his knees.

Causing pain seemed to be Carl's power of choice, Aiden noted. But it appeared as though he could only inflict it on one person at a time. They needed the upper hand—make it so that Carl had to face them all at once. There'd be no way he could incapacitate them all.

But first, Carl's goons and their guns had to go.

Aiden eyed the men holding Lindsay and Marissa. If he could get rid of their weapons, the men would be easy to deal with. He toyed with the idea of blowing up the pistols, but the girls were too close; they'd be hit. He had to find a way to put more distance between them.

A plan was starting to form. Now, how to let Marissa know? Aiden's gaze swung to Hannah.

"Hannah, baby, can you hear me?" Aiden pushed his thoughts out to her.

"Yes, Poppa."

Perfect. *"Hannah, do you think you can talk to Aunt Rissy's mind like you do mine?"*

"I think so. She has magic. That makes it easier."

"Can you do that now, and tell her exactly what I say?"

"Yes."

"Okay, here's the message."

Aiden watched Marissa closely and caught the slight widening of her eyes when Hannah first made contact. Her focus darted to Hannah and then to Aiden as she got the steps of the plan. When she nodded slightly, he knew she understood.

They were about to enact the most important game of witch's skeet they'd ever played.

Aiden was ready to fire at will when Marissa used her powers to launch the guns out of the men's hands and into the air. The sound of the weapons imploding in on themselves was startling, and it had the desired effect. Carl released his hold on Jack, and his men were disoriented long enough for Marissa to subdue the two henchmen, while Aiden advanced on Carl.

Aiden reached out and grabbed him by the front of his collar. Carl may outweigh him, but he was taller. Using that to his advantage, he stepped in close so Carl would have to look up at him.

"You may think you have me," Carl taunted. "But I will have what I want. *No one* stands in my way."

"That's where you're wrong," Aiden declared. "It's not just me in your way. It's Lindsay too. And Jack and Marissa. And if by some chance you manage to get through us, you can count on each and every member of my family stepping up to stop you from getting your hands on that baby."

Aiden tightened his grip and lifted, causing Carl's head to tip back. "Do you really want to go up against the entire Marquand line? You have no hope of beating us all, and we won't rest until you're put down for what you've done to not only Lindsay and her baby, but also to Margaret, Steven, and Lauren. Your reign of terror is over. It stops here and now."

"You honestly think you can take me on?" Carl sneered.

"Yes." Aiden let the confidence ring true in his voice as he raised his hand, a fireball dancing merrily in his palm.

Carl's eyes darted to the flickering flames before his gaze returned steadily to Aiden. "Well, think again."

Carl pushed off hard away from him, and Aiden gasped as his head exploded in agonizing pain. He dropped to his knees, the burning orb snuffing out of existence.

Through the haze of torture, he saw Lindsay and Marissa clutching their heads, doubled over in torment.

He could hear Jack cursing behind him and knew he was suffering again, too. Aiden had misread the situation; Carl could dispense his special brand of punishment on multiple people at once. And that mistake was going to cost them all their lives.

Fuck, it felt like his head was in a vice. None of them would be able to withstand this much longer.

Carl was killing them.

Aiden's thoughts were becoming more and more disjointed.

The horrendous pressure in his head was more than he could bear. His vision was closing in, and soon the blackness of unconsciousness would take him, and then he would be gone.

He needed to think and find some way to make it stop, but it was too overwhelming. Aiden felt himself being pulled under and wished it had all been different.

32

As abruptly as the pain had started, it was gone.

Its sudden absence made Aiden dizzy. When he recovered enough to raise his head, it was to find Carl's lifeless body on the floor in front of him.

There wasn't much left of his face.

Aiden's stomach rolled at the grisly sight, and he quickly looked away, his gaze drawn to Margaret.

In one hand was Hannah, held close and protected, while in the other was Jack's gun. Carl had neglected to take it from her after collecting it.

From the condition of Carl's face, Aiden surmised she'd shot her husband through the back of the head, killing him instantly.

And she'd done it to save their lives.

"There sweetie, it's all over now," Margaret cooed to Hannah.

Lindsay was on her feet, crossing the room to where the older woman was standing.

"Margaret?" Lindsay approached her slowly. "Please give me the gun."

"What?" Margaret glanced down, almost surprised to see it in her hand. "Oh yes. Here, take it."

Lindsay took the gun and quickly passed it back to Jack.

"Margaret, are you okay?" Aiden asked, approaching her.

"What? Yes, yes, I'm fine," she told him.

Margaret handed Hannah back to her mother. "Here baby, let's put you back where you belong."

"Margaret, I'll never be able to repay you for all you've done," Lindsay told her.

"Just take good care of that sweet little girl." Margaret brushed a hand over Hannah's little fuzz-covered head. "She's the last of my family."

"We will," Lindsay smiled.

Aiden and Lindsay had asked Margaret once before to come and stay with them, and now he put the question to her again. "We would like you to come back to Marquand Manor and stay with us. I'm sure our parents would love to see you, and you can stay as long as you'd like."

Tears came quickly to Margaret's eyes. "I'd like that, but I've just killed my husband. I'm sure the police will have something to say about that."

Jack stepped into the conversation. "I'm sure after we all explain what happened here, and what everyone, including the police, knows of Carl's history, they'll understand that it was justified."

<p style="text-align:center">~~~</p>

Several hours later, it was just as Jack had predicted. No charges were brought against Margaret for shooting and killing Carl. It was declared self-defense, and finally they were able to leave.

After a brief stop at the motel to gather their belongings and a quick call to let everyone know all was well, they headed back to Margaret's house.

With Carl gone now, she didn't have to be afraid anymore, and she could enjoy getting to know her granddaughter in the comfort of her own home.

Jack and Marissa decided to leave that night. They had

pending cases which needed to be finalized before their upcoming wedding.

Aiden, Lindsay, and Hannah stayed at Margaret's for a few days before they caught a flight back home.

Margaret had so much to do to straighten out Carl's holdings that she wouldn't be able to join them for a couple of weeks, if not longer.

With a promise to call every day, Margaret stood on the porch and waved goodbye until they drove out of sight.

They hadn't made it a mile down the road when Lindsay turned in her seat and spoke. "With everything that's been going on, it slipped my mind, but there was something I was wondering about."

"What's that?"

"What was that back in Milly and Wyatt's motor home? Was that supposed to be a proposal?"

"Uhhh." He'd been dreading this conversation. How could he explain what he'd said, when he didn't quite understand it himself?

Lindsay continued on before his thoughts came together.

"Because if it was, it sucked. I mean, if you think my daughter and I are going to spend the rest of our lives with someone who can't properly ask us, then you'd better think again."

He pulled the car off the road and stopped. This moment was too important to all of them, and he wanted to do it right.

Once they were stopped, he removed his seatbelt and turned to face Lindsay.

"I hadn't planned for that to pop out of my mouth like that. But when Marissa was floundering for a way to describe our relationship, I suddenly knew exactly what I wanted.

He couldn't tell what she was thinking, so he continued. "We hadn't discussed anything permanent, so I wasn't sure how you felt about it, but in that moment I knew I loved you and wanted to marry you."

"So that wasn't a proposal—it was a slip of the tongue?" Lindsay asked with a suspicious light in her eyes.

"No, that wasn't my proposal, but this is." He cupped his hand against her cheek and laid his heart at her feet. "Lindsay Donnelly, I was lost before you showed up in my life. I didn't know where I was going, or what I'd do when I got there. Having you in my life has brought me more than I could have ever wished for. You helped me finally accept who I am and embrace it fully. You make me stronger and more fulfilled than I could have ever thought of being. You have trusted me with the most precious gift possible, your daughter. I love you both to the center of my soul. Will you marry me and share that beautiful little girl with me?"

Lindsay's tear-filled eyes smiled up at him before she turned to speak to Hannah in the back seat. "I don't know, baby girl. What do you think? Would Aiden make a good daddy?"

When Lindsay gasped and turned surprise-filled eyes up to him, Aiden knew exactly what had happened.

He grinned. "What did she say?"

"How . . ." Lindsay was stunned.

"Her powers grow every day," he reminded her, pulling Lindsay across the seat and into his arms. "So, did she say yes?"

Lindsay smiled up at him. "You know she did, Poppa. She said you'd make a great daddy."

"Then there's just one more thing I still need to hear."

"What's that?"

"A yes from you."

"As if I would say anything else." She leaned into him and kissed him with all the passion he'd come to love in her. "Yes, Aiden. I will marry you."

EPILOGUE

Aiden and Lindsay had been back at the manor for a couple of days when he realized he had yet to see his sister. Searching out his parents, he asked them about her. "Where's Amber?"

The look that came over their faces caused a feeling of dread to settle in his stomach. His father's reluctant admission confirmed it.

"We're not sure."

"What do you mean, you're not sure? Is she missing? Have you called the police?"

"She's an adult," Becca told him. "And, technically, she's not really missing. We know she's been here, but she's avoiding everyone. And you had so much going on in your own life, we didn't want to burden you with this, too."

"I remember you being worried about her when you came to the cabin. But it must have gotten a lot worse since then if you're *both* worried about her now. Tell me all of it," Aiden demanded.

His mother cleared her throat, her eyes downcast. "She comes and goes at odd hours and won't tell us where she's been or where she's going. I know she's a grown woman, but I'd still like to know what's happening with my daughter. Her behavior is very erratic, and she's completely shut us out."

"I'll see what I can do," Aiden promised.

~~~

Upon their return to the manor, Lindsay's parents came up for a long-overdue reunion with their daughter and new grandbaby. Over the next few days, while Lindsay and her parents got caught up and marveled over Hannah, Aiden did what he could to find out what his sister was hiding.

He didn't make much progress.

Even after speaking with her friends, he still didn't know any more about the situation than when he'd started. All they'd told him was that she'd met some new guy none of them knew. And, since then, she'd stopped getting together with them.

About a week after he and Lindsay had returned, Amber finally showed up.

He watched her from the hallway as she silently made her way to her bedroom. Seizing the opportunity, he followed right behind her.

She still hadn't noticed him when they'd reached her door.

Since she hadn't closed it behind her, Aiden stood at the threshold and watched as she crossed the room.

"What the hell is going on with you, Amber?" he demanded.

She ignored him, bypassing him to walk to her closet. He was shocked by her condition. She'd lost weight, she had dark circles under her eyes, and she looked unbearably sad.

"I take it you got everything straightened out with the Donnellys?" she asked him over her shoulder. "How are Lindsay and Hannah doing?"

She was deliberately avoiding his questions. "They're both fine. Though, I'm kind of surprised you even know their names." He continued when she didn't acknowledge the dig. "You know, I kept expecting you to show up. Especially when Hannah was kidnapped. But no. Not a call, not even a text. Why was that?"

"Something came up," she said flippantly as she pulled clothes from hangers. "I knew you could handle it. And you
~~~

did."

"Yeah, we came out of it whole and healthy, thankfully. But now, instead of spending time with my girls, I'm here trying to find out what's going on with you."

"There's nothing going on with me."

"Don't lie to me, Amber," he demanded.

She turned and headed back towards her bed, her arms full of clothes, shoes, and duffle bags.

"Damn it, Amber. Mom and dad are worried about you. Since you refuse to tell them what's going on, you can explain it to me." He closed the door behind him with the solid thump of a jail cell door closing. "We're not leaving this room until you do." He folded his arms over his chest.

"Okay, there *is* something," she finally told him, as she stuffed jeans and shirts into the bag, "but it's no big deal, I'm taking care of it."

"Yeah, you look like you're taking care of it," he countered. "You've lost what—ten pounds? You don't just have bags under your eyes, Amber, you have the whole damn set of luggage. You look like shit."

"Thanks, love you, too." Sarcasm dripped from her voice.

He used the only thing he'd been able to learn. "Does it have anything to do with the guy you've been seeing?"

Her breath caught, and she swung around to face him fully for the first time. "How did you . . . ?"

"Since you didn't see fit to tell anyone what was going on, I did a little detective work on my own. I talked to some of your friends. You know," he tilted his head slightly, "it really pays off having a private investigator in the family. You pick up all kinds of neat little tricks." Aiden pinned her with his green eyes. "Who is he? What has he done to you?"

She didn't answer him.

"Amber." He dropped his arms to his sides and gentled his tone, as he took a couple of steps closer to her. "I know we haven't had a chance to really get used to this brother-sister thing yet, but you can talk to me. I can help."

She was silent for so long, he didn't think she would tell him. "Amber, sweetie, Let me help you."

"My powers are gone," Amber blurted out, turning to sit on the edge of the bed. "All of them. They're just *gone*."

"What?" Aiden couldn't believe what he was hearing. "How?"

"I don't know." She wouldn't look at him.

"What do you mean you don't know? Who did this to you? This new guy?"

Amber nodded, still not meeting his gaze.

"Who the hell is he?" Aiden took a step forward in his anger.

When she held silent for too long, some of his impatience slipped through. "Amber, tell me who the hell he is."

"I can't tell you!" she cried out, dropping her hands to her lap, and finally raising her head.

"What do you mean you can't tell me?" he ground out, his face a solid piece of granite. "This asshole has stolen your powers, and you won't tell me who he is?" Aiden was holding himself rigid. "Amber, he can't get away with this. Give me his name."

"I can't," she said again, imploring him to understand.

Aiden tried. He took a deep breath, releasing it slowly as he knelt down in front of her. He reached out and grasped her hands in his. "Is he threatening you? Is he threatening the family?"

"No." She released one of his hands to wipe at the last of the tears on her face.

He reached up and caught one she'd missed. "If he hasn't made any threats, why won't you tell me?"

"If I tell you who he is," she whispered miserably, "you, and the others, will feel obligated to hunt him down."

Aiden's confusion changed to shock as he stood to his full height. "You're protecting this jackass? This man has stripped away the magical abilities you were born with. He's taken away what makes you who you are. And you don't want him *hurt*? My God, do you hear yourself?" He paused and looked down at her. "This isn't like how Marissa and I grew up. We may have been *born* with abilities, but they were bound when we were so young, we didn't know any different. Not to be callous here, but do you even know what it's like living without power?"

"No," she admitted.

"And yet you still protect him. Why? Help me to understand."

She locked her emerald green eyes on his. "Because I still love him."

Misha McKenzie has been an avid reader since learning how at four years old. Countless books later, she still loves to immerse herself into the lives of the people within those pages. After graduating high school, she went on to earn a degree in Business Administration, married her high school sweetheart, and had two beautiful boys. At thirty years old, while working as an office manager for a construction company, a family of witches began to brew, and The Magic of the Heart Series was born.